For my wonderful daughters

'Strive not to be a success, but rather to be of value.'
Albert Einstein

1

Flora

When I was nine I saw a clip on *Newsround*, or some other magazine show, about the Dionne quintuplets. The footage was blurry, shades of grey, the girls (they were all girls) tick tock toddled in their pen as a steady stream of Lowry-like stick people jerkily funnelled past them. Natural quintuplets born to farmers in rural Canada was pretty special in the 1930s and the authorities acted quickly to supportively snatch them away from their parents, build a zoo and charge hordes of visitors a fortune to ogle the little tots playing, eating, napping before streaming the sightseers into the Dionne merchandise store to spend more money that was quickly syphoned into a few 'good' men's pockets rather than stowed away for the girls' futures as promised.

Naturally, none of this was reported in the clip that I watched, bare legs crossed, sitting too close to the TV, ensuring the development of square eyes or the threatened destruction of my vision, or so my mother constantly warned me. No, all I took in was five near identical girls in their enclosure, and all those people who wanted to look at them. So many souls who had travelled for hundreds, maybe thousands of miles just to see those little dolls.

The next day I corralled Heidi, Pam, Lou and Netta into my new game. 'We have to dress the same,' I yelled, my voice high with excitement as I threw the few clothes I possessed out of my wardrobe. 'Find anything that looks like it almost matches. Next time you can bring stuff from home. And we're pretending it's winter.' There was snow on the ground in the film in Canada. Lots of snow. I wanted the game to be as realistic as possible. I wanted to be a Dionne Quintuplet. I didn't want to go to school. I didn't want to live in an ordinary house. I wanted to live in a zoo where thousands of visitors could press their palms up against the glass and look and look at me and wonder at the miracle of my very existence.

'Hurry up! Get dressed!' I barked into the puzzled faces of my friends, 'We're going to be stars!'

Their expressions made me want to slap them all. Why couldn't they understand? I knew I would be the only one who truly enjoyed the game and by the next day we'd be back to riding our bikes, single file, round the stony track circling the allotments or trotting up the bare metal steps of the slide over and over again down at the park. I didn't know it then but what I wanted most was to escape.

'I don't want to push yet! My hair looks like shit! Shy, stop filming. Cut, cut!' I yell.

Shy looks up from the camera but it's still running. 'We haven't stopped filming for the past seven years Flo, are you sure?'

My head crashes against the pillow, I can feel the familiar fury of my childhood bubbling as the next contraction overwhelms me. Why is it happening so quickly? It wasn't like this last time. I had hours. This isn't how it was supposed to be. They said because I'd had so long in between it would be like having a first birth again. All I can feel though is the force, the undeniable force, that this baby is bloody well coming and I want Tia here, now, to do a quick up-do.

'Where the fuck is she?' I bellow to the ceiling and then grit my teeth as my belly hardens and my chin goes to my chest, which I know is not a great look, and I can't help but push and push. There's no pain now, just the urge, the power, the necessity of this baby to be born. I am nothing but a giant muscular womb contracting and constricting and pulsing and pushing my daughter into the world.

'Wait Flo, wait, pant now, pant. Give me a moment. The cord's around the baby's neck,' and I dutifully pant, looking over to Shy who has the camera tight in on the midwife's concentrated energy.

I smile through the lapdog breathing. My mind floats away from the gruesome reality of my body's contortions and imagines the comments, the reactions, the subscribers racking up. Shy pans back to me and the smile is wiped. Panic replaces it. I know how to work the camera.

'Okay, big push with the next contraction for me now darlin', lovely big push,' the midwife encourages.

I plump my sagging hair with my drip free hand, lick my lips wishing I'd had time to apply a little nude gloss and bear down as the next contraction washes up and over me.

The baby is bloody and swaddled on my discreetly bare but voluptuous breast. Shy has handed the camera to Milk, my other camera guy, and is sitting in the early morning light in a huddle by the window, wiping a tear away. 'It's a miracle,' he's saying to Milk who's still on the baby. 'I'd no idea I'd feel like this.' Men are so soft.

'Thank God they agreed to a home birth,' I yawn and stretch extravagantly, 'In a moment,' I say to camera, 'my gorgeous dula is going to take Treasure for a little bath and you're all going to be there for that as well. How precious. I'm going to stay here and re-charge for a moment or two,' and I wink a tiny wink of self-congratulation.

Right on cue, Jan, the dula arrives. Unfortunately she's missed the birth; she claims it's an unreliable Fiat Punto that was reluctant to start in the freezing temperatures of a January night that has forestalled her appearance but I'm pretty sure I can smell wine on her breath. Anyway, she's here now.

As baby, dula Jan and Milk disappear, I heave myself up onto the pillows and attack the toast and tea the NHS midwife has made me. Shy moves to sit on the edge of the bed. 'You were amazing,' he says softly.

'Where's Meryl?' I splutter through the mouthful of toast.

Shy looks shifty. 'I'm not sure she's home yet. I text her when your waters broke. Maybe her phone's out of battery…' He's never been good at covering up my firstborn's shortcomings.

'It doesn't look great her not being here. Find her and get her home, will you?' I abandon the toast, set down the tea and reach for my phone.

'Sure.' Shy understands when he's being dismissed. He waits at the bedroom door, 'Congratulations, Flo,' I hear him say but I'm lying down, head turned away, eyes on the screen.

I've never felt the need to offer anyone answers.

2

Meryl

'You're always telling me to stop doom scrolling and look at you!' Tyler sounds tetchy, tired and pissed off and I know I should put my phone down but I can't. Besides if I do all the anger that is currently percolating through my veins could well be misdirected towards Tyler, the goon. I blink and fix again on the live feed of the yellowy-pink, slippery, mewling creature weakly turning its head this way and that as it receives a bath from the dula.

I can hear Jan's irritating sing-song nasal whine in the background as she narrates what is happening. Not that much as it happens. An infant is getting a wash.

The reactions are through the roof though. And the comments too.

As I read, `I wish I was that babe being born into your perfect family #miracleoflife`, I let out an involuntary yell and throw the phone down the bed where it pitches off the end and bounces onto the floor.

'Chill out, Mare!' Tyler flinches. He'd shut his eyes and is startled out of a little hypnogogic reverie by my uncharacteristic shout. The weed is making him sleepy, bet he thought he'd grab a kip if I was going to give him the silent treatment. Again.

'I'm going,' I decide and I'm up and out of the bed, pulling on jeans and tugging on a jumper as Tyler props himself up onto his elbows.

'Shit,' he stammers, 'You can go on your phone if you want. S'nothing to me really.' He clambers clumsily towards me, the grubby duvet bunching up between his knees and halting his progress. 'Don't go. I'll get some food. You hungry? I'm hungry.'

'You mean *I'll* get some food,' I mutter grumpily as I tug at my tangled hair and scan the chaotic room for my keys, 'You never have any money.' I sound mean. I am mean.

'Woah, harsh Mare, not cool!' but Tyler is grinning as he flops back against the pillows, 'Go if you want to babe, I ain't your jailor.' He reaches for his vape and I catch the scent of bubble-gum from the pale cloud he exhales.

'Flora's had her baby. I should go.' I have my hand on the door, exiting the room as I speak. I catch Tyler's shout of congratulatory laughter as I dart down the stairs summoning an Uber en route.

Tugging on my thick wool jacket as I step out into that particular stillness of the hour just before dawn, I look towards the threads of colour just struggling to light the sky. For a moment I am calmed and tranquil as I take in the suburban quiet, the curtains closed, houses dark and all inhabitants tucked up in warm beds, cars cold and still, cohesively opaque with frost on driveways, no movement, no sound, not even a fox nosing a dustbin to break the spell.

My phone pings.

The Uber is announcing its arrival.

I pull my jacket tighter against the chill and move out onto the road to wait.

3

Flora

I saw *The Truman Show* when I was eighteen. The first time that is. Since then, I've watched it too many times to count. It is my perfect film. A perfect world, a perfect life, a perfect idea. When I saw it, I wanted to live in *The Truman Show*. I wanted to be Truman except I would have been happy, no honoured, to be any character on *The Truman Show*.

Milk said there was something weird about him filming me watching it. Especially when he thought about all the viewers watching me at home or on their commute or in offices, and then they would be watching me watching the film and watching the viewers watching the show in the film. Milk said it was a meta moment. I said it was a dream come true.

Truman is the star of a reality show but he doesn't know it. He's adopted at birth by a TV corporation and placed at the centre not just of a fictional family but a fictional world. A wonderful world as far as I am concerned. A world with nostalgically beautiful exteriors and interiors and beautiful people and perfect weather and plentiful food and little misery or despair. And everyone watches him all the time through tiny hidden cameras. Everyone shares in all his greatest moments. Except Truman can't ever leave.

Why Truman wants to leave once he realises what is going on is a bit of a mystery to me. Who would want to live in the real world if you could live in a perfectly constructed one?

If I couldn't be a Dionne quintuplet, I could create my own *Truman Show* and that was what I'd pitched seven years previously. My following was big by then on all the socials, I mean impressive. So many, many steps taken to get to the place where I knew I could rely on those hearts and ticks and clicks every time I posted a bowl of cereal or a lipstick or a couple of seconds of a walk by a pond, but I had made it happen.

'Yes I want cameras in every room and I want the viewers to be able to choose the angle. Like they can edit the view. You know like in a video game you can turn around and see what's going on. I want it to be like that. Plus, we'll have a handheld following me when I'm out and about,' was how I pitched it to the group at the studio.

'Isn't it a little invasive Flora? How will you live your life?' One of the more benign execs, Tim, leaned forward, concerned.

'It's supposed to be like that,' I had snapped, 'That's the whole point. I live my life on camera. The viewer sees it all. Or they choose what they want to see.'

'What about when you're sleeping. I mean that's not exactly great TV, is it? You want us to run this continually but will there be enough good footage?' This time it was Deborah, an emaciated woman with thin hair and too many teeth in her broad mouth. I had done my research though, I knew Deborah was the one who had the final say so.

'Viewers have to sleep too. It's opt in, opt out. I think if they get hooked they'll get into my routine and live their lives alongside mine. That's the dream. And we can have playback options. So highlights can be rerun, viewers can catch up on events if they've had other stuff on. But yes, in answer to your question, some of it will be dull but that's life isn't it? The whole point is that everyone can escape from their lives into mine and I will make them feel welcome. They will know me. They will want to come and be with me and see what's going on and how Meryl is doing and who I'm dating and what colour I've chosen for the tiles in my kitchen. They will show up because they're interested.'

'Or nosy,' Deborah replied archly.

'What does it matter?' I replied mildly, 'As long as they're there and we have the figures.'

'And revenue streams?' Deborah clicked onto her laptop to appraise my pitch in detail. This didn't worry me; I'd spent hours on it.

'The usual advertising and sponsorship with product placement and endorsements with different price points for covert and overt. If we reach the figures I think we could, then every brand is going to want their stuff on the show.' I smiled warmly hoping that this time my words would translate into some sort of reality.

Deborah paused and looked up from the screen. 'You have the experience, Flora and the face for it, and there isn't anything else like this at the moment. I do like to be the first. There seems to be quite a lot to iron out. I want to check with legal about Meryl's involvement - do the same laws apply about filming children et cetera - but in principle I think we have a show, people.'

In reality, I couldn't quite believe they'd agreed but contracts were drawn up and in a few short months a house was found and a launch date decided upon.

One of Tim's research assistant's heard about the property. It had been built by a premier league footballer in Hertfordshire to his wife's exacting specifications. She had a love of period dramas but hated old properties so it was a new build suffused with Georgian elegance and so perfect for all the cabling required for the high spec cameras and mics required to get the best quality footage for the Show. Luckily for me, but sadly for the footballer he'd run up a lot of gambling debts fuelled by a serious cocaine problem and was selling quickly post-divorce on the down-lo. The house was a steal for what it was and already had some excellent security built in to keep passionate fans out.

The only rooms with no cameras are Meryl's bedroom and bathroom. She has been filmed in there but by Milk or Shy on the handheld and only by her invitation. It was a stipulation of the legal team; they didn't want any comeback in the future from Meryl and they certainly didn't want anything unsavoury appearing online.

Eight years or 2927 days of continual filming ago *The Flora Show* had gone live and Meryl and I were catapulted into super stardom.

4

Meryl

The camera picks you up at the gates, so, despite myself, I do an automatic hair check and clear my throat even though I have no intention of speaking just yet. I'd made it through the usual huddle of creeps at the bottom of the lane. The show's success had necessitated the purchase of the lane as a buffer zone; too many gawpers and 'enthusiasts' aka stalkers hoping for their fifteen minutes of fame were stretching the security team and Flora's nerves. Despite the early hour, a few are already there clutching teddies and a handful of foil balloons, the better to welcome the latest addition to the programme. I ignore them all; what losers show up at this ungodly hour for no good reason? There was no way Flora would be out to do a Meet and Greet having just given birth. Idiots.

Shy opens the door before I have time to get my key in the lock. As he hugs me he whispers into my hair, 'She's not happy. You should have come home. She needed you.'

'Lies,' I breathe back into his neck.

'OMG you've got a baby sister!' Shy pulls away, holding my shoulders the better to tilt me towards the camera pointed down from the cornice so it can pick up my reaction. Shy's okay but if he thinks I don't clock exactly what's he's doing he's a fool.

'I know,' I keep my voice flat, dead. I don't smile. No reaction here, pal. 'I'm exhausted. I'm going to bed,' and feel Shy watching me helplessly as my feet drum up the stairs to my room.

'Uh oh. Perhaps we've got a case of sibling rivalry already?' he says. I'm sure he's thinking how can I not react? How can I not want to see my sister? But Flora had taught him to think on his feet and I've watched him instinctively spin any situation to their advantage. Viewing figures and followers were ever-present gnawing shadows hunched on his shoulders; he watched Flora's world through their combined eyes, not his own.

Checking my phone, sure enough the responses are empathetic - `I feel for you Meryl, never could stand my brother` - or spoiling for a fight - `Choose the baby Flo, Meryl's grown she don't need you no mo #selfishbrat`. Shy will see it as the start of a useful thread.

I know I'm right though. My mum had not needed me tonight. Flora has never needed anyone.

My rooms are on the corner of the house. At one side I have a view of the drive and, depending where people park, I can monitor departures and arrivals, if I can be arsed. At the back I overlook the courtyard which is the access to the annexe. As I peer out of this window now, I watch Shy appear from the main house and jog across to his quarters. I can tell that he too is exhausted. He's moving fast, yes but his head is down and his shoulders are dropped.

He and Milk share the converted outhouses that were converted for 'staff' when we moved in at the start of the show. Flora would never use the word staff though; we are family. You don't pay your family though, do you?

There are no cameras in the annexe. Flora says it's to protect them, Milk and Shy that is, but, as I watch, Shy strips off his T-shirt, inhales the night air deeply and runs a hand across his lean abs just before he disappears through the door; we all know the no camera policy is because she doesn't want anything distracting focus from her, from *The*

Flora Show. That guy is always too hot, he's like a radiator. It's January! How can he bear to be bare-chested, even for a second, in the dead of night at this time of year. Unsurprisingly, he has his own little coterie of fans, and Flora hates it though she pretends she doesn't. Shy's meant to be behind the camera, unseen, a ghost who records and nothing more. It's hardly his fault that he is accidentally drawn into some 'scenes' and that he looks good in front of the camera too.

    Milk is good looking too but he is more reserved than Shy. Milk is mixed heritage. He's shown me pictures of his parents, a tiny Senegalese Mum and a white blonde Swedish father. He has blonde hair and pale blue eyes that are mesmerising like his dad but his hair is thick and curly and his skin is the colour of caramel. He is tall and broad and, if he wasn't so bashful, he could be a model, but he hates people looking at him. Except Flora. He worships Flora. He wears glasses too and when he was little he had round ones with gold frames and he was called the Milky Bar Kid by his class mates. I looked this up. That dude doesn't look nothing like Milk but you know what kids are like and some tags just stick. So he became Milk and he accepts it. His dad is dead but even his mum calls him Milk. Weird.

    I bet Shy won't even make it up to bed tonight – he'll just flop down on the sofa and sleep there. God knows how many hours he's been filming her. There's no such thing as a proper contract here. They keep going and going, switching between the two of them like some micro Hollywood sweatshop.

    Knowing Shy, the arrival of the baby will still be running through his brain, the drama and tension but more than that, the reality of it. He doesn't say much but he feels everything really deeply and the birth was a real life wonder. An amazingly intimate, private moment where a life hung in the balance. Yes, I'd watched it all. How could I not? 'The chord's around the baby's neck,' the midwife had said and Shy would have felt his stomach turn. Like I did.

In that moment he won't have cared about the show or the network or the lighting for the shot, his head will have been full of the emotion of a life snuffed out before it started. A chord tightening and stopping the heart.

I wonder if he felt the same terrible suffocating panic I did. What was he going to do if the whole thing ended terribly? If the first live birth on air in a mainstream show ended in a death, what would happen? How could he record it? Had he felt the tears in his chest like I did too? Real tears. Not just tears actually, wracking sobs.

I know this baby is very much a part of his life. He'd recorded the first scan and pulsing grey heartbeat, he'd watched Flora's belly swell and I've clocked him keeping a track of her food and water intake, seen him suggest she take a nap, silently push a footstool towards her to put her feet up if he couldn't persuade her to go and lie down. Yes, and Milk was the same. The pair of them quietly doting on all Flora's maternal needs. Hell, either of them might as well have been the father. In fact she'd have been better picking one of them rather than some random donor. They are great guys. They love her. God knows why.

I picture him nudging his shoulder into a cushion and feeling the tension easing from him. Sleep will be coming after such a wild night. I feel mean. We should have talked. I didn't think about him or Milk; they'd probably have liked to celebrate Treasure's arrival. To mark it in some way. Yes, there are plans for the show, but Shy probably now gets why fathers light a cigar in the waiting room, affirming the arrival of their progeny.

Except that Treasure isn't his. Or Milk's. Or even really mine. She's Flora's and The Show's.

And Shy's just the cameraman.

We must never forget to stick to our parts.

5

Joyce

When Flora was ten, she discovered the child star Shirley Temple. Those chubby cheeks and long lashes, pouty smiles and the total adoration which surrounded her were a source of constant fascination to Flora. In her films, everyone adored her, everyone was charmed by her halting singing voice, her adorable tap dancing, her cheeky retorts.

Flora wasn't a difficult child and, as there was just the two of us, life should have been uncomplicated. Truth is, I'm not sure I ever understood her. She had, well, obsessions. And I soon learned it was easier to give in to the obsessions and just let them run their course.

'Look at Shirley Temple, Mummy, no one sends her away because it's, 'Grown-up time', no one tells her to, 'Stop making such a racket!' when she sings. Quite the opposite in fact. Everyone loves her. All the adults adore her. She is perfect.'

Flora was right. Throngs did appear before Shirley as soon as she opened her mouth, all delighted by the precocious and perfectly packaged bundle before them, but this was a film not real life. Flora found this fact hard to take on board.

'I need tap dancing lessons,' Flora had announced to me. I was recently divorced, following a separation of several years. I was working in the local library. Full-time. A permanent job but not well paid. We were not a family of means.

'You didn't really take to ballet Flora, what makes you think tap dancing will be any different?' I reasoned with her. I remember the first time she brought up the tap dancing I was sorting through a pile of bills and Flora must have known she didn't have my full attention. She was always wily though, Flora. It was a shrewd move. There was a chance I'd say yes just to get rid of her and be able to focus on stretching the family finances a little further.

Flora pouted darkly at the mention of the ballet lessons.

It was true however. Flora had believed that she would be perfect for ballet. She adored the feel of the starter tutu I had purchased at considerable expense, and she marvelled at how light the soft, leather ballet slippers felt in her hands and on her feet. She'd have worn the whole lot to bed if I'd let her. In class, however, Flora found it hard to pay attention to the teacher, Miss Seville, and couldn't stop herself from running across the polished boards of the studio at full pelt in front of the mirrored wall at any given opportunity.

Ballet is all about discipline and practice and Flora had neither. She wanted to pirouette on pointe shoes before she knew all the positions her feet should start in. I'm embarrassed to say she just wanted to stare and stare at herself in the mirror, and stare at her face, her expressions, not her body, rather than concentrate on the repetition of the exercises Miss Seville wanted her to do.

Anyway, after a calamitous collision during one of her forbidden and much disapproved of runs across the studio just as Mrs Granger the piano accompanist was nipping out for quick loo break, Flora was persuaded that ballet was not for her. She protested at first, but I reminded her of Mrs Granger's broken wrist and the hiatus in piano playing that Flora had caused. Flora shrugged and said perhaps she'd learn the piano instead.

'I think if I start now, I'll be good enough for films in a couple of years,' Flora had pressed me, thinking this argument might clinch the deal.

'I'll look into it,' I'd agreed. Like I say, I'd learned that it was better to indulge her obsessions and let them run their course.

So ten-year-old Flora was fitted for tap shoes, dull black, not the far too expensive shiny patent leather favoured by Shirley Temple she'd hoped for, but they did however make the most excellent sound on the right surface.

Term was a few weeks in, and many of the other girls were both much younger than Flora and had got the hang of the basic steps. I could tell that this annoyed Flora before she'd even attempted a shuffle ball or a timestep.

It turned out Flora had neither the lightness of foot nor the sense of rhythm required for tap. And she grew tired of the dancing lessons before I gently suggested she abandon them. For a while, she watched Shirley Temple with her hands snug in her tap shoes and danced them on the slate hearth as Shirley flicked and twirled and grinned her way across the screen, tight little curls bouncing and shining in time with the music.

Eventually the shoes ended up, squashed and dusty, in the back of Flora's toy cupboard and, when they were re-discovered during a spring clean, they no longer fit. Hurling them back in, Flora announced to me, 'I'll just have to find another talent. I'm bound to be good at something.'

'Of course you will be Flora,' I'd encouraged warily as I'd reached back in for the shoes and dusted them off, ready to sell them on second hand as I had her ballet garb.

However, it transpired that Flora was not miraculously talented. She couldn't sing, dance or even act as she later discovered when she participated in her first high school production. The school was lucky enough to have a thriving drama department and Flora saw the possibility of the annual Shakespeare as a gateway to discovery and thence, fame. She would chatter on about it endlessly as if becoming famous was the only future available to her.

Flora had to wait for a couple of years to get beyond the general crowd or party scenes. Not that she really minded; she liked being backstage, she said, gossiping and larking about and wandering around the school corridors after dark, much more than she enjoyed being on stage.

I think it was hard for her not to be bored by the repetition of the rehearsals; she never did have a very good concentration span and she didn't understand all the old-fashioned language. She wished they could put on *Grease* but then I reminded her she couldn't sing.

Anyway, at fourteen, she was cast as Lady Macbeth's Gentlewoman. She liked her costume, full skirts, a cap and apron but the scene with Lady Macbeth sleep-walking she found interminable. A pretty girl called Hester McInally was playing the wicked queen and she *loved* the scene. Hester was in the year above Flora; she was striking and talented with sharply glinting, greenish eyes, cloudy, soot-black hair and magnificent breasts. As Flora stood patiently at the Doctor's side while Hester washed her hands and declared her guilt in a translucent nightgown that revealed her shapely form in all its glory, Flora felt diminished by her flat chest, her sandy hair and most of all by the flat, monotonous delivery of her own lines.

Flora would come home with tales of notes and ideas the director, Mr Day, had given her. But try as he might, once on stage, Flora's delivery was dull as ditch water. And Flora, to her credit knew it. She knew the drive and tension seeped from the scene as soon as she opened her mouth. Mr Day, an intelligent but not very tactful enthusiast, saw Flora backstage recounting some silly tale of a missed bus, a muddy puddle, and unsuitable shoes. As the crowd she was entertaining burst into appreciative laughter, Mr Day piped up, 'Why can't you bring that energy and animation to the stage, Flora?' Flora said he sounded genuinely cross and stomped off before Flora could respond. Unfortunately, it appeared that when pretending to be someone else, Flora's vitality disappeared. She transformed into a cardboard cut-out.

If anything I always found Flora a little too chatty, a little too much. Is that a terrible thing for a mother to say? I'm a quiet person. I like peace. Silence. Calm.

People say their teenage children shut them out and never say a word. Flora shared everything. She would draw breath as soon as her eyes opened and never stop talking until she shut her eyes last thing at night. It was exhausting. I used to lie in bed praying she would draw the line when she became sexually active; I did not want any details. I wanted her to hide things the way I would have hidden everything from my mother.

When I look back at our time living together, I think the words I most used to Flora were, 'Quieten down a little now,' or 'Haven't you finished that story yet?' I feel like I was always trying to silence her or rush her to the end of her everyday tales of her teenage dramas.

Funny that.

'If I can't be an actor, I'll just have to be famous for being myself,' I remember fourteen-year-old Flora saying lying, belly-down in front of the beloved TV, clicking her feet together as she watched the trailer for the first episode of *Big Brother*.

6

Flora

I have already made the decision not to breastfeed Treasure. I fed Meryl myself but that was partly due to having no money and my essential tendency to laziness. I couldn't be bothered with all the washing and sterilising when I could provide everything on tap with very little effort. It is a different matter with Treasure though. Now I have a team and, most importantly, my wonderful housekeeper Morag and nanny Marsha so I won't have to sterilise a thing. Also, I have to get back in shape and part of the programme planning is going to focus on this; if I was breastfeeding, and I'm sure this must be true, I would have less energy for my PT and be more sleep deprived and the whole process would just take too long. Plus, my product placement of baby formula is already proving to be extremely lucrative.

Milk watches me through the camera as Treasure finishes the tiny bottle that has been warmed for her. I keep smiling up at the camera and mouthing words like, 'Precious,' and 'So cute,' then gazing back down at the baby. Even if I do say it myself, I am looking pretty fantastic considering I gave birth less than twenty-four hours ago. Tia has been and gone and I am now sporting relaxed but bountiful curls. I've changed into a blush pink coord which is a luxurious silk and jersey mix. The baby's blanket is a pale, apple green which matches her little knitted cap. Framed by the expansive bed, made up with freshly laundered bed linen sprinkled with tiny apricot and lime flowers, are mother and child; I'm sure we make a perfect picture, calm, harmonious, flawless.

If I know Milk, he will have allowed himself a tiny personal bet on how long I'll be able to keep up the glow of early motherhood. I'm guessing a tight ten minutes before I summon the dula, nanny or Morag but he forgets I've done this all before. On my own.

I lift Treasure up to a sagging sitting position to burp her, tucking a manicured hand under her chin. I check in again with the viewers, smile and rub the tiny, curved back of the little parcel that is my daughter, then smile demurely at the camera again. I think I am feeling contentment.

Treasure effortlessly pukes an impressive quantity of milky drool onto the blanket, my leg and the bed linen. 'Bloody hell,' I momentarily snap, then gaining more control add, 'Is that better, sweetie? Didn't want that in your tummy, eh?' I look around me, 'We really wouldn't have bothered to change everything if we'd known you were planning on doing that.' I ineffectively mop at the sick with a muslin square.

'Jan! Jan?' I raise my voice and Jan the dula and Marsha the nanny both appear. As I lift the baby towards both of them, I say sweetly, 'I'm going to have to change. Will one of you just hold Treasure while I do that?'

'Of course,' Marsha says as she takes the baby.

'Do you need anything?' Jan adds as I head towards the en-suite. I don't bother to reply. Does she think she's going to bathe me too?

As I peel off my soaked pants I flick on the screen in the bathroom. I mute the sound, so I hear Marsha in my bedroom as she mouths the words on screen. 'You know, in hospital, they often move the babies to the nursery so the mothers can get some sleep and recover from the birth,' Marsha is gazing into Treasure's face and rhythmically swaying with the confidence of a woman who has handled many new-borns.

'It's important for mother and baby to stay together, Marsha,' Jan tersely replies, 'We don't want any attachment issues.' I sense Jan has raised her voice so I can 'overhear' her. Good move.

'I don't think that would be a problem,' Marsha replies mildly.

'Forgive me, Marsha, but how would you be able to judge that? There are children who cannot settle into secondary school because they didn't sleep in their mother's bed in the early years.' Jan is now jealously regarding Treasure; Milk zooms in on her fingers twitching at her sides. Nice touch, Milk. Really, he's a frustrated movie director.

'Is that a fact?' Marsha answers, looking straight at Jan, not bothering to hide her scorn.

'Yes, a well-documented fact, actually,' Jan answers.

'Is that so?' Marsha replies, she is back to gazing at Treasure who now has her eyes closed and is still and soothed by the gentle motion. 'Shall I take Treasure to the nursery, Flora? She's dropped off. I can wake you for her next feed if you want me to?' Her voice is raised but somehow sing song and relaxed.

I pop my head back out of the en-suite door. 'That sounds like a lovely idea, Marsha. I might just grab a quick shower or maybe a soak in the bath might be nice? Jan, could you ask Morag to make me a salad? I'm famished,' and I retreat to scrutinise the screen.

'Come on then bubba, let's go and settle you down,' Marsha turns from Jan, whose mouth tightens as she is demoted to messenger, and leaves the room. Jan turns to Milk, or rather the camera, and raises a tetchy eyebrow then stalks out after Marsha.

I peep out and can just see Milk. He allows himself a little smile as he checks the camera. It had been his idea to bring Marsha in from the word go. She'd come for the interview, and he knew that her no nonsense attitude expressed through a willingness to share her forthright opinions even at interview, would provide some excellent on-screen conflict with Jan's alternative attitudes. He said as much. He was bang on the money. I check my phone and the comments are flying in as to where Treasure should be and with whom. Result!

Programme planning is carried out in short, medium and long term strategy meetings. When I came up with the idea of a pregnancy coupled with a live birth, the biggest problem was keeping it a secret from the viewers until it could be revealed with maximum impact. The trick is to have something absolutely riveting or deadly boring going on to distract them or allow for some flat time when planning could happen. Then there is a lot of WhatsApping on the group chat with the producers and legal, so nothing is said out loud to give the game away. Milk and Shy update the programming mood wall in the staff quarters and photo it and send it to me for changes.

My decision to follow the IVF route lead to another boost in viewing figures and the reveal was beyond amazing. We'd been trailing, 'big news' and a, 'life changing event' but me walking into the hyper-smart clinic for my first consultation during prime time viewing on a Saturday night was genius. It had taken some organising and agreement with the consultant to see me out of hours, but everyone agreed it was gripping TV.

'Don't mind the cameras. Is it okay if they film?' I had smiled winningly at the professionally efficient looking woman sitting behind the desk.

'No. No filming,' was her abrupt reply.

Not to be put off, I immediately countered, 'What if they only film me?'

'Okay, that's acceptable.' Dr Eckhart still didn't crack a smile.

'Super! We can work with that,' I effused, nodding discreetly to Shy.

'So, how can I help you today?' Dr Eckhart started.

'I'd like a baby. Well, another baby. I have a daughter already. She's sixteen.' I flicked my hair, a reflex really, waiting for the usual, 'You don't look old enough to have a sixteen-year-old,' response.

It was not forthcoming. Bit of a knock back but anyhoo. Dr Eckhart clicked the top of an expensive pen and prepared to make notes. 'And was she conceived naturally?' was the first question. So, this was to be all business. I could do business. I sat up straighter.

'Yes,' I replied. I hoped that gave me a tick in a box.

'And apart from your daughter, have you had any other pregnancies?' She wasn't really looking at me, just waiting for the answer.

'No.' Frankly, if I had I'm not sure I'd have shared that truth without thinking about the implications first.

'And your age?'

'Forty.' Again, no gushing, 'You don't look it,' response. I was wishing the consultant had been a man. I get on better with men. Sometimes.

'And are you aware if you are still ovulating? Do you have regular periods?'

'Er, yes, still regular, yes.' I replied truthfully.

'And have they always been regular?'

'Yes.'

'Okay, good.' At last, a glimmer of the positive.

'And your personal situation. Your partner?'

'I don't have one and I don't want one. I've read that I could have a donor, is that possible?'

'Yes, of course. Who needs men? We have sperm banks in the UK which are fairly limited but access to banks in the US too. There's a charge obviously.'

'Yes, of course. That's not a problem. Can I ask, can I choose the donor? Can I request … certain attributes?'

'Absolutely. What did you have in mind?'

'A singer maybe? Or some type of performer?'

'I see.' Clearly, this wasn't the answer Dr Eckhart was expecting. If anything, her manner shifted to that of further detachment; an eyebrow slightly raised, a minimal flare of her nostrils. I was watching her closely and now I was a little relieved we hadn't been given consent to film. 'Every donor fills in a questionnaire and some may say they can sing.'

'And is this verified as the truth?' I tried to keep my tone light and smiled warmly at the camera.

'No, Ms Tatton. We accept the questionnaires at face value. They are not verified. There is not an *X Factor* panel to check whether someone who says they can sing, can actually sing.' Dr Eckhart's tone was now unmistakeably edged with irritation.

'Perhaps there should be. Ha ha!' I tried a little wink to camera this time, hoping the audience weren't getting the impatience in this tightwad's tone.

Dr Eckhart sat back in her seat and looked directly at me as she laid her pen down. 'May I ask what your background is Ms Tatton?'

'Please call me Flora. Yes, of course. I'm a performer of sorts, well, I'm on television, reality television.' It was unusual these days, rare you might say, to come across people who had no idea who I was. The Show played 24/7 across the world and had done for seven years. Where has this woman been?

'I see. So, you'd like your baby to be a performer too?' I sensed Dr Eckhart's disapproval. She probably thought I was some pushy parent with silly aspirations to give birth to a child star.

'Look,' I said, leaning in, trying to connect, 'It would just be lovely for him or her to have some talent. You see, when I was little, I would have loved to sing or dance but I was hopeless and my daughter, Meryl, she has no visible talent either. I mean, she's a wonderful girl but she can't hold a tune. Just like me.' I never could quite shake the desire for everyone to like me, to warm to me, to approve of me.

'Your daughter, Meryl, after Meryl Streep?'

'No, no after Truman's wife in The Truman Show. Have you seen that film? I love it.'

'Yes I have.' She didn't sound particularly enthusiastic.

'Well I'm Flora from The Flora Show. My whole life is filmed, and millions of people watch it. Frankly, I'm a little surprised you didn't recognise me.' Perhaps it was time to flaunt my status and celebrity a little.

'I don't watch reality TV, Ms Tatton,' she replied instantly dismissing me and my life's work, 'So, going back to your question you could select a donor who lists the ability to sing but then there is the question of whether singing is actually genetic.'

'Oh, I see.' The sound of my mother's lovely unwavering, high soprano voice, rarely heard and never seen as a gift by her plays in my mind; certainly, I had not inherited that. 'At least they'd have a chance if the father could do it though? Maybe?'

'Perhaps. So, I think the first step is for you to have counselling.'

'Counselling?' Not what I was expecting.

'Yes, it's standard when you're going to use a donor. It's called Implication Counselling and is entirely confidential.'

'Okay, great. Can we film it?' This sounds like gold.

'Absolutely not. The counselling aims to make you think about your family, Meryl, the implications for the future, this is not for public consumption.'

'Dr Eckhart, I don't think you quite understand my whole life is for public consumption. It's a commitment I've made. I want this whole process, including the birth, to be filmed and if that's going to be a problem perhaps I need to find another clinic.'

'Hmmm,' and I am treated to another arched eyebrow, 'I personally would strongly advise against it. IVF can be extremely difficult emotionally. We'd obviously have to get consents from all parties. Counselling on camera is not the norm.'

'How soon can I start?'

'Within the next two weeks.'

'Super!' I beamed at the cam.

'If, at the end of the counselling, you still want to go ahead with the donor then there's your treatment.'

I turned back to the lens, 'Phew, there's more! Maybe I should just do it the old-fashioned way,' and I winked saucily.

'With respect, Ms Tatton, at your age success via that route is going to be extremely unlikely.'

'Okay, so what's next?' I said quietly. I was beginning to think Dr Eckhart could do with working on her bedside manner. I made a mental note to check who had screened her suitability for The Show.

'Just to be clear, I recommend no purchase of donor sperm is made before you've gone through the Implications Counselling. Then if you want to go ahead we'll do a blood test to assess how many eggs you have left which at your age frankly isn't likely to be many. The other consideration for your age is the likelihood of embryonic abnormality.'

'Ooh, I don't like the sound of that,' I said, trying to keep it light. This woman really was a pill.

'If we get to the point of fertilised embryos, we can genetically test them before we transfer which will reduce the risk of abnormality.'

I was silent for a moment. 'How can I avoid abnormality altogether?' I asked.

'You can't.' I heard Shy shift and looked up at his alert face so engaged with the monster the other side of the desk. I bet he liked this woman. Liked her direct answers, liked that there wasn't any sugar coating, no spin, no changing the story. I bet *he* found it refreshing.

'What about if I used younger eggs?' I asked, trying not to wince.

'Donor eggs?' Dr Eckhart confirmed.
'Yes,' I nodded.
'Yes, you could have a double donation.'
'And could the egg be a singer too?' I asked.
Dr Eckhart sighed.

7

Meryl

Marsha is napping in the nursing chair when I ease through the nursery door. Her head is lolling backwards and her mouth, normally a tight line of disapproval, is now a startling curve of grubby, charcoal fillings edging the dry ridge of the roof of her mouth. I sneak across to the painted grey crib to inspect my sister.

The whole nursery is monochrome. The focus groups had been very clear about not pressuring Treasure to conform to any gender normative preconceptions. I find the room chilly and cheerless, like I've stepped into a black and white film.

The baby stares straight back at me. She's lying quietly, expertly swaddled, in her ivory cotton blanket, a cocoon, a pod with delicate features, cloudy eyes blinking in honey skin. A perfect little human.

We look at each other.

Neither of us cracks a smile.

I scoop her up and pad out of the room. 'Let's get some breakfast,' I whisper to the solid little bundle that smells of milky hope.

Later, we're lying on the living room floor behind one of the sofas, and I'm feeding Treasure a bottle. I know all the spots the cameras can't pick you up; they are few and far between.

I also know that the online forums usually hunt me out so, just like in *The Truman Show*, if I duck out of view for too long, some version of Truman's supposed best friend, Marlon, will appear with a metaphorical six pack of beer to lure me out, cheer me up, calm me down. Whatever is required to continue the façade of Happy Families that we have to maintain. I've been alone with Treasure a long time in *Flora Show* terms, a little under an hour, but it's after four in the morning. Viewing figures are low and there are even fewer people who have the energy to be posting at this time. A significant number of viewers overseas watch The Show in sync with their own time zone, so they feel like Flora is living her life with them; another protection for us from interference.

I tickle Treasure's tiny palm and feel the delicate fingers grasp surprisingly tightly around mine. The strength is impressive. 'I hope you're a fighter, Treasure,' I whisper, 'You'll need to be.'

The baby stops sucking at the rubber teat and half opens one eye to look at me. 'Are you saying you are?' I smile back at her and the other eye opens in surprisingly alert attention.

'Or maybe this is just wind?' and I sit up, cross-legged to pat and rock the baby, still shielded by the sofa. I hum quietly as I do so (the mics are sensitive) and I feel unusually calm. Almost happy.

The thundering footsteps racing down the stairs break the little reverie I've slipped into. Treasure is relaxed and sleeping quietly against my shoulder, and I'm slumped, leaning onto the back of the sofa, head tilted, eyes closed.

By the speed of the steps, I guess it's Marsha rather than my mother; Flora would consider the alacrity of this descent far too ungainly. Whoever it is whips through the living room and into the kitchen and I hear the back door in the utility room unbolt and open. She must be heading over to the boys.

I stand up as gently as I can and steal back to the nursery. Treasure wriggles and snuffles a little but settles back into slumber moments after she's back in the crib.

As I'm pulling the door to behind me, Marsha and Shy appear. Shy has the camera, red light on of course. It's not a surprise how quickly they've managed to get back inside the house.

'What the absolute fuck is going on?' Marsha hisses.

I can picture the angle Shy will choose tight close-up on me because I'm trapped by them and I avoid the camera so much that this golden opportunity must be plundered for all that it is worth.

'I gave her a bottle. She's asleep now,' I reply quietly keeping my eyes down and I push past them and heads towards my bedroom. There's no point trying to soften the blow, trying to say, 'The baby woke up,' or 'I heard her crying,' because I know someone will check the footage and then there will be more trouble.

'You can't just waltz in there and take the baby anytime you please, young lady! I thought she'd been kidnapped!' Marsha seethes.

I sigh and look at the ceiling but maintain my silence. There always comes a point where they want to take me on. Some reach it sooner rather than later. Looks like Marsha was going to be one of those.

'My job is to look after that child. My priority is that infant. You have no idea the havoc you have created.' Marsha crosses her arms. She is angry but probably more because she's worried about Flora's reactions rather than mine.

'What havoc, Marsha?' I say quietly, 'How long have you been looking for her? Ten minutes?' 'Don't you take that tone with me, young lady,' Marsha starts, abandoning the whispering. I don't care for the repetition of the term 'young lady'. Where are we? In some 1930s fucking boarding school story.

'Or what?' I want to not respond but her jutting chin and mouth like an arsehole just gets to me, 'You'll give me a spanking?' Straight away I'm furious that the words have left my mouth as I picture the memes and comments that that phrase will generate. My temper is rising, as it does from time to time. 'There's barely any chance of Treasure being kidnapped, Marsha – there's a security gate, plus a 24-hour security detail and the house is fully alarmed. I don't know why you would even think that that's what could have happened to her. However, I did manage to walk into the room with you sitting in the chair right next to the crib, and take her from under your nose, so, if you are the guard dog, we'd better get a new one.' And I turn away and open my bedroom door.

'Well I have never been ...' Marsha starts.

I turn back. In for a penny, I guess. 'Spoken to like that? I'm surprised. Genuinely. And I'd also like to point out that I am 'the infant's' sister. Her closest living relative, in fact, aside from my mother, and if I choose to come and get her, at any time of the day or fucking night, to do whatever the fuck I want to with her, then I will. I don't need your permission, Mary pissing Poppins. I'm her sister! Okay? Now I'm going to bed so would the two of you kindly leave me the hell alone.'

Inside my room, I shake my head and slap my hand on my forehead over and over, furious with myself for giving them so much useable footage, but that Marsha needs to back the fuck off. Over the years, I've had my fill of production assistants, researchers, runners and hair and make-up telling me who or what I can say and do. I'm at the end of my rope. I have to make it stop.

the.real.flora.tatton

daily contemplation: Be the reason someone feels welcomed, seen, heard, valued and most importantly loved.

Liked by **hatchet_man** and **2,818,419 others**

nowayback
Meryl wants a spanking lol

fuckeduphuman
"mary pissing poppins" comedy gold Put these two in the ring. I'd pay to see them fight it out #merylforthewin #catfight #smackdown

bobbyboombastic
sending calming energy across the ocean

1974999
why does M think she can do whatever she likes? Living life in the shadows #creepinaround

lilpiggywenttomarket
so much negative energy around a newborn bad energy guys #peaceout@theflorashow

cheesywotsups
no no no. FLra does not want this. Heart breaks to see this tension. #meditatetodissipatethehate

8

Flora

Meryl was six when I bought the house in France. 'Your father's dead,' was the bald announcement down the phone from my matter-of-fact mother one bright February morning, 'He's left you some money.'

I hadn't seen my father since I was four and, in my memory, he was muddled with Dirty Den from *Eastenders*, who I barely remember but mainly seemed to grab his car keys and leave in every scene, and a towering, spindly vicar from the Sunday school I went to for a while with Lou after he'd left us. In my mind he was just a tall, dark figure with light behind him, a face that refused to come into focus, a voice I couldn't recall.

There were a few blurry, orange-toned photos of him which were unceremoniously stuffed in a drawer, but neither I nor my mum were given to sentiment, and he was rarely mentioned. Perhaps that's why he left. I have no memories I can attribute to him. No notable events, no days out, birthdays, Christmases. As far as I'm concerned, I never sat snuggled in his lap and listened to a story, he never bathed me or fed me or made me laugh, we never sat under the sun or the moon and stars together, we never walked down a muddy lane or through a wooded path; we didn't sit cheek by jowl on a grumbling bus or speed through the clouds in a plane. Sifting through my early years, he was a shadow, a shape, a haze of smoke. Nothing more. He had been in my life for four years and I shared half my DNA with him, but he meant little more than that to me.

That he had died was a surprise. To have someone who should have been so close, slip out of your life without even knowing he was ill, was a little staggering.

'He was very successful apparently. That's what the solicitor said. Didn't show any signs that he had that in him when he was with me,' Mum huffed down the phone, 'If he had, maybe I'd have thought twice. Anyway, can't be helped, what's past is past. Did you catch *Eastenders* last night?' And that was that.

So it transpired my father had left my mother and his four-year-old daughter and moved to Australia of all places and set up a very successful production company specialising in low price sanitary ware. Bargain loos or budget dunnies to be precise. He'd sold the business when he retired, despite having a couple of strapping sons from a second marriage but had generously made some provision for me in his will, despite his lack of contact over the years.

When I heard all this, I briefly imagined a life in wonderfully warm and colourful Australia as I looked at the thin, pale leaves of the first snowdrops braving the biting, easterly wind while I waited at the school gates for Meryl. As my daughter appeared, chin down and frowning, hunched and crow-like in her thick coat and skinny legs, I wondered what our life would be like with wide, flat beaches and a swimming pool in the garden; with vibrant, crunchy salads eaten outside in flimsy clothes day in day out with the sun warming our skin. As Meryl slipped her chilly little hand into mine (she'd lost her third pair of gloves of the winter), and we trudged back under the low iron-grey sky, I schemed about that money that was awaiting me and an idea hatched.

'I'll do up the house and you film me. The whole point is there won't be much money. It's all going to be done on a shoestring so we're showing that everyone potentially could do it. It could be anyone's dream come true. That's the hook. I'll show everyone how to make it look fantastic but cheaply. I'm going to do most of it myself. Obviously.' I pitched the show the following week. 'But I want to be a producer; I've got to make some money from it, this time.'

I handed over brochures from the houses I was looking at. Beautiful, dilapidated, ramshackle rural places with sprawling, tangled gardens in France.

'You've seen what I can do,' the producers, Tim and Petra nodded, acknowledging my win on the Reality TV design show, *Time for a Change* and my brief stint presenting the home makeover show *You **Can** Make a Silk Purse!* I knew the cameras loved my direct attitude and there was no doubt I was a grafter. It was a new century, and the hunger was for cheap TV and real people.

'I want Meryl to be on the show too,' and now I played my trump card, 'I want this to be an aspirational show for all single mums out there. If we can do it, anyone can do it, no matter what your family looks like. Bollocks to the social stigma – I want it to be a celebration of my life with her.'

Tim had met Meryl. He liked kids. Didn't have any of his own despite his success and easy-going manner. At six, Meryl was a charming kid, bright, funny and good-looking. This was going to be a winner.

'So, to clarify, you're buying the property,' Tim said.

'Yep,' I replied, 'but there will be expenses for programme content obviously,' I added evenly. My father's money couldn't bank roll the whole show.

'I think this might work,' he said.

'I'd watch it,' I said grinning.

'Yes, but you watch everything,' Tim replied.

As I drove the small van into the gaping mouth of the ferry at Portsmouth with a perky Meryl strapped in the front enjoying the high view, a stone of doubt solidified in my stomach. My French was basic, I knew no one and my only holiday abroad had been a three-day French and History combined school trip to the Normandy beaches when I was fifteen. And that was grim.

We'd spent most of the time in an airless coach, yelling at each other, drawing rude pictures and swear words on the steamed-up windows, and drinking too much warm coke which made us want to pee. It had rained relentlessly, and no one had brought the right clothes expecting to bask in sunshine as it was June. We'd returned to Dover dejected, sleep deprived and hating the French for no reason other than teenage misery and frustration. It was a wash-out.

As Meryl climbed the steep iron stairs by my side, up out of the exhaust fume filled car deck, my anxiety increased. In my head I rattled off the list of jobs needing urgent attention on the house and married them with my skills. There were gaps – worrying gaps.

The house, hurriedly purchased while Tim and Petra were still keen on the show, was old, mainly nineteenth century. It was a long, low building with bedrooms in the eaves and a sizable chunk of land including an orchard and a small lake with a tiny shingle beach and an old wooden jetty, plus a scattering of outbuildings of varying sizes and in varying states of disrepair. Half-hearted renovations had been started and abandoned over the years. The roof needed attention and there was no proper heating, just open fires and wood burners. It was going to need a new septic tank, or fosse as the French called them, and the re-wiring, started in one half of the house, had to be completed. I could turn my hand to a lot, but I wasn't a qualified electrician or a roofer. What was I thinking taking this on?

Meryl instinctively tugged me towards the deck and as we stepped out into the salty wind that whipped my hair across my face, I yelped with surprise and delight and scooped up my daughter who looked a little startled. I'm not given to spontaneous acts of affection; I try but it doesn't come naturally. My mum is what some would call a cold fish and I think I might be too.

Anyway, on land, we'd been enjoying a warm afternoon but, up on the exposed deck, it was cold. Really chilly. We cuddled together and watched the solid, drab sea. 'I can't see France, Mummy,' Meryl shouted against the noise of the ferry's engine and the weather, her face was close to mine, her arm tight around my neck. I think she was aware of how surprisingly high we were above the ocean.

'We haven't set off yet, it's a long way away,' I said, still waiting for my default optimism to return and the lump in my stomach to dissolve.

'I'm hungry,' Meryl said, 'Are we going to see dolphins and whales and sharks in the sea?'

'No, babe. I don't think so. Let's go and get a croissant. We'll be having them every day from now on. And then let's find the film crew,' and I dropped Meryl down and thought the film crew will cheer me up and I don't need to think about things too deeply. It's an adventure. If it doesn't work out, we can always come home. The voice in my head didn't sound that convinced. The voice in my head sounded a bit babyish and fake. I shut it down and looked at Meryl instead. 'Croissant and hot chocolate to warm us up.' I smiled at her, and we moved back inside as the water around the ferry began to churn and froth as the engines roared ready for the off.

In reality, croissants from the local boulangerie were far too expensive to eat every day and I resorted to buying them in bags from the Intermarché. The other reality was the difficulty of the building work. Everything had to be cleared by the village mayor or Mairie and, even though I did my best to charm and chat my way through the bureaucracy, nothing moved as quickly as I would have liked. As I had plans to renovate the outbuildings, this constituted change of use and I wanted to put in French doors to access the garden from the kitchen, so this was an external change definitely requiring the Mairie's approval. With the refurbishment moving at a snail's pace, that first summer we spent more time lazing in the garden, half-heartedly digging a veg patch and neglecting to water it and mowing and cutting back the small orchard than we did in the house. We acquired some chickens and a belligerent goat we named Maurice who we moved around the garden pegged on a chain to keep the grass short and, having swept out and painted the rough plaster in one bedroom, we just lived in that together sharing a big old iron framed bed that was left in the house.

In truth, neither of us had ever known sunshine like it, days and days, back to back, very occasionally interrupted by a short, sharp deluge from a thunderstorm. So, we woke up each morning and walked out, barefoot, onto the already warm stone flags and stretched and yawned and tilted our heads up to the rising sun, closed our eyes and gave ourselves up to the day. It was glorious.

Meryl liked to paddle in the lake, but I didn't like the thought of what might be swimming in the brackish water. I couldn't step in beyond the first few inches, so I bought a large pop up pool and we lounged in that, sipping long, icy drinks with chunks of cucumber or handfuls of berries bobbing at the rim. We just got lazier and lazier, though Meryl read her books in there too, practically submerged or hanging over the side. I fetched vivid, grainy slices of grinning watermelon cold from the fridge which we gobbled greedily washing the pips off in the water, and our bodies darkened and our hair lightened, Meryl's almost to white and Tim called the crew back to the UK as there was nothing worth filming and scheduled a reshoot once all the applications were finalised. Secretly, I was relieved. I would walk barefoot through the cool, coarse grass in the orchard late at night and I couldn't believe the house was mine. I wanted that summer to last forever.

Mum and I had never had much money and I was used to eking it out. Even after I left school, work was never constant so I could make a little bit of cash go a long way. That summer, Meryl and I lived like peasants. Almost like hermits. We hardly left the house except for food and essentials. I blamed the heat and adjusting to the new way of life but really, I just didn't want to do anything. There was no rent to pay. My father's money was just about covering the bills and expenses and it was the first time I didn't have to worry or plan. I didn't have that sense of scrabbling for mine and Meryl's future. The only luxury were Meryl's books regularly shipped over by my mother.

I wasn't stupid; I knew it couldn't last.

'Enough's enough,' Tim said tetchily over the phone, 'The crew will be back in ten days. You need to email me your plans or we're going to re-think.'

I opted to pull my finger out and, as Meryl was going to be starting school soon anyway, the show swung into action.

The first series was moderately successful. Meryl was the star, however. There were endless shots of her backlit by the sun, hair a golden halo as she plucked apples from the lowest branches in the orchard or ran through the garden down towards the chickens or just read at the kitchen table or sat tucked up under a blanket on one of the old lawn chairs as the sun set. They made her look like a star. The house was slowly, slowly transformed and I got to know more locals and my French improved. It was never as good as Meryl's though.

Viewers loved the drama best. And it was an incident in the first few episodes of the first series, which bumped up the viewing figures significantly, and set me on my path.

I'd bought an old rowing boat at one of the Brocante or flea markets, clearly not that exciting in itself. Meryl loved it nonetheless and it was all I could do to keep her from sleeping in it. The footage of the renovation worked well. I sanded and sealed the hull and named it, The Good Ship Lollipop in a nod to my childhood love of Shirley Temple; I talked about her as I painted with meticulous precision the curling font in brilliant white and cobalt blue on the now gleaming boards of the prow. In the edit, they interweaved fuzzy footage of plump cheeked Shirley singing the song as the more beautiful Meryl looked on, eager to set sail in our modest little craft. It was divine.

Hair and make-up had a field day preparing us for Lollipop's maiden voyage. Usually, I was head to toe in ancient overalls or paint spattered T-shirts and shorts. I know I can look good, and I know you have to use that sometimes. I knew that Finbar, our location producer had to resist the temptation of pointing the camera at my arse as I climbed onto the roof to re point the chimney. I know the way the world works, and that I am aesthetically pleasing enough to merit being on TV all the time.

That day, we were dressed in Victorian costume, all crisp white frills and far too much lace and broderie anglaise. The get-up worked well, however. The nipped in waist and low neck made my naturally boyish physique, curvaceous and appealing. The white against my tanned skin was both dramatic and somehow alluring. This definitely had the makings of better TV – not just looking down the hole where the new septic tank was going to be sited. I'd already readied some delicious morsels for us to eat in an on-the-water picnic, more mouth-watering footage as I'm an accomplished cook. As the champagne bottle was smashed on the hull and we were launched giggling onto the glittering lake, it felt like the show was finally hitting the spot.

I rowed powerfully towards the centre of the lake with the crew in a rented inflatable dinghy with a small outboard motor in pursuit. 'We could invite someone to row for you,' Tim had suggested.

'This is about Meryl and me,' I'd replied sharply, 'I knocked down a partition wall with a sledgehammer last week. I think I can row a boat!'

The lake was calm, and the sun was high. I put up the lacy parasol, pulled up the lazily dripping oars and we settled back, top to toe, against the large stripy cushions I had sewn and stuffed to make the little boat more attractive and comfortable as the craft gently rocked us. We closed our eyes, and the only sound was the buzz of the dinghy circling us as the crew chased the best shots of this idyllic moment.

'What do you think, baba?' I said, and I opened one eye and peered at Meryl who was leaning over the side, lightly tracing the skin of the lake with the tips of her fingers.

'It's cold,' Meryl said, 'The water's cold, not like the paddling pool.'

'It's because it's deep. The sun has to do a bigger job to heat it up. There's not so much water in the pool.' I shut my eyes again and wondered how long we had before the dairy in the picnic started to spoil.

'Are there fish in here?' Meryl asked, leaning further out.

'Yes, probably loads.' I adjusted my position carefully trying not to be too obvious. My mic pack was digging in.

'Flora! I think we're going to re-shoot you rowing out to the middle again, think we'd be better on the other side, we'll get a better shot with the house in the background,' Finbar was on the loud haler. He bloody loved that loud haler. When I was up on the roof or in the trees, he took every opportunity to use it, all delivered in the grave tones of a hostage negotiator or as if he was talking down a jumper from a motorway bridge. 'Flora, think we could all do with a fifteen minute break, let's take a solid fifteen everyone.' 'Flora, could you angle your face towards us while you're speaking, if at all possible, haven't got the best shot down here, but we'll work with what we have obviously.' 'Flora, just noticed that hammer's right behind you if you step back, just be careful, okay?' 'Flora, Gerard is going to the village, do you need anything? It's really no trouble for him to get anything for you. Am I right Gerard?' 'Flora, did you see that bird? It was massive. Big and black. Not sure what is was. Some type of hawk perhaps?' And so on and so on. I suspected he'd liked to speak through the megaphone at all times. He certainly carried it with him everywhere.

Finbar generally loved to control everything, and I'd watched his real agony as he'd realised he couldn't quite manage the outboard motor and the loud haler as well. His beloved megaphone had won out however; he'd relinquished the boat to Pearl (general runner and dogsbody), presumably so he could bark at us relentlessly and ruin what I was hoping would be a blissful afternoon.

I was used to the re-shoots. Nothing was ever right with a first take. Or even if it was, they always wanted to do it again. And again. And again.

'Okay baba, we're going to go again. Back in and row out. That okay?' And I sat up slowly, pushing my hair back and smiling into the sun. It was likely they could use anything in the edit, so I was always conscious of the camera, even then.

At that moment, Meryl leaned further out, trying to peer deeper into the water, looking for an elusive fish no doubt, and her wide-brimmed hat tipped off her head. The shock made her recoil and, as she snatched to grab it, she caught the water instead creating an effective ripple and swirl to push the hat just beyond her reach. Climbing onto her knees and stretching further, she said the words, 'It's okay, Mummy, I can get it,' and I watched, feeling the smile freeze on my face as the equilibrium of the boat shifted as Meryl tipped the lip a fraction too far. The water was suddenly way too close to the side as Meryl stretched out across the lake, and rather than lean the other way to provide an opposing force, I jerked forward to snatch at my child who was now three quarters over the dark water, fingers reaching for the hat which continued to gently bob and glide away.

My movement was all it took. The boat tipped over, and, in an instant, I was underwater. Not in beautiful, clear, clean water either but murky, shockingly cold water. The opposite side of the boat slammed down hard on my shoulder as it upturned and pushed me fully under. My ridiculous dress billowed and tangled in my legs and up around my face and arms, as I kicked back up to the surface and towards where I thought Meryl had gone in.

Coughing and panting, I broke out of the water, to see the dinghy heading straight for me, then sharply turning away. The parasol was marooned a little way off and the picnic basket was slowly sinking, but as I turned and turned in the water, there was no sign of Meryl. I dived back down cursing the stupid dress, squinting through the green and brown, waiting for my eyes to adjust to the murk. My breath didn't last, and I was forced up again too quickly. As I broke the surface, the dinghy was by me, and someone dived in. 'Who?' I managed.

'Pearl,' Finbar replied as I gulped another lungful and pushed back down through the water. This time I knew I was deeper. The water was colder and darker, and I willed myself to calm down, to slow down, to properly look for Meryl. There was no sign of Pearl, but I caught a glimpse of something paler below me, and made for it.

Meryl was floating, suspended, like some ghostly apparition, her dress ballooning around her. I snatched at her, unable to look at her sleeping face and pulled up and up. At one point the effort became easier, and I looked back to see Pearl behind Meryl, helping. The hull of the dinghy was above us. I focussed on that and put my bursting lungs out of my mind.

When I allow myself to relive those moments, or when I dream about it, it's as if the lake is hundreds of feet deep. As deep and fathomless as one of the great lochs in Scotland, deep enough to conceal a monster. Or as deep as an ocean, as deep as the ocean we crossed to get to this place. In reality this must have been impossible. But even if it was only thirty or forty feet, that's some depth to get to.

We hauled Meryl into the dinghy, the fabric of the dress clinging onto her tiny frame, the lake water puddling and pooling around her in the bottom of the boat. We clambered in after her and we headed for shore with me administering the kiss of life as we went. Once at the small, wooden jetty I dragged my child up to my chest, like she was a sack of grain and squeezed her hard against me, Meryl's head and neck falling lifelessly over her shoulders. I felt a glug of warm water release from her body and laid her down.

'Come on, Meryl, you can do it,' I breathed at her as I started to breathe into her still mouth again. It was odd. I didn't feel any hysteria, or panic running though me. There was just a job to be done.

Finbar and Pearl watched and waited in silence. Shy filmed it all.

Meryl, pale and cold and rigid, at last spluttered back to life and, in no time, the paramedics and gendarmes arrived.

Rather than hug her to me, I slowly stood back to let the professionals do their work and stepped out of my soaked and filthy Victorian garb, leaving it in a soggy heap at my feet. I stood in my bra and knickers and looked on while the medics attended to my daughter. No one noticed. No one cared.

When the episode aired comments were mixed. Was this brave or tasteless? Exploitative or groundbreaking? Triggering or necessary? Whatever it was, it was great TV. It was real life. Life and death, unplanned.

Fortunately, or unfortunately depending on whose point of view you look at it from, Meryl survived the next series with no near-death incidents and the viewing figures tailed off a little. We limped through a third but what had really taken off was my social media. I was posting a lot, and was loving the next best thing after *Facebook*, the new place to be, *Instagram*.

I made the decision to move back to the UK just after Meryl turned nine. My plan was always for her to get through secondary school at home; besides by that time I'd had the idea for The Show, and I'd already pitched it to Tim.

9

Joyce

Everyone thinks it must be a dream to have a celebrity daughter. 'You must be so proud,' is the usual response when people find out. And then their beady eyes peer around my modest bungalow and I know they want to ask why I don't have more of Flora's money. 'Don't you get on?' Is what they want to say but what no one understands, including Flora, is that I'm content with my life and I don't need money poured all over it to make it better.

I don't really watch The Show.

I don't really like Reality TV as they call it. I prefer more serious programmes. I was never very interested in real life.

And as far as I'm concerned, the Flora on the television isn't really my daughter. I don't know who she is.

It was odd when they moved to France. I don't like the heat. I was never much attracted to travelling – lucky really as we could barely afford a holiday when Flora was growing up. I look at her life now, and Meryl's, and it is a different world to mine.

My parents were quiet people. My father was shop floor foreman at a small warehouse who reached up to sound the horn for the end of the shift one Thursday afternoon and dropped dead of a heart attack. I was twelve, nearly thirteen. My mother, a secondary school history teacher, soldiered on but was hit by a drunk driver on her way back from work two years later.

I arrived at a small children's home called Burnley Place in an area of town we didn't often visit the following day, as I had no other living relatives, having spent a bewildering night at a neighbour's. I kept going to the same school and I have no real horror stories to tell. I shared a room with two other younger girls. We were well fed and cared for by kind, youngish youth workers but, from the day my mother died, I had a sense of being untethered. I was no one's responsibility. Everyone who looked after me was paid to do it and even when they smiled at me, I felt like they were doing it because they were good people not because they particularly liked me. I became my own person, a sense of the solitary I had always possessed, settled over me, overwhelmed me really. I'm not sure I've ever been able to rid myself of it. Though now I don't know that I would want to.

There was a communal rec room in the home. It had a rickety table football, a couple of long wooden refectory tables and chairs for eating and board games or drawing for the younger kids and a large telly which always had the volume on at maximum, surrounded by three large, tattered sofas. No one bothered too much about what programme was on and there was always talking so the TV was a constant blaring buzzing that made all the chat and arguing even louder. It was a kind of house policy that we should all spend time together; they thought it was good for us. There was talk of a 'family ethos' and some of the youth workers believed that. Looking back, I think it made supervising us a bit easier and that's okay. If we were all up in our rooms, how could they know what was going on?

I hated rec room time. The noise, the blaring telly. The boys wrestling with each other, winding each other up. The whispering behind the hands of the girls or the blatant shrieking taunting. I wanted to do my homework. I had wanted to go to university. I was clever. In the home, no one realistically had time to encourage school or its value.

One way or another, none of the kids had had an easy time and there was always something for the workers to unpick or deal with so who could blame them if they weren't on top of providing quiet space for the one or two who wanted to hand in their work instead of getting yet another detention.

Before my parents died, Mum and I would sit end to end on our polished oval dining room table and do our homework together before tea. She would splay all the exercise books open at the right page first and have them in a pile at her left and then, as she worked through them methodically, an increasingly large pile of closed books would appear at her right hand. She marked with her head tilted a little to the right too, and a small smile on her face, like she enjoyed it, not like it was a chore. Even when she tutted at the state of a particularly dog eared book, or there was a quick progression from left to right indicating missing work, the good humour never left her face.

I would sit at the other end and work away at my tasks, stretching my tasks out as long as I could, just to stay with my mum until the last possible minute. There was nowhere else I wanted to be. After tea, there would be reading together or sometimes a game or television at the weekend, but Dad was there then. I liked the time when it was just the two of us. I especially liked when I had history homework, and I could pretend to be stuck on it. Then she would come round to my end of the table and leaf through my pristine exercise book and pull up a closer chair and explain the answer to my question in far more detail than was necessary, and I would sit and gaze at her and think that she was the cleverest person alive.

At Burnley Place, you had to watch out all the time. I never felt I could relax. This might have been me rather than them. It just felt like something was always on the verge of happening. Something out of my control, obviously; I was just a child.

Years later, after Flora left home and I was sitting reading a book one afternoon in early spring, I realised that even though the home was called a home, I never really felt like it was. For me. I never felt At Home. I don't know if any of us did. I felt like my emotional bags were permanently packed there. Like I was on a platform waiting for a train, unsure of my destination. Like I say, untethered.

Then I met Robert.

I never made it to university.

I got a job in a shoe shop instead and moved into a bedsit with a damp patch in the ceiling and frightening scrabbling, scratching noises under the floorboards.

Robert came in one day to buy a pair of brogues.

I should have known then that it wouldn't end well.

10

Flora

'The health visitor said it was a blocked duct. That's why I haven't done anything about it. To be honest, I tried to avoid too many conversations with her because she made me feel so guilty about not breast feeding, but it just wasn't for me. I mean I fed Meryl. For bloody months. It's not like I haven't done my bit. She was nearly two when I stopped.' The consulting room is small, and Shy is squashed up against the wall to get a good enough angle. Marsha is outside with Treasure.

The GP is young, a lot younger than me. 'How old is baby now?' he asks, fingers poised over the keyboard, ready to add to my notes.

'Treasure,' I say pointedly, 'is coming up to six months,' and I smile back at the camera as a reflex.

He turns his full attention to me. 'Well Ms Tatton, you're very low risk for breast cancer; you've had a child in your younger years, you breast fed, you're a non-smoker, you're under fifty and there's no history of hormonally driven cancers in your family as far as you're aware though we're not so clear about your paternal side, are we? As the health visitor said, if there is a lump, it's more than likely a blocked duct and will just dissipate over time. Now let's have a look, shall we? Top things off, including bra and lie on the couch please.'

I move confidently to the couch as the doctor briskly washes his hands.

Shy and I have agreed beforehand that all filming will be non-explicit, but everything verbal will be recorded.

I catch Shy focusing the camera on a rather dull sculpture sitting next to some books above the doctors' desk. It is abstract, a fluid shape with an oval hole in the centre, a matt, rusty red glaze. It's a good choice for a neutral backdrop.

'Can you just sit on the edge of the bed there and just let me look to see if there's anything noticeable?' The doctor sounds relaxed and calm. Though he is young, his tone implies he's done this many times before.

'Sure,' I reply, and I look up at the plastic rings holding the curtain in place to stop thinking about this young man staring at my breasts. I resist the temptation to count them. I have a tendency to do that. Count things, that is.

'Have you noticed any changes visibly? Any alterations in shape? Puckering? Dimples? Or discharge?'

'No, nothing.' I'm relaxed too, my voice light.

'Arms up above your head please, like this. Perfect. Thank you. Okay. Let's lie you down.'

He cups my elbow to help me even though there's nothing really wrong with me. I'm pretty sure Shy will be able to hear the thin paper sheet on the bed shifting. A slight creak of a modern spring. The doctor's feet shifting position. It won't be completely dead TV.

'So where do you think you can feel the lump?' he asks, remaining calm and relaxed.

'It's here,' my hand goes straight to my right breast, just under the nipple. 'I first felt it in the shower. I wasn't sure at first, but it hasn't gone away. That's when I mentioned it to the midwife, and she said about the duct. I think it's grown though. I even wondered whether it might be infected, perhaps.'

The doctor palpates my breast and stares unseeing at the wall. There is silence. A long silence as his hands explore my arm pit and up around my collar bone and my other breast. He returns to the lump.

'So, when did you first feel it?' The doctor's voice is quieter.

'Oh, let me think, well Treasure must have been about six weeks old. Maybe less. I'm not sure.' I'm still sounding bright, but I feel a slight shift in the doctor's attitude. Like he's really concentrating. It's as if all the energy in the room, no the whole building, has been sucked into his hands. I hope it's some kind of healing energy.

'And she's six months now,' the doctor says.

'Yes,' I answer contentedly and shift my mind from the troublesome lump to Treasure's sweet face.

'I see,' he says, 'Well that's quite some size, isn't it Ms Tatton.'

'Is it?' and I feel and sound breathy all of a sudden, 'I have no experience of this sort of thing. Unlike you.'

The doctor takes my elbow again and I sit up. He is frowning.

'Okay, pop your things back on and let's assess,' and the doctor slips out past the curtain and back to the sink.

When I come back out Shy is refocusing onto the keyboard as the doctor starts to type and I slip back into the patient chair.

He turns to face me, and his demeanour has unmistakably altered. It is impossible, but his more serious demeanour seems to have aged him. 'I'm going to refer you for a scan and biopsy, Flora,' he says gently.

'Okay,' I reply slowly.

'It's a fourteen-day target, meaning you should be seen within two weeks ideally. It's an urgent referral.' He is looking directly at me.

'So you think it's something serious?' I say not quite taking in what he's saying.

'You'll have to wait for the tests, Flora. They'll want to do a mammogram, an ultrasound and a biopsy before anything can be confirmed.'

'I notice you didn't answer my question.' I try to smile, I really do.

'Where are you going now, Flora? What are you doing?' He looks up at Shy. 'Did you drive Flora here? Can you drive?'

'Er no, but I can. I mean, sure, I don't usually, but I can. Drive. Usually I film, I always film,' Shy mumbles.

The doctor turns back to me. 'Maybe just go somewhere, get a cup of coffee, take a beat, if you have to drive. You've had a shock.'

'Have I?' I say. I try to sound in control, but it feels like things are unravelling.

'And remember we're here, once you get your results, if you need anything, or you don't understand anything you can always get back in touch with us.' The doctor is onto the keyboard and fixed on the screen. 'I'm going to do the letter right now. You'll get something through in the post in the next few days.'

When I stand up, I catch Shy properly looking at me. I must look like shit if his face is anything to go by.

We walk back up the washed out blue, generic corridor. 'What just happened?' he says to me.

'I think he was telling me I've got cancer,' I answer staring straight ahead.

the.real.flora.tatton

daily contemplation: Not every day is a good day but there is something good in every day.

Liked by **bellydancerbabe** and **26,942,643 others**

nowayback
Cannot stop crying. Lost my great gran to cancer. Bringing it all back.#lifeisshit

fuckeduphuman
holy hell did not see this coming I mean is this a wind up? Can't be true right? #fakenews #conspiracy #nowayjosé

bobbyboombastic
sending power and love across the ocean

1974999
That doc looked like he didn't even finish school yet. It's no big deal. You'll be fine Flo. #survivor #scaretactics

lilpiggywenttomarket
makes you think about the importance of a regular breast exam. Have made appointment to get checked out today. You may have saved my life. #tearsofgratitude

cheesywotsups
Heart breaks to see this. #somuchloveforyou

11

Meryl

Baby's first Christmas is supposed to be magical, isn't it? Not one where hygiene is paramount because the mother is undergoing chemotherapy; not one where you have to be careful not to get the sharps bin in the background of Christmas lunch photos from Mother's daily steroid injections which she has to have to stop the chemo from killing her; not one where Mum has to drag herself out of bed to open the presents and can't wait to crawl back again at the earliest opportunity. No cracker hat for Mama over her bald head (far too cold and flimsy); no Christmas turkey served when Mother is in the room as the smell induces at best a dry heave, at worst vomiting and, as even water tastes vile, there's little point in her attempting to actually eat any. Besides, her mouth ulcers make anything other than sucking on an ice lolly or a slice of pineapple almost unbearable. No, poor little Treasure's first Christmas is far from ideal.

Interestingly, viewing figures have never been higher.

'You can't keep going with The Show, Mum,' I had pointlessly argued as Milk had filmed 'the family' round the kitchen island the day after we got the biopsy results.

'Of course, we bloody can, Meryl,' Flora had flared back at me, 'I've made a commitment. This is like a marriage – for better, for worse, in sickness and in health. I can't just stop because life gets difficult. That's the point, isn't it? I'm sharing everything.'

'For fuck's sake Mum, it's not just about *you*, is it?' I looked down at my hands gripping the marble top, my fingernails were white. I didn't want to be angry with her. I wanted, no, I *longed* to hug her, to fold her into me, to wrap my arms around her and never let her go but instead my shoulders were rigid, and I held on to that worktop as if my anger might cause me to fly up to the ceiling like some malevolent spirit to hiss and spit on the assembled company and cast vicious curses on the lot of them.

'What do you mean?' Flora seemed genuinely surprised. She was unbelievable.

'You're my mum and Treasure's mum and you're going to have to go through this horrible treatment and we don't even know what ... And we're going to have to do all this with ... Holy hell, I can't believe I'm having to explain to you how fucked up this is.' Milk would be able to see that I was fighting back tears; I never cried publicly. Why couldn't my own mother sense it? Why couldn't she let it go?

'But that's the whole point, Meryl. Think of all those kids who are going through this alone. You can help them. You have the opportunity to share your feelings and connect with them and let them feel like someone else understands what they're going through. That's what it's about for me. There's so many women who are diagnosed with breast cancer. Bloody hell, so many of us will get some form of it. One in two, in fact. Isn't that what the statistics are? We're showing people, we're giving people the chance to see inside the reality of one family's journey through this show. In real time. No editing, no soft soaping. It's real life. That's what we've always done.

'I think it's going to be a comfort to some people, an education to others. Some people won't watch and that's fine too. And yes, my experience won't be the same as everyone else's but if it helps one family come to terms with it, it's worth it.'

The tears were shining in her eyes by the end of her speech. I'd be prepared to bet everything I had that Milk had helped her shape the words via the WhatsApp group the night before, I'd seen them work up moments like this so many times over the years. To her credit, it sounded spontaneous and from the heart. No. Wait, is that to her credit? Why couldn't this moment be real? She'd just told me she had cancer for fuck's sake.

'You're full of shit,' my voice was low and menacing, 'All you care about is the ratings. Your ego won't allow you to stop. You disgust me.'

Flora gasped. She hated any reference to ratings or viewing figures live on air. She wanted the façade to be maintained at all times, like *The Truman Show*. I knew she would have been uncomfortable about even having this conversation - it would all be far too emotional for her, but she knew it would come up, she knew I would push for something more.

'You're upset, Meryl,' Flora changed tack, 'That's understandable. Anyone would be. This is a momentous event for any teenager to process so, of course, you're going to lash out. And why wouldn't you lash out at me? This isn't something you can control. None of us can. We just have to get through it,' she paused and inhaled as if to steady herself, 'together.' What a bullshitter.

'Can't you be real for ten seconds? This is incredible? I mean, is this all in the script? This was not in the plan. Okay, a bit of redesigning your bedroom and arguing with your personal trainer is one thing, but going through *cancer*? Mum! It's a horror story. It's ghoulish. It's not what people want to see.' I felt myself looking round the room for objects to hurl at the cameras. Yes, there are times when you forget you're being filmed but other times the phrase rabbit in the headlights makes total sense.

'Why don't we let them decide, eh?' Flora was trying to sound light but there was a waver in her voice. I knew I was right; murky, seeping, twisting, terrifying cancer snaking into her beautifully curated, pastel-coloured harmonious life was not the plan.

She wouldn't relent though, and I felt my face set into stone cold fury. 'Okay, do what you like. You always do. But I'm out. Don't expect anything from me. I'm not participating. This is sick. Fucking warped. And Tim needs sectioning too, allowing this to be broadcast. You're fucking weird.'

As I started to leave the kitchen, my mother had turned to the comfort of the silent, blank camera, visibly composing herself to close the scene. 'I don't want any of you to be distressed by the path I have to follow over the coming months. If you need to take a break, I completely understand. Ultimately the treatment, the surgery, the recovery is something I have no choice but to do alone.' Flora glanced deliberately over to me as I hesitated at the door, 'But I will share my thoughts and feelings with you, if you want to check in on me from time to time. I'll be here, I'll show up. Every day. Like I've said before, and I will keep on saying, no matter what, I made a promise to share my life with you, all of you, so, I will be here, through thick and thin.' She managed a brave smile and turned back to the kitchen counter and reached for her phone.

I was in the hallway as she started on the first step guiding her loyal fans along the pathway. She managed it seamlessly, no hesitation.

'First adjuvant chemotherapy session at the start of the week, so I'm off to the clinic now for blood tests and so on to check I'm fit for it. Adjuvant means it's designed to shrink the tumour pre-surgery, by the way. Come along but make sure you use the blur out button if you're squeamish. I'm getting weighed too. That'll be fun, won't it? I think we'll stop at the drive-through and pick up some coffee. Think the pumpkin spice is in for autumn.'

The whole episode only served to see engagement increase, however. Flora was perceived as the victim and messages of support flooded in on every social media platform - #ungratefulbrat was attached to me at every opportunity and ratings rocketed. It was fucking great.

Three months later and Mum has faded fast; the chemo has been punishing but I've stuck to my word absenting myself from conversations and only interacting with Treasure and Morag. It hasn't been easy but what choice did I have?

The typical Christmas hysteria that Flora usually manages to generate has been noticeably absent. She didn't make it downstairs to decorate the tree; we could hear her puking as Marsha put the old angel Flora had treasured since I was a baby on the top.

Yeah, it's really been a merry fucking Christmas.

12

Flora

What I couldn't fathom was how Meryl never appreciated the cause and effect of *The Flora Show*. It was our bread and butter. My career had provided Meryl's school fees, holidays, her first car which she was currently enjoying, her extensive wardrobe, the ability to develop and pursue any hobby in which she expressed even the slightest interest. In short, she had a damn good life. Her whining because, for example, she had to do a re-take or two opening her Christmas presents or be told what her birthday gifts were in advance, so the reactions were right for the camera, were a small price to pay for everything that my career path delivered. Yes, our privacy was compromised but oh how I wished I could transport her to my childhood where day to day, me and my mother scrimped and budgeted and eked out a scrawny piece of meat to three or four meals and then boiled the bones for soup and stock; where we trudged every Sunday morning to the launderette to complete the weekly wash as we couldn't afford a washing machine. Meryl's clothes disappeared from her bedroom floor where she discarded them and reappeared clean and pressed in her wardrobe thanks to the housekeeping talents of Morag.

No point listing any of this to Meryl though. She would just throw it all back in my face. 'I'd rather live like that any day. I hate this life. I hate the cameras. I hate you,' was how our spats usually ended.

Christmas is not going well. I'd failed to wrap the Christmas presents, finding the fresh inky smell of the wrapping paper such an assault on my senses I spontaneously puked into the wastepaper basket. This was worse than morning sickness; at least with that there was a baby at the end of it. As I lie like a limp rag on my bed, bones aching now as the chemo has moved on from my soft tissue to ravage my cartilage and skeleton, I try to remember that I am going through this to stay alive and that I won't always feel like this.

'Do you want me to put on some music?' Milk is at the foot of the bed. The house is quiet.

'Where is everyone?' I ask.

'Treasure's gone down. It's past eight. Meryl's out. Gone to meet Tyler I think.'

'I missed the whole day,' my voice is barely more than a whisper. I hope the mics can pick it up, I can't be bothered to raise it any higher.

'There will be next year,' Milk says gently.

'Doesn't feel like it,' I sound tiredly truculent.

'Come on, it's Christmas, less of that. Do you want something to eat? Some soup? What about I ask Morag to bring up some of her split pea soup, eh? You love that.'

'No. Nothing. I can't face any of it. I think I need another adjustment on my antiemetics. I'm not keeping anything down again. I feel like crap.' I roll over and look down towards Milk, wiping my hair back from my face. It's true. I can't remember the last time I managed to eat anything substantial, and my stomach is sore from the constant throwing up. Maybe I've picked up a bug.

'I can call the helpline now. We don't want things to get out of hand,' Milk rests his one hand on my foot and with his other I see him surreptitiously texting. My guess is it's Shy.

'I dunno. I can't decide.' I close my eyes. It's too hard to make a decision and every time we call the helpline there's always an intervention of some sort.

'Try and sip a little juice. It might perk you up. And then I'm going to check your temp, okay?' Milk moves to the bedside table and offers me the tepid diluted apple juice that sits there. I can't drink plain water anymore – it tastes revolting, and currently, apple juice is the only flavour I can manage. Bland. Fresh. I sit up with the awkwardness of the bedridden and chronically fatigued and manage a meagre mouthful. I see Milk take in my dry skin and cracked lips. I know my eyes are shadowed and sunken. Not a scrap of make-up today. No make-up for days and days.

He sits carefully next to me on the bed as if even that act could cause me terrible pain, and hands me the thermometer to place in my ear. I roll my eyes, but I obey.

Shy appears with his handheld camera and immediately takes in the scene. Milk takes out his phone again ready to dial the on-call doctor and places it on the nightstand.

There is silence and stillness as I hold the thermometer, waiting for the tiny beep. The house is seldom so quiet. Every other year we would be celebrating, friends over, family, games and drink, and shouted quips and laughter until the early hours but this year, the house is holding its breath, tense, on edge, trying to hold firm whilst under siege.

Milk takes the thermometer. 'It's up, Flora. I'm calling, okay?' He makes it sound like I have to agree before he acts but he's made a decision. Shy texts Meryl but we all know that whether she replies is not a foregone conclusion.

When we arrive at the hospital, there is already a gathering at the entrance. I've had a couple of admissions, nothing too serious and to be expected but each time the fans have shown up. As I step out of the car, the shouts of support are a barrage in the glaring artificial light. Involuntarily, I duck and squint against it and Shy thinking I'm collapsing, grabs me round the waist, 'You okay, Flo?' he asks.

'I'm fine,' I pull myself back up and take a breath, 'Just a bit of a shock. The noise.'

Thankfully the hospital has erected a temporary barrier to keep everyone at bay though this is not exactly convenient on Christmas Day evening when they only have a skeleton staff. Better this however than being inundated with a mass of people who apparently have nowhere else to be on the happiest day of the year than a hospital to briefly glimpse a sick woman and bellow their good wishes to her in the hopes that they might feature on a TV show.

Once I'm set up on the ward with an IV to replenish my fluids and some antibiotics to fight off an infection that's brewing, I perk up. Shy films the crowd out of the window; the messages flood in as people tag themselves and achieve fleeting fame.

'It's lovely of them to leave their Christmases to come to check up on me,' I smile weakly.

'It really is,' Milk agrees, but I catch him making a 'loser' sign at Shy who, to his credit, raises an eyebrow at him.

Shy pans back round to me, taking in the room as he does so, a nice establishing shot, 'Are you feeling better yet?' Milk asks.

'Much better,' I say bravely.

'Really?' he presses.

'Well, a little bit better. I feel happier to be here. I need to be here. Just need a bit of extra help at the moment,' I turn to camera, 'You've seen how much I've been puking haven't you? So sorry everyone. Not what you want to see, is it? Not what I want to be sharing. Too much, isn't it? Feel like my insides have been grated tbh. But I'm here now to get a bit of care and a reset. Back home really soon I think,' and I manage a wink, which without my eyelashes and my usual sparkly eyes I'm sure probably looks a bit odd, but the sentiment is there. Don't think I'll do it again though. On the other hand, this is why I have so many followers, the honesty, the open access, and, let's face it, the oversharing.

I shut my eyes and think about the millions of people who have witnessed the vomit that has come out of my body, have seen me physically puke live over and over. And they still keep watching.

Weird.

the.real.flora.tatton

daily contemplation: Just because someone carries it well doesn't mean it isn't heavy.

Liked by **bellydancerbabe** and **1,201,409 others**

nowayback
no need to be lonely this xmas - thinking of you always

fuckeduphuman
Flora will keep on fighting #tough #powerful #cancercandoone

bobbyboombastic
sending seasons greetings across the ocean

1974999
Watch out for mono and MRSA. Why are hospitals so minging? #germwarfare

lilpiggywenttomarket
you'll feel better soon keep on fighting #weneedyouflora@theflorashow

cheesywotsups
you are my whole world. take my heart. fight beautiful Flora.#keepstrong

13

Meryl

I'm lying on Tyler's bed and looking at the patterns on the cracked plaster ceiling. Tyler has not bothered to celebrate Christmas. 'When you've never had a Christmas, it's no big deal,' he chuckles offering me the excessively big bag of tortilla chips he is intending to work his way through.

'Must have been crap,' I hate that I feel uncomfortable when Tyler talks about his childhood. A childhood with a young addict mum, a squat, living in a car sometimes, in shelters, finally a grim flat, a whole group of users, in a high rise.

'It's alright. No big deal. Just got used to it. At least we didn't have to go to school the next day and write the 'What I got from Santa' shit stuff for the teachers.' Tyler was the youngest of three. 'You had a while to work out what you were going to make up. I love this bit,' He's watching *Die Hard*, and Bruce Willis is about to blow up a lift shaft and save the day. Tyler's TV screen is cracked in one corner, but he doesn't care. There was no TV growing up. 'Nothing ever happens up there, does it?' he reasons. When I look at it, that's all I can see, the creeping split, the fissure, the imperfection.

'Where's your Dad, Mare? You in touch?' Tyler asks. It's a surprise. We don't have too many conversations like this. I can count on one hand the number of times I've spoken out loud about my dad.

'Dunno. Never met him.' I start to count the grimy plaster swirls, each thin crust highlighted by Tyler's bare bulb.

'Same. You ever think of tracking him down? Especially now.' Tyler has a mouthful of chips. He casually wipes the spray from his mouth that's spattered onto his chest, onto the sheets.

'What do you mean, especially now?' I can hear my voice harden.

'With your Mum ill n' that,' Tyler is only half aware of what he's saying, *Die Hard* has him transfixed.

'Do you mean she's going to croak so I'd better find another parent to replace her?' I'm up to 138 circles. I might have counted a couple of them twice.

'Yeah, I guess so. I mean, it's better if you've got someone around who's got your back, innit? Woah! Love that! Go John, go John!' and he whoops as the telly flashes with explosions and gunfire and tiny anonymous silhouetted people fly through the air.

'What happened to *your* dad?' I deflect, trying to control my anger. There's nowhere obvious for me to go if I piss Tyler off as well.

'Dunno now. He was in prison at first. That's what I was told,' Tyler shrugs. 'They both were. You know addicts. Nicking and that I think. Or possession. Not sure. No one to ask now really.' He crams in more chips.

'Right. Sounds rough. Would you want to see him? Now I mean?' I've lost count of the circles, imagining a life with addicts for parents. The chaos and insecurity. The anxiety and jittering constant misery.

'Nah. He's a stranger, ain't he? What's he gonna tell me anyway? Probably want *me* to provide for *him*. Too much aggro, you know what I'm saying.'

'So why do you think I'd want to know my dad?' I say, my voice spiky, 'I mean as far as I'm concerned, he's not much more than a sperm donor.'

'Okay, don't know your story. Perhaps he'd want to be more than that. You know. With your mum n'all.'

'Stop fucking implying she's going to die, you stupid fucking arsehole' I sit up and stare at Tyler.

'Shit, Mare, like, sorry, I wasn't saying that. I was just saying she was sick, and you could do with, I dunno another… I mean, like, someone who could… who might, like another adult, that's all. I wasn't saying she was going to die. She's a fucking warrior. If anyone can beat this, it's her.'

'Okay. Just as long as we're clear on that then,' and I decide to relax back on the bed and start to count again, trying to put the image of my mother's grey face, so monochrome against the brash table decorations, across from me at the dinner table earlier in the day.

My phone buzzes. It's Shy telling me she's been admitted. Nothing life-threatening but Flora would like to see me. I would like to see my mother too if I could do so in private. I roll over onto my stomach and reach for the bag of chips.

'How many times have you watched this film?' I ask Tyler.

'Loads,' he grins, 'Best Christmas film ever.'

14

Joyce

There are several sub-groups on *The Flora Show*, fan hubs and access via separate cameras that contribute to the success and revenue streams of my daughter's whole set-up. For example, Flora's walk-in wardrobe is on an interactive camera so I believe you can click on links to look at each item in more detail and, if you wish, buy it for yourself. The same goes for Treasure's clothes and nursery items, though Meryl has now banned camera access to her outfits. There was a rather difficult situation that Meryl found most trying with Meryl lookalikes. They bought up everything she wore and congregated at the bottom of the drive waiting to catch a glimpse of her on the way to school. In some ways it might not have been so bad if they'd all been Meryl's age, but some were middle-aged women or boys or old men. Meryl began having nightmares and the links were cut and Meryl began to customise her clothes and rarely wore anything more than once. The Merylikes are still going strong, but they have to work harder at it.

There's also a permanent feed in the fridge and a matching group obsessed with what the household eat and what is going to go past its sell-by date. A link takes you to any new purchases as well, so you can immediately grab anything *The Flora Show* inhabitants are consuming. As a result, food and beverage suppliers will go to extreme lengths to get their new products into that fridge and endorsed by Flora or, even better by her formidable housekeeper, Morag.

Morag is Scottish, now just into her sixties, she has worked with Flora since Meryl was little and they were in France, the second series I think, and had taken on the role of housekeeper with relish. She is a magnificent cook, as, to be fair is Flora, but her real strength is in managing the house, the removal of stains, the organisation of tasks and objects, the care of furniture and soft furnishings as well as being a talented gardener, flower arranger, jam and bread maker. She is briskly efficient and extraordinarily energetic and can turn her hand to anything. She is also a fount of knowledge and, as such has a large fan base and separate online presence from the kitchen or her staff annexe via the handheld, where she presents regular little tutorials or bake-alongs much to the delight of her fans, of which I count myself one.

Whilst Flora tacitly tried to restrict Shy and Milk in front of the camera, keenly aware of their youth and musculature or possibly deliberately teasing the audience with the glimpses they managed to steal of these beautiful younger men, with Morag she was not in any way threatened and they often teamed up together. Morag is one of those women who has always seemed much older than she is. Her stolid little body, short wiry grey hair and traditional, somewhat old-fashioned dress sense is no competition for Flora's glamour. Morag favours tweeds in winter and heavy cotton, floral print tea dresses in summer. She almost always wears an apron of some sort, sometimes a full house coat. She favours wellingtons for any outdoors activity and her only jewellery is her wedding ring from her husband Sandie, lost in a car accident in his early thirties, about whom she very rarely speaks.

'I've been giving some thought to the stain in this rug,' she will start in her soft Edinburgh brogue as she reaches for bicarbonate of soda and lemon juice rather than any fancy cleaning product.

'Someone's put down a glass and it's left a nasty water mark on this wood, so I'm going to lift this out with an iron and some newspaper,' she'll frown into the camera, her pleasant face scrubbed clean, not a scrap of make-up in sight and the magic will begin.

'There's a nasty snag in this garment and I'm going to rectify this with a wee bit of pulling at the threads a little lower. Just easing the snag away. Takes a bit of time but at the end of it you won't know it was ever there. Once I've steamed it out, it'll be good as new,' and she'll peer with concentration and, even though it is menial, it is utterly absorbing.

Perhaps for viewers it is seeing all the possible solutions to the blights in their lives; perhaps it is her no-nonsense approach. It doesn't matter that they sit on their sofas, staring at their screens and never bother to deal with their stains and snags and blemishes, Morag is a hit. A comfort.

When I come to stay, I have to admit, I spend more time with Morag than I do with Flora and, for some reason, the viewers love this, so I am told.

'I'm just finishing the turkey pie, we'll have it with bubble and squeak,' Morag calls to me as I come back through to the kitchen from the downstairs guest suite.

'Have you added tarragon again?' I ask hopefully as I stack a few stray plates in the dishwasher.

'I have. I managed to get some of the French variety growing in the garden last year and it's thrived. I froze some in October before it wilted in the first frost. Just taken some out and chucked it in.'

'Delicious. Would never have thought of it but I'm a plain cook, me. Shall I start on the bubble and squeak?' When I am with Morag at least I can keep myself busy. With Flora there is never actually anything to do. We are supposed to just 'chat'; I mean what on earth do we have to talk about?

'Why don't you pour us a wee tot? There's no sign of anyone yet. No word that she's been discharged even. I'll no put this in until we get word.' Morag wipes down the marble work surface and moves the impressive pie over to the fridge.

I fetch whisky and tumblers. We both love a dram and usually wait until after dinner but there's no guarantee the pie will even make it into the oven. The last two days we've prepared food and then settled for cheese and biscuits or turkey sandwiches neither of us with much of an appetite. We have, however, managed to make a serious dent in the whisky.

We settle by the unlit log burner. 'Shall I light it?' Morag asks as we stare at the smoke-stained glass door.

'Don't bother on my account. This house is far too warm,' I answer, 'I usually only have the heating on to dry the towels in the morning and then to take the chill off around teatime. Seems a waste to have it on all the time. What happened to putting on an extra jumper?' I glug my whisky cheerfully. I know Flora's not well, but this really has been the most enjoyable Christmas I've had for years.

'It's the wean. You've got to keep Treasure warm, can't freeze a baby, can you?' Morag smiles.

'I never had the heating on all the time when Flora was tiny. I couldn't afford it. And she survived,' I huff, 'I mean, it's stifling in here. Yesterday, I had to open the back door and go and stand outside. Does no one ever open a window? It can't be healthy.'

'I suppose I've acclimatised. And Flora's ill too, remember? She can't maintain her temperature at the moment. Gets freezing in minutes, seconds even and takes forever to warm up again.'

I raise an eyebrow. 'I'll give you that. Hospitals are always far too hot, aren't they. Even now after austerity. Everyone just lying around all the time, they have to be kept warm. I'll just remember to pack summer clothes next time,' and I have another swig.

'And maybe we should lay off this stuff, Joyce, alcohol raises your body temperature you know.' Morag opens her denim blue eyes wide, deadly serious.

'Oh Morag, now you're being ridiculous,' I frown, and we laugh as I reach for the bottle to top up our glasses.

We settle back into the comfy chairs and stare ahead. It's not often we are quiet in each other's company despite our different upbringings. In Morag's company, I can relax and chat in a way I just don't find easy with my daughter. Morag and I have shared stories of our youth, past loves, swapped favourite recipes and books, dug out holiday snaps to show each other, baked bread and forked over the borders and planted bulbs, side by side. I know we both look forward to seeing the other and miss one another when my visits come to an end.

Secretly, I know in my heart that if Morag wasn't in the house, I wouldn't come to stay as often as I do. I have little interest in my surly elder granddaughter – she has barely uttered a civil syllable this visit – and, whilst my younger one is fine to dandle on my knee, the ever-present nanny hovering in the background as if I've never dealt with an infant, is tiresome and a battle I can't be bothered to take on. Yes, without Morag to natter to over a whisky, I would stay put at home and leave them all to it.

'Is there cancer in your family, Joyce? Or is Flora the first?' I love how direct Morag is. There is no beating about the bush; she has a question, she just asks it and, if I don't want to answer, I just say so and Morag doesn't care a jot.

'None that I know of. Can't speak to her father's side. Or I can't remember. Seems like another life when I was married to him. I do remember a poorly auntie, but I was young and she seemed ancient at the time. I don't think I paid attention to what she had. You don't, do you at that age?' I look at Morag who is staring intently over my right shoulder towards the kitchen.

'Oh heavens, it's not another spider is it, Morag? You're such a capable person. It's hard to believe that spiders are your Achilles' heel,' and I turn to look, a glance really. I have had to deal with everything on my own –

wasps, mice, even the occasional rat. A spider is no big deal.

It is with some surprise that I see not a spider but a man standing in the doorway of the utility room. He's dressed in black. A zip up jacket, hooded. It's hard to see his face. I can see he's tensed, ready for action.

I turn back to Morag. 'Well this is interesting,' I say calmly, 'Would you like a whisky, dear?' I raise my voice to the intruder.

'There's a glass in the cabinet. Plenty in the bottle. Come and join us. You've probably got about three minutes before you're rumbled,' Morag joins in.

I hear him step into the kitchen and the cabinet door open. Glasses chink against each other. A good sign I think.

'You've done well to get into the house. We haven't had anyone achieve that for a long time. Good lad,' Morag says picking up the bottle and meeting my eye.

'You'll know that Flora's still in the hospital if you've come to visit her,' I take up the thread and the man appears in front of us, a crystal glass in his hand.

'Why don't you take a seat, pet?' Morag indicates the chair next to her, 'You look a bit done in.'

He does indeed. He's young, late-twenties maybe older. Thick, blonde hair flops forward under the hood and, as his cloudy blue eyes focus on the whisky going into the glass, his skinny, greasy-jeaned knee begins to jiggle, and he nibbles at the skin on the corner of his grubby finger nail. He nods a thank you and takes a polite sip.

'Have you had a good Christmas?' I ask as if it is perfectly normal to be sharing a drink with a potentially dangerous stranger after dark in my celebrity daughter's house.

He shakes his head and stares at his glass.

'Us neither,' Morag sounds matter of fact, 'You'll have seen what's been going on. Not much reason for a Holly Jolly Christmas this year.'

We look at each other and then at the man who is furtively staring around the room. At least there is no obvious sign of a weapon.

'Did you come by for anything in particular? Would you want a signed photo? Or a T-shirt maybe? They're lovely quality. Wash super, you know,' Morag tries again.

The man glares at her.

'How rude! We haven't introduced ourselves. I'm Joyce, Flora's mother and this is Morag. And you are?' I sound like I'm coaxing a reluctant animal, my voice low and lilting, all its usual hard edges evaporated with the arrival of the unwanted guest. I hardly recognise myself.

We watch and wait. The man says nothing.

'How did you get in? Must have been quite difficult,' I try, hoping the man's ego will want to make him share, make for a bit of to and fro and a connection of sorts no matter how frail. 'So much security and the cameras. You must be quite the expert. Not your first time breaking in somewhere would be my guess!'

For a moment he looks horrified and then takes a bigger gulp of whisky. His voice is tentative, 'There weren't many there. Guys. I just ducked in. With the delivery truck.'

We both respond with amazement and incredulity. 'Brilliant!' I say.

'Great plan!' Morag chimes in.

'And then you just walked up the drive?' I say as if he is a genius.

'I laid low until it was dark. Came up then. It was easy really.'

'Why don't you have another top up?' Morag clanks the bottle against the glass.

'Have you travelled far?' I try a different tack; my tone is every day; we could be two visitors chatting at an art exhibition.

'Not too far no. I come down quite often. As often as she tells me to. It's not always easy but I do my best for her.' He goes back to gnawing his finger.

'Oh, I see. You have a ... connection with Flora,' Morag says, nodding slowly.

'Yes,' the man answers quietly.

'How lovely,' I lean forward, 'How long have you had this connection?'

'We've been together for over ten years now. Since France. But it's had to be a secret. You know what it's like.'

'Of course, of course,' I too nod encouragingly, 'Why is that? Are you married?'

'No!' He looks at me directly for the first time, brow creased with dismay, 'We're *going* to get married. As soon as she's better. No. We can't tell anyone because of the mix up with the courts and that. No one understands except me and Flora. They want to keep us apart, but we won't let them. We *won't* let them, see. Flora knows I won't let anything happen to her.' At this point, he reaches into his pocket and pulls out a large hunting knife which he lays on his thigh. The blade waits, glinting, fat and dangerous.

'Now that is an impressive weapon,' Morag pipes up cheerily, 'It's very similar to one my da used when he went fishing. Used it to gut the fish. He would clean it and sharpen it at the kitchen table and my ma would get onto him saying it was filthy and to do it outside,' and she lets out a peal of laughter which I join in with, but my stomach has lurched and my heart is racing.

'Yes, it is a magnificent knife. The sort of knife which would make short work of any whittling project. Have you tried whittling ... sorry what was your name?' She is staring at him again.

'Whittling? Like making stuff with wood? No, I've never done that,' he looks confused, 'It's Dean. I'm Dean.'

'You've never whittled with a magnificent blade like that in your possession?' Morag jumps up from her chair and reaches a sturdy piece of kindling from next to the burner. She hands it to Dean. 'Here, have a look at this.

Just try stripping it away with the knife. The wood will tell you what it wants to be.'

'Yes,' I join in, enthusiastically 'And the smell of the wood as you cut it, is *heavenly*. Go on Dean, have a go.'

'Grasp the wood in your left hand and whittle with your right. If you're right-handed that is. Stroke away from you. Don't want to cut yourself.' Morag encourages the lad to push the blade into the kindling and peel a few tentative strips away.

'That's it!' I say, 'Use your thumb as a guide. Now isn't that calming? Would you like a sandwich, Dean? You must be starving. Waiting all that time outside. I can easily make you one.' And I'm up and out of my chair and opening the fridge muttering 'Where the hell is everyone?' into the fridge cam as I grab butter and ham and mustard and slam the door shut.

'You're really making progress. Now you can carve out more detailed shapes as well. Like little nicks and chinks so you can fashion a proper object. A wooden sculpture. Have a go at that.' Dean is clumsier at this stage however and the knife snags and catches and Morag can see he is finding it frustrating.

I watch with admiration as she reaches over. 'Here let me give you a little demo. Sometimes I find it's easier if someone shows you how it's done,' and she gently takes the wood from his hand and then the knife as I fill his suddenly empty hands with a plated fat sandwich.

'You just need to take little chunks. Don't work it too hard. See? Better to go at it a wee bit at a time and then it comes away easily and before you know it, you've whittled out a whole piece. There, that section's nearly done, look.' And she relaxes back in her chair and whittles away fashioning the wood into a tiny totem pole, expertly carving a couple of tiny animal heads in minutes as Dean works through the substantial snack and the hot, sweet milky coffee I have made him. He is mesmerised by Morag's quick work, idiotic great lump that he is, and when

I take his empty plate and mug, he smiles up gratefully at me.

'You're such lovely people. I can't wait until we're all one happy family.' Dean is visibly relaxing. He is captivated by Morag's hand working deftly with the knife and wood. I can see that Morag has noticed that he's looking a bit woozy. She looks quizzically at me, and I can't help smiling smugly back at her as I settled back into my chair.

'Tramadol in the coffee,' I whisper as Dean's head lolls forward.

Blue lights flash at the windows. Morag tops up our glasses and we chink them together and impatiently wait to be 'rescued'.

Later, in Shy and Tyler's annexe, Tim argues with us that we were never in danger. 'Did you see the size of that knife, you gobshite?' Morag cries, 'Security should have been in here the moment he set foot in the premises. You have a duty of care.'

'But nothing happened, Morag. You're both fine, aren't you?' Tim is trying to sound calm, but he was pulled away from a red carpet premier to be here where he'd already had a few too many drinks plus, by the looks of him, some recreational chemicals to make what looked like a fairly flat evening sing. He is clearly finding it hard to take the situation seriously, his giant tipsy skeleton looms over us reducing us to tiny fidgety old women.

'You took a massive fucking risk with your gravy train's mother, you fuckwit. That's what you did. Okay, Flora's not up to hearing that now but you know she will be soon and she will review all the tapes because that's what she does and when she sees that you let Dean Argyle in here and within five feet of one of the handful of living relatives she has with a fucking hunting knife knowing he has a court order against him and you didn't step in because it was 'good TV', well Tim, you'd better have a good argument organised. Fuck, you'd better have a good fucking lawyer organised. You're fucking history pal.' Morag's usually pale cheeks are by now flaming. She looks about twenty years younger.

'But you disarmed him. You drugged him. You took the knife off him using *whittling* as a decoy for Christ' sake. Nothing happened. It showed how ineffective he really was. And the ratings were through the roof. They're showing it on the national news. This is better than the intruder breaking into the Palace. I don't see what the problem is.' Tim slaps his hand against his forehead which is slick and clammy. His hand is shaky. It looks like he needs a drink. We both huff with exasperation and fury.

'Great! And what if he'd slit our throats on live TV eh? What then? Because you decided to see how it played out?' Morag shakes her head at the stupidity of the man in front of us.

'Well, I suppose it would have been a first.' There is an awkward silence before Tim groans and collapses to the floor as my fist makes efficient contact with his groin.

'I could never trust a tall man,' I say looking down at him, curled up on the floor, 'They always think they are naturally superior even though they had absolutely nothing to do with their height. You grow and then you stop growing. Big deal. It's been an irritation all my life. Flora's father was tall. He literally and metaphorically looked down on me. I didn't care for it. And you are far too tall. You need to take more care, my lad.' I turn to Morag, 'It's been what my mother would call a trying day, time for bed I think?'

'I agree,' and Morag nods, 'And you,' she says to Tim as we walk away from him, 'can fuck off out of here.'

'I bet your mother never spoke to people like that,' he says through gritted teeth due to the pain from his groin still swimming in the pit of his stomach as he tries to sit up. Most satisfactory.

We turn as one to face him.

He raises a hand and bows his head, 'I'm sorry, I didn't mean that. You're both right. I'll sort it. I'm an idiot,' and he rolls back to the floor as Morag slams the door shut as we leave him to his misery.

the.real.flora.tatton
daily contemplation: Push yourself because no one else is going to do it for you

Liked by **underthefunsun** and **1,055,923 others**

nowayback
woah that dude is wack he goin to spend sum time reflectin on his crime

fuckeduphuman
Flora will kick the shit out of Dean Argyle. He is insane #nutjob #stalker

bobbyboombastic
sending good vibes across the ocean

1974999
Where were the security? Are they for real? What if Flo had been there? #headsmustroll

lilpiggywenttomarket
no one is safe. wot if he had a gun? #bringbackcapitalpunishment

cheesywotsups
OMG I am praying for your safety. you and your beautiful little family are all I think about #norightnojustice

15

Flora

Meryl's father was a one night stand. I mean I knew him. Really well actually, but I didn't want anything from him. I didn't want a relationship, a family, the commitment. I couldn't see how I could fit into that.

When I was younger and I went round to friends' houses, I found their fathers … complicated. Or more the idea of them. Mostly they just seemed absent. I mean they lived in the houses but more often they weren't there. Or they were arriving and departing, making announcements and then disappearing. 'Just nipping out, back in half an hour.' 'Going to go through the papers for work tomorrow. Keep the noise down, will you?' 'Watching the second half of the match. City are up 2 nil.' A head and shoulders appearing through a doorway, a suited generic figure wandering into the garden – a few brief words, a masculine scent, sometimes cigarettes, sometimes drink, then they were gone. They never stuck around. They were never that involved. I baked cookies with Netta's mum, we piled into Lou's mum's car and went swimming, Heidi's mum let us have the run of the house, actively encouraged us to dress up and create and make a mess which she cheerily dealt with. And we were fed and watered as and when needed by those women. I'm not saying these mothers were interested in us; we all entertained each other so made their lives easier I guess, but I was more comfortable around them. At times, more comfortable with them than with my own mother.

We didn't often play in my house. In winter it was cold. My mother didn't like noise and she didn't have squash or snacks. She couldn't even pretend to be interested in my friends and would be shooing us out to the park as soon as she could. Sometimes almost before we'd all made it through the front door. And there was no one to argue with her. 'Leave them be, Joyce, it's freezing out, they'll be good, won't you girls?' No, my father was on the other side of the world, sunning himself on some paradise beach.

When I was older and I realised that some men like the attention of teenage girls, I paid more attention to some of the dads. Once I was more grown up, they stopped looking through me and I could hold their attention if I jutted my hips in the right way or flicked my hair or pulled my T-shirt down or stood just a little bit too close to them. I found it funny the way Pam's dad's neck went all red and blotchy as he pretended to talk to me about school. Or the way Lou's dad would run us all home and I knew he was planning the route so he could drop me off last.

Like I said, I usually get on with men better.

But when I was little, I didn't know what to make of those fathers. Sometimes they were over jolly. Like they were putting on a show or had slapped on a mask or pressed a hyper button to make them what they thought a dad should be. It was like they didn't know what to do when faced with four little girls. I hoped for my friends' sake that they were better when they were on their own with their daughters – more themselves.

I always knew where I was with my mother.

So when it came to Meryl, I didn't really think I needed a man around to bring her up. I figured I had managed without a father so why shouldn't she? The pregnancy was a surprise though. I was well on the way before I even realised. It just didn't occur to me that I could be 'with child'. It was absurd. If I'd found out earlier, I don't know what I'd have done. Probably not gone through with it. I like to take the easy route when I can.

I was living in London.

I'd just finished shooting *You **Can** Make a Silk Purse* and I was looking for something else. The show had been fun, but it was doubtful they were going to run another series. We'd been all over the country marching into all sorts of drab little houses and tarting them up with the help of interior designers of differing levels of talent. I was a bit sick of the smell of paint and sawdust to be honest and some of the makeovers were grim; shoddy finishes and dreadful colour combinations but the homeowners were generally jolly or tearfully grateful or sometimes disappointed but hey ho. I had lugged furniture and scraped walls and painted tired bedside tables under tarps in tiny gardens with grey rain dripping down my neck and shepherded the hapless victims around and around until I was heartily sick of it.

There was a big post-wrap party. A lot of drink. One thing led to another and the next thing I was looking at a very cross little bundle and my mother's matching older face at the foot of my bed in a hot ward in July. 'The things you do for attention, Flora,' Mum said evenly, shaking her head.

I had laughed. I was looking forward to motherhood. I was going to strap Meryl to my chest and carry on doing everything the way I had before.

The funny thing was Mum never asked about the father. Never suggested marriage and never questioned how I was going to manage as a single parent. She made a few comments about the remarks and looks I may get being on my own, but she obviously didn't think even that amounted to much. One thing sticks in my mind though.

'I'm not grandmother material Flora, so don't expect anything from me. I've brought you up and that was enough child-rearing as far as I'm concerned. So don't think you can depend on me. I won't be responsible for the baby. Or you. Anymore. I want to make that clear. I need to be on my own now.' She was folding Meryl's little vests and sleepsuits at the time. Teeny doll clothes that you think would melt anyone's heart.

Apparently not.

'Okay, Mum,' I said. And in some ways, I admired her honesty.

Like I say, I always knew where I stood with my mother.

I never told the guy I was pregnant. I've been deliberately evasive with Meryl. We're alright on our own. I mean there have been times when another pair of hands wouldn't have gone amiss, but I look at some of the relationships around me and I couldn't be arsed to be involved in half of the negotiations and effort they take day to day. Meryl has more material stuff than most girls her age. And I don't have to ask anyone's 'permission' to do anything.

When she was about seven, Meryl asked why she didn't know who or where her dad was and why she couldn't meet him. 'There are some mums who are fabulous enough to be mums and dads combined,' I told her, 'We don't need a dad.'

'You might not need one,' she said, 'but I'd like to have been asked.'

'It wasn't really like that. We don't want a dad stinking up the house, with smelly feet and beer and curries, do we?' Meryl had a heightened sense of smell so I thought this might work.

Her mouth had turned into a squiggle. 'You like curry and beer and why do dads' feet smell?' she asked.

'Some dads don't change their socks very often.' She always was impossible to argue with.

'Why not? Don't they have enough?' Now she was frowning as well.

'I'm not sure, but luckily we don't have to deal with that do we?'

She shrugged. 'I wouldn't mind too much. I could put up with it. I put up with things about you.'

'That's not a very nice thing to say, Meryl. What sort of things?' I didn't know whether to be offended or impressed. And I didn't know if I wanted to hear the answer to my question.

'Um,' Meryl looks at the ceiling, thinking hard, 'I know! You watch the TV very loudly and you talk all the time while you're watching so sometimes it's hard to hear what's going on. Even though it's on really loud. Also, you often say you don't want any sweets but then you want to eat mine. Why don't you get your own? Also, when you sit with your feet up on the sofa, you tuck them into me and I don't like it. It's squashy. Also, you rush me out of the bath sometimes and I like it in there. Also, you come in and want to chat when I'm reading my stories in bed and it's usually when I'm at a good bit and I have to wait until you've finished chatting until I can get back to my book. Also ...'

'Okay Meryl, you've made your point!' I interrupted, 'I am very difficult to live with!'

'I'm not saying that Mum,' she replied patiently, picking up a stray teddy from the floor and patting it absent-mindedly, 'I'm saying that I wouldn't mind putting up with smelly feet.'

16

Joyce

I notice Flora's hair is starting to grow back in. It's been a while since I visited. She was in and out of hospital over Christmas, so I saw more of Morag than I did of her. I was back down for Easter, and she looked really drawn, in the flesh. It's odd being able to check in at any time of the day or night and see how she's getting on.

Not that I do that often.

'I bet you have the telly on the whole time,' my busy body neighbour Rita two doors down says every time I fail to avoid her on my way in or out. She's a true *Flora Show* fan. She brought round flowers for me when Flora announced her diagnosis on the telly. She never knew Flora before she became a celebrity; it's not like she grew up in this house. And the stupid woman stood and cried in my kitchen.

I didn't know where to put myself.

I stood looking at the disappointing bouquet all crispy and garish in my sink and Rita blubbed and rattled on like the tap that was filling the vase. 'How could it happen to her? How can life be so cruel? And what about poor little Treasure? What's to become of them all? I barely slept a wink last night. I'm sure you were the same. You should have come round. We could have cried together. Those poor little mites. Motherless. And she's so young. And so beautiful. And what are we going to watch now? I said to Les, I said "What are we going to watch now?" And his eyes welled up and he's not one for tears, our Les. No. There's not many occasions when a tear's been shed in our house. No. But for Flora. For that angel. Yes. He was welling up.'

'Well, chin up Rita, she's not dead yet and it's not terminal, is it? It's an excellent prognosis. I don't think there's any need to be thinking in terms of the "motherless mites" at this point. And if the worst comes to the worst - which it won't - she's not short of a bob or two,' I countered, in as brisk as way as possible, combining this with shutting off the tap and walking over and opening the back door, despite the chill wind outside.

'You're so strong, Joyce! Like mother, like daughter. A pair of warriors. I'd be in bits if I were you,' and for a terrible moment I thought she was going to try to hug me again as she lurched towards me, blinking back yet more tears. On arrival, I'd managed to ward her off by grasping the flowers and using these as an adequate if flimsy barrier. Now I was unprotected. I side-stepped instead, squashing myself into the wall and opening the door widely.

'I'm expecting a call,' I said with an unashamedly unsubtle hint of sub-text.

This brought Rita to her senses. 'Oh yes, of course, do pass on my love, won't you? She knows how much I care about her, doesn't she? She's like a daughter to me.'

As I closed the door on her I considered the lunacy of the woman's behaviour. If she caught a whiff that Flora was in the area, it was all I could do to stop her marching into the house, behaving like Flora was the prodigal son returned. To her credit, Flora dealt with her unctuous over-familiarity with grace and good humour. I'd have slapped her pawing hands away and shooed her out, but Flora was warm and welcoming; giving the sense of having all the time in the world whilst actually only really offering a few minutes. To my horror on one occasion, I awoke to find a double sheet draped over my privet hedge, with a crudely painted 'Welcome Home Flora' blaring out in tawdry pink.

Rita was standing proudly next to it with Flora's face printed on her cheap T-shirt.

I forbade Flora to reveal any planned trips up north after that.

I burnt the sheet in my brazier in the back garden.

I saw Rita watching from her upstairs window.

I didn't care.

I have checked in with the family on the show this week though. I find it's better to be forewarned. As I say, there's a little bit of hair returning. Well, all the treatment is over, and I have watched Treasure toddling about a little. Quite boring. Meryl is a shadow who flits across the screen and is gone. It's like she's been miscast. She's a ghost, or more like a ghoul from a horror film occasionally flashing a scowling, sallow face at the camera. She has no place in the pastel, sweetie shop world Flora has spun and fabricated.

I hope Meryl keeps out of the way while I'm there. I can do without the drama.

An excessively large and very clean car arrives for me at the allotted time to transport me to my daughter's house. Despite my protests, the driver, Michael, insists on carrying my bags even though I am perfectly capable of managing the job myself. We are almost to the car when Rita bundles down her drive and out towards us.

I reach for the handle, but Michael gets there first, the infuriating man, blocking my escape from Rita. Another irritation of a celebrity off-spring is the impossibility of travelling any distance on the train. I too am now recognised and besieged with questions by every man and his dog as well as a never-ending stream of requests for bloody selfies. The car is a begrudging compromise on my part paid for by Flora.

'Joyce, wait, wait!' Rita pants and she waves a wrapped package at me, 'I knew you were off to see our darling girl, so I've got her a little treat. Something to pep her up. Some of those luxury smellies for the bath,' and she puts the parcel to her face, shuts her eyes and inhales deeply. 'Mmmmm. Gorgeous,' she breathes, 'I love her bath and I think she'll love this fragrance. It's magnesium and amethyst and,' she says proudly, 'it's vegan.' She gives the package a gentle kiss then keeping her head bowed, hands it over to me as if we are performing an ancient ritual.

Ridiculous woman.

I shove it into the top of my handbag.

'Thank you, Rita,' I say and glare at Michael who promptly opens the car door.

She stands on the pavement and waves and I watch in Michael's wing mirror as she wipes away a tear with a small, white hanky.

Once we're just out of town heading towards the motorway, I wind down the window and throw the parcel out of the window. I hate littering but hopefully someone will pick it up; it's a popular route for cyclists.

I simply can't be bothered to carry it and it's already stinking up the car.

17

Meryl

There are some advantages to this whole *Flora Show* trip. As soon as I turned seventeen, I got a car and a crash course in driving and, yes, there were cameras there when I passed my test, but the freedom to drive was something else.

It went to my head I guess, and I don't know why I thought it would be okay.

I just thought Treasure deserved a bit of normality, a bit of reality, and I didn't think there'd be any harm.

What surprised me was how straightforward it was to leave the house with her. I literally picked up her car seat and went and plugged it in to the car. Then I just circled back and grabbed her changing bag and scooped her up. No one bothered. I'm not sure who was supposed to be watching her. That happens quite a lot. It's fuzzy. There's no strict timetable. It's what you might call fluid. And there was a bit of chat going on between Morag and Marsha and Shy and it was all a bit of a gift.

To be honest I don't have much of a plan. Not a real plan. The gate opened as always, and I just drove out. I don't think anyone even bothered looking at me.

'I'm coming to get you,' I tell Tyler, 'We're going to the park.'

I check for photographers while I am driving but no one is very interested in me. I never do anything that is any fun.

'Hello Princess,' Tyler grins into Treasure's face, 'This is a surprise,' he says to me.

'Isn't it? We want to go to the park, don't we, Trumpet?' and I nuzzle into Treasure's neck and make her giggle.

Tyler is wearing old joggers and nothing else. 'Give me five,' he says.

The park is quiet despite the warmth of the May morning. We've driven to the edge of town; you can almost see countryside. In the distance. The parks around where Tyler lives are a bit grim.

Treasure likes the swing best. Every time we try to lift her out to try something else, she squeals and straightens her legs so we can't get her out past the bars. She relaxes as soon as we start pushing her again though and tilts her head up to the sky and squints at the sun, a tiny smile on her face.

'Do you want kids?' Tyler asks eventually. We're taking it in turns to push, a couple of minutes each. He's pushing her quite high. It's bit scary. I take over when I can't stand it any longer.

'Don't think so. Too much responsibility,' I say focussing on the soft hair on the back of Treasure's head.

'I do. Loads and loads,' Tyler breathes deeply and grasps me around the waist, cheek flattening against my shoulder.

'You're soft,' I say, pushing him away. I spend quite a lot of time doing this. In fact, the feeling of putting my hands onto unwanted limbs attaching themselves to me is a constant in my life. I've never liked cuddles or hugs. Or people being too close generally. Flora sometimes grips onto me for the camera, and I loathe it. I extricate myself as quickly as I can. It's not just because it's fake, it is the sense of another person too close, their breath in my breath, their skin on my skin. It creeps me out. The only person I love to touch is Treasure. And she is always wiggling away, desperate to escape to something better that catches her eye. Just like me. I can't blame her. I love the feel of her plump, velvety arms and her tight little belly and she smells good. Always. I don't even mind if she has a full nappy. Even that is somehow, pure. I love to be with her. To hold her. To play with her. To sing to her. If the cameras weren't there, I'd have more time with her for sure.

I succeed in levering Tyler from around my middle. He's used to it. He knows he needs to give me space.

'I think I'm gonna be a great dad,' he announces.

'I'm sure you are,' I say, biting back the desire to point out he's had no role model, is a fundamentally very lazy boy who could sleep for England and has little or no means to provide for any kind of family let alone 'loads' of kids.

'Thanks, sweet,' he laughs. I'm aware that it's also rare for me to be kind. To anyone. 'Maybe you'll change your mind, and we can a have a whole football team together,' and he runs round to the front of the swing and tickles Treasure's tummy as she swings towards him. She shrieks and giggles at this new game. It makes me smile but I feel a little sad too.

'I think we should be getting back,' I say, 'You know, before they launch a full search and rescue.

We're nearly back at the car park, which is small, isolated, at the edge of a scrub of trees. I'm carrying Treasure as I couldn't be bothered with all the palaver of the buggy. We're chatting to her, she's telling us animal noises and we're being amazed at how clever she is, when two guys in dark clothes are standing in front of us stopping us walk any further.

'Scuse mate,' says Tyler in his easy manner but I am ready for a fight. Who the fuck do they think they are? No doubt they're fans, and they'll want selfies, and to chat and be all pretend pally and already I'm getting angry that our precious snatched hour is running the risk of being ruined.

I look at their faces. Neither of them is smiling in that slightly desperate way that fans do. No. One is tall and broad. A lot taller than me and he has his chin tucked into his solid chest and his hands held together in front of him, kind of relaxed but like he would be good to go at any time. He's got small pale eyes and very thin, short hair and he's staring at me. Not in an obviously threatening way. Just focused. Attention all on me. My face.

The other one is shorter, stocky. Muscular too but in a more compact way. Thick black hair, neatly cropped and faded at the neck but full and tidy on top. He's got one of those black bomber jackets on. It's pretty cool. I've got one quite like it. He's looking at me too, but his eyes are laughing at me, like he knows the punchline to a joke I'm about to tell.

We stand there for a moment and look at each other. Or rather the two of them look at me. With intent.

'Look guys,' Tyler takes a half step towards them, and I don't even see the big guy's fist make contact with Tyler's face, it's so quick. I hear the crunch of bone on bone though and Tyler is felled like a tree. And I mean by that he falls straight back and lands with a heavy thud. I look at him on the ground, head lolled to the side, eyes firmly shut and blood trickling from a nose already starting to swell and bruise. 'Tyler!' I gasp but as I stoop towards him another arm hooks into mine, jerking me back towards the fucking idiots in front of me. My grip tightens on Treasure. 'What the fuck did you do that for?' I say and I lurch at the thug who is staring impassively back at me.

A van screeches up next to us and the side door opens.

'You've got to be kidding me,' I yell.

We're sitting in the back of the van. Me and Treasure and the grinning moron who thinks whatever plan he's come up with is going to work. There's another chump sitting next to him. He was driving but the thug who punched Tyler took over. This dweeb can't be trusted with that job is my reading of the situation. He looks really young. Same age as me. Thin, scrawny neck and loads of black hair too. Masses of it. Lank and unwashed. Like him. He apologised as we were bundled into the van, even after I kneed him in the groin. Not a dyed in the wool kidnapper is my bet.

I think the van must be used for landscape gardening, there's little piles of earth where they've run together with the movement of the road between the metal grooves on the floor. There's a coil of faded, frayed and tattered rope in the corner. Looks like it's been there years rather than being part of this grand plan.

I'm trying to keep track of where we're going, where we've turned and I'm pretty sure we're on the A road heading out of town. I can't see much through to the front of the van and out of the windscreen but it's definitely a dual carriageway. The only issue is I'm not sure which direction we're heading, except we went all the way round the roundabout.

They tried to take Treasure away when we first got in but she bellowed so loudly they gave her back. Good girl. Now we're just biding our time.

The grinning fool is desperate to speak. He wants to tell me how pleased he is with himself. That he's got us in the back of the van, that is. His pal is looking more and more forlorn the longer we drive. He is behaving like a turtle. His head is slowly retreating into more and more hunched shoulders and his eyes are getting bigger and more frightened as every second passes. I occasionally fix him with a glare or a sneer and he sinks further down into his bony shoulders.

We're playing Chicken. I think The Fool would like me to beg and plead and be hysterical. When my knee made solid and well-timed contact with Scaredy Turtle he should have known I was never going to play the damsel in distress.

The Fool gets out his phone with an exaggerated flamboyance and an even more superior curl of his lip. It is hard for me to say nothing but luckily The Turtle jumps in.

'What're you doing?' he sounds like he's going to blub. It's pathetic.

'I thought I'd send a message,' The Fool replies slowly.

'Oh God, what do you mean?' The Turtle sounds appalled. I really hope he's not going to pee his pants. Or worse. Where did they get him? Perhaps it's some kind of intern or apprenticeship post? He's certainly not cutting the mustard at the moment as my granny would say. I half smile at the thought of this and think that Tyler would find that funny. This rekindles my anger; I'm worried about Tyler.

'I mean I'm going to send a message,' The Fool says raising the camera on the phone towards me and Treasure.

Instinctively, I hunker down and pull Treasure's head into mine. I will not be filmed. Not like this.

'Oh thank God, I thought you were going to do something horrible to them, like cut the baby's ear off or …'

He is silenced by the look The Fool is giving him. 'Jesus Dwayne! What kind of a sick brain have you got?' he says like he's speaking to a dullard.

The Turtle looks like he's been slapped. 'My name,' he hisses, 'You used my name.'

'Relax,' The Fool doesn't sound particularly relaxed, 'There are millions of Dwaynes.'

I stare at him, hoping he can see that I think he is an idiot.

He gets the message.

'Don't look at me like that, you silly little bitch. You think you're so clever but who's the one in the van with three rotters, eh? We're not on the way to your prom, you know?'

'Good!' I snarl, 'I never went to my prom. I hate all that crap. Now why don't you tell Dwayne here what your plan is? Because this seems a truly inspired heist so far.' I sound brave. I sound strong but my heart is thumping against Treasure's chest. I hope she doesn't catch on how scared I am and start wailing again.

'And I thought you were clever,' he grins back at me, 'It's all about money little Miss Meryl. We've already set up a GoFundMe page on TikTok and the money is pouring in. We don't even have to ask Flora, we're tapping into the Gen Pub and Ker Ching, everything's coming up roses.'

He turns his phone to me and there is a reel of battered Tyler's face and me and Treasure huddled in the van and blaring, blatant requests for money to get us back. It's working; you can see the figure rocketing up in real time.

'Not such a bunch of nitwits after all, are we?' and he and Dwayne smugly smirk into each other's faces.

'So, what's your endgame?' I ask, 'Are you going to kill us? Up your crimes from kidnapping with menaces to murder? Not just murder actually, infanticide. Is that your grand plan?' Dwayne starts a bit at this.

'You never said we was killing the baby, Trev. You never said that,' and he clutches onto Trev's jacket sleeve in a surprisingly tender way, like he's his son.

Or his brother. I take in the same thick, black hair; the glinting blue eyes, the dimple in the chin – weaker in The Turtle's but there nonetheless. They have different builds, different mouths but they are related. No doubt.

'Oh Trev,' I say, 'This is low.'

Trev looks at me, not smiling this time.

'What is?'

'Involving your kid brother in such a dirty scheme,' I shake my head in gentle disapproval as if they have stolen a few penny sweets from the corner shop rather than kidnapped two innocent sisters.

'How do you know?' Dwayne can't keep his mouth shut. He has no future in crime.

'Shut it, Dwayne, she doesn't. She didn't.' Trev's mouth tightens. 'Just shut up,' he shouts at me, 'Not another word unless I ask you to speak. Got it?'

'But Trev…' Dwayne tries.

'And you too, you prick. Just shut it. You told her. Now the police will be looking for two brothers called Trev and Dwayne. How long's it gonna take for them to get to us, eh? Be quiet and let me think.'

He checks his phone and I pull Treasure closer, realising from her stillness and heaviness that steady thrum of the van combined with her burst of wailing and all the fun of the park, has sent her to sleep.

'The money's clocking up nicely. I said it would work,' Trev mutters to himself as he scrolls and clicks.

He looks up sharply. 'I've had a brilliant idea,' he says, 'We need to bring this to a hasty conclusion. Let's do a live. Now.'

'You're joking?' I say, 'If you've watched the show at all you'll know I haven't said anything on air for months. Why would I start now?'

'It's true,' Dwayne confirms, 'Flora's tried everything, but Meryl said she'd have no part of it since Flora decided to keep going with the telly once she had, you know,' he lowers his voice, 'cancer. And she won't go back on it. She's determined to make her point even though everyone thinks she's cold and heartless.'

I roll my eyes and glare at him, the puny cretin.

'Alright Alison Hammond, we don't need a full-blown critique of the show. She may *choose* not to speak on *The Flora Show* but this is different.' He is calm, soothing almost and thinks he is being charming.

'Why?' asks Dwayne, genuinely perplexed.

'Because if she doesn't do it, I'll chuck the baby out the back of the van,' he says and his eyes aren't laughing, they are steely cold and terrifying.

Icy terror washes over me.

Perhaps he will kill us both.

He edges further towards me, fiddles with the phone and turns it towards me.

'What do you want me to say?' I say quietly.

'I'm sure you'll think of something,' he says with a sneer of menace.

I see myself in the camera. I look like some kind of ghoul. My make-up has smeared and run down one side of my face and my hair is wild.

'Can I just tidy myself up a bit,' I say.

'It looks better if you're a state,' Trev answers mechanically.

I adjust Treasure so she nestles into my lap giving me two free hands. 'Look,' I say, 'Give me the phone so I can adjust my hair at least and we'll have a practice before we go live. That way I'm not going to piss you off. I won't be able to call anyone – you'll be able to see. I might as well do it the way you want it.'

'I'm not giving you the phone, end of,' Trev replies.

'Didn't you say my sister's life was at stake?' I say, 'I'm not going to risk that, am I?' and I look beseechingly at Dwayne. 'This is a big deal me saying anything on camera.'

'It is Trev, it is. If she does it, this'll make the news. Deffo.' Dwayne sits up in anticipation and Trev licks his lips hungrily at the thought of the notoriety he's about to achieve.

'Okay,' he says, 'No funny business. I'm watching you.'

As he hands me the phone, I press the live feed and begin to scrape at my make-up and hair with intense concentration.

'So, Trev, what do you want me to say? I won't mention you or Dwayne for a start, no? Or the thug who knocked out Tyler who's driving the van?'

Trev and Dwayne grin at each other.

'No definitely not!' says Dwayne smiling.

'Pleased Treasure's asleep. She was worn out from the park. We go there a lot you know. Or did you see us there before? So close to the A120 isn't it? Handy for us. Ooh that's looking a bit better now. Bit of a criminal mastermind are you, Trev? You must be because I didn't see a dark blue Transit van in the car park, or any of you hanging around. Come on Trev. Let me in on your secrets…'

I leave a pause.

Trev just raises an eyebrow at me. 'Okay,' I say, 'You did say you'd throw Treasure out the back of the van if there was any funny business on the Live so let's practice. How about I do a bit of 'Help I'm terrified? Please give as much as you can to secure the safe return of me and Treasure to our perfect lives with our beloved mother. Would that work?'

Trev nods but is looking suspicious and angry again.

I flick off the Live.

'Okay, let's go,' I say mock wearily, 'Do I press this button?' I turn the phone back to face him and he nods, 'Despite what you might think, I've never done this before,' I mutter, and I press it. In my head I plan to fake tears but as I look into the camera Treasure sighs and shudders a little in her sleep and I realise I have just taken a massive risk with her life. I catch Trev's eye over the phone, and he is leaning closer towards me. I see his hands, all hard knuckles and a few coarse, black hairs. I look into the phone and catch my image; a stupid seventeen-year-old who thinks she's invincible. A sob bubbles in my chest and real terrible tears erupt. I can't stop and it is all I can do to hold the phone and let the moment be captured forever.

'Please help us. We have been taken. We are terrified but unharmed. Please do whatever you can to ensure that my sister gets home. Please. Please save Treasure. She is so tiny and hasn't had any life yet. Please,

please help us and do anything they want you to. For Treasure.' The short speech takes ages. This is partly by design and partly because of my constant choking sobs.

I figure the longer I can keep the feed going the more time they will have to find us. The more chance I have of stalling Trev from looking at the comments and seeing what I've done.

I can feel genuine hysteria building up inside me. I'm panicking about giving Trev the phone and being caught.

'Thank you,' I say, 'I can see so much money, coming in, more money than I could ever have dreamed of.' I turn the Live off and turn the screen to Trev so he can take in the sum. He is astonished.

'I can't believe it!' he shouts, 'We've done it! We've bloody well done it,' and he and Dwayne hug each other with greedy exhilaration.

I hold his phone high, out of his reach. 'I hate that you made me do that,' I say, 'I hate that the whole world saw that. I hate technology.' I throw the phone on the floor and smash and grind it under my shoe.

We all look at the shattered phone in silence.

'Oh my God,' I say, 'I'm so sorry. I don't know what happened. I just...I don't know what to say...I got so emotional doing the live,' and a small sob escapes me.

Dwayne looks terrified, casting looks between me and Trev, not knowing what will happen next.

Trev looks at the phone and then at me.

He exhales loudly. 'Doesn't matter,' he says lightly, 'You did brilliant. We reached our target and more. Way more. We can buy as many new phones as we want,' and he starts to laugh, a loud, open-mouthed greedy laugh that takes up all the space in the back of the van and Dwayne joins in and I hope I have bought us a little more time.

I cuddle into Treasure who, if I put my head really close to hers, is snoring softly.

It takes the police about half an hour to find us. I hear the helicopter first, then the sirens.

It's all over very quickly.

I only wanted to take my sister to the park. And look how it ended.

18

Flora

I couldn't have Meryl move out. Not after everything that happened. I just thought it was more important for her to stay close to me. Where I could protect her.

She didn't see it that way.

'If it wasn't for your Show we would never have ended up in the back of that van,' she'd shouted at me when we went to pick them up from the police station. Yes, they could have been brought home but I couldn't wait to see them and so we raced over.

Didn't take long. It wasn't far. Turns out the kidnappers were more or less circling where they'd picked them up and were going to drop them back off once they reached their 'target'.

'Just give me ten minutes alone with those bastards. You don't wanna mess with this mama bear!' I joked with the Chief Superintendent after we'd done the press conference. Turned out she was a fan, so it was a good day in more ways than one for her.

'I can't be a part of this madness anymore, Flora,' my daughter had said to me.

'Do not call me Flora,' I said, 'I'm your mother. There are only two people on this earth entitled to call me Mum and that's you and Treasure. Call me some form of that Meryl, do not use the name that everyone else does.'

'Don't you get it?' she rounded on me, 'I don't want to be your daughter anymore. I'm moving in with Tyler. I just can't deal. I've had it.'

She packed that night, and I watched her car disappear up the drive.

Like I say, I couldn't have Meryl move out.

I've opened an account for her and Tyler. There's a lot of money in there. I deliberately put it in joint names. I spoke to Tyler and said as far as I was concerned, he was taking on some of the responsibility for Meryl and for that he should be recompensed. He was hesitant at first but then he came round to my way of thinking.

They say every man has his price. I'm more interested in how Tyler behaves with the price he is paid. He comes from nothing. How will he fare with a big chunk of money burning a hole in his pocket.

I want my daughter back under my roof and I want her here on my terms. I can afford to be a little patient.

19

Meryl

'Why do you keep spending it, Ty? No matter how much you spend, it'll just get replaced. Don't you get it? But the more you spend, the more she owns you. I don't know how many times we have to go through this.'

He's looking at the flimsy silk shirt in his hands like he doesn't know how it got there. No, he looks guilty, like a poacher who's bagged a beautiful, rare breed and now regrets the loss of life he's caused. The silk is sumptuous, and the print is wild but Tyler will never wear it.

'I never had anything so soft,' he says quietly, thumbing the fabric, 'And it feels so good on my skin.'

He's sulking.

'Keep it then,' I say and climb out of his new bed with the fancy high thread count bedding (whatever that is) and past the rowing machine and the mountain bike propped against the wall, below the set of framed movie stills. I catch my shin on the pedal of the bike. Again. 'Shit!' I spit out.

'We're going to need a bigger place,' Tyler says, moving to squash his new shirt into the second new wardrobe he's bought.

'Not if you stop buying stuff we're not,' I say rubbing my shin.

He turns on me. 'Why can't I get myself some gear Mare? Why're you so harsh all the time? You've had this your whole life. I'm just getting myself to a point where I feel like I've got what I need, okay?'

'Whatever,' I say and go to shower.

The reality of living with Tyler isn't all I thought it would be in my head. But that's life isn't it. One big disappointment after another. It's easier to lower your expectations.

'I can't believe you moved in here,' was how he greeted me but when he proudly presented me with one long drawer and one short drawer for all my stuff, I did pause for thought. When I realised I'd have to wash my own clothes and Tyler had no washing machine it was a reality check, but I liked the clean soapy smell of the launderette, *Suds Away*, and ignored the chipped floor tiles and the homeless woman napping the corner and the fag butts huddling by the entrance. I had the time to make a weekly trip here.

Food shopping was another experience. We *Deliveroo*'d a lot of stuff but there were things like loo roll and shampoo and breakfast cereal and milk that we kept running out of. 'We need to go to a supermarket, Tyler and get some stuff in,' and, as we pushed the trolley round, me in sunglasses and hoodie up, again I thought I have the time to do this. It's no biggie.

Everything continued to run out though. And you keep having to decide what to eat. And Tyler kept asking me. Like I was his mum.

'What did you do before I lived here?' I asked belligerently.

'D'you know I can't remember. Funny that,' he smiled back at me, oblivious to the annoyance he was causing.

'I don't care what we eat,' I snapped, 'I'm going to college.' I slammed the door as I left. Through all this I was still studying. A levels in psychology, biology and maths. There was work to do. On my knee on the bed. I'd started staying later at college and working in the library to get stuff done there. It wasn't that I couldn't work at Tyler's; I didn't want to.

He was messy. I knew this about him. Why shouldn't he be? But the flat was small, I mean tiny, and he didn't have much stuff but he never put anything away if he didn't have to.

All in all, living with Tyler wasn't great, then Flora opened the joint account.

'He deserves a break,' she said, 'I wish I'd had someone to look out for me when I was his age. Your granny never gave me a penny. Too bloody mean.'

'We don't need all that money, Flora. It's too much. He's got the rent covered. Why do we need so much?' I argued.

'Perhaps it'll give him a head start. There's enough there for him to manage a little start up maybe? I mean he can't work in a shop his whole life can he?'

Tyler's flat is an HMO or house of multiple occupancy. He'd got it when he was working but had been made redundant pretty soon after. The landlord let him stay on even though he went onto Universal Credit – good of her really, she could have kicked him out. He can't work more than a certain number of hours or his benefit is cut. He works part time in a bike shop to keep under the hours and keep his flat, but he says he's looking for something full-time again. He's also supposed to be doing a college course in something but I don't know what and I've never seen him go or seen any sign of him doing anything, so I guess he's dropped out of that.

Flora knew all this when she set up the account. Having the extra money jeopardised his Universal Credit and his flat.

'This is a win, win, babe,' Tyler said hugging me too tightly when he got off the phone to Flora.

'What about when she decides to stop paying it?' I said, 'Where will you be then?'

Tyler is an eternal optimist. 'We'll be okay. With your brains and my looks, we don't need her money,' he countered.

'Exactly my point,' I said, 'If we start spending it,' and by 'we' I meant 'him', 'we'll get used to it and then if it's not there we'll miss it.' I was speaking by this time from bitter experience. I had had an unlimited credit card that I had tried not to use since leaving the house. It was unbelievable how often I reached for it from habit. Previously, I probably made ten impulse buys a day, maybe more, without giving it a second thought, because I'd never had to.

All that was over now.

When I said she might stop it, it looked like that at least registered with Tyler and nothing more was said. For a couple of days.

His spending was fairly low key at first.

And he made it look like it was for me. Or to make my life easier.

A washer dryer was practical and money saving in the long run. And part of his brief was to keep me safe and weekly trips to the launderette made me an easy target.

A dishwasher followed which I argued was pointless as we barely cooked. Tyler said he was going to start.

Then there was a whole run of kitchen appliances which filled up the already cluttered kitchen; an air fryer, a bread maker, a barista coffee machine, a fondue, a rillette, a waffle maker, a panini press, a rice cooker, a four-slice toaster. We never ate bread! He unpacked each one like it was Christmas, his long fingers running over the chrome or enamel surfaces, and he used them, once or twice. Then they just sat there. In the way.

He bought all new china and cutlery and saucepans and towels next and then he started on the 'soft furnishings'.

'Are you gay?' I said as he cooed over a goose down duvet that had arrived.

'What a horrible homophobic thing to say,' he recoiled, hurt I think, that I would say something like that, not that I was being mean to him.

'You're right. I'm sorry,' I said, 'But what the hell is going on?' I indicated the new scatter cushions and scented candles, the deep pile rug and the wall art. The place was unrecognisable.

'I've been watching The Show,' he said, 'I wanted you to feel at home.'

'What are you talking about?' I said.

'When you're at college I watch The Show. *The Flora Show.* You know you can buy everything that features. So I thought I have no idea what to buy. Never really bought anything in my life. So I watch The Show then I go online and find the links in the chatrooms and order it. I also figure I'm giving your mum back some of the money.'

I was so gobsmacked I couldn't respond.

'I mean she gets a cut doesn't she, so it's a bonus for her too.' He turned his attention to the matching pillows.

'I didn't want any of this,' I said, 'I moved out to get away from it all. Why are you recreating it here?'

'But it's such sic stuff,' he said, 'Have you smelled that candle? I mean, yes, it was eighty quid, but it transports you to a higher plain.'

'Are you listening to me, Tyler?' I said, 'You used to live on £80 a week and now you're spending it on one bloody candle. What the hell is going on? I hate this. I hate all of it.'

He looked really hurt that time.

Again, the packages stopped arriving for a few days and nothing more was said.

Then he started spending the money on himself.

And here we are.

Surrounded by, wading through, drowning in, all kinds of meaningless shit provided by my mother.

Cheers, Flora.

20

Joyce

Morag and I have been busy with *The Times* crossword but now we're back to more mundane jobs. We have taken the crossword up on my recent visits and neither of us are particularly good at it, but it keeps us amused, particularly moaning about the impossibility of the clues and enjoying congratulating ourselves if we can solve one or two. We have a *Sunday Times* delivered in preparation for my arrival and that keeps us going for the whole visit. As I say, neither of us has much talent for it.

'We're both too straightforward, Joyce,' says Morag.

'Agreed. We'd be hopeless as detectives,' I reply.

'Oh I don't know about that. That's piecing together clues in a different way. You're putting together a story there. With a crossword it's like someone jumbles all the letters up and tosses them in the air. You're on a hiding to nothing.' Morag is working out a blackcurrant stain from one of Treasure's favourite dresses. She's bent over the sink and concentrating hard.

'That's true. You've just got to put the science and the stories together as a detective and most people are dreadful when it comes to committing crime apparently.' I am peeling peaches for a cobbler. They've been soaking for half an hour in boiling water while we fretted over a clue (Idiot made hate fashionable?) and now the skins are slipping away easily from the flesh. I wish the clue had worked so well. Neither of us had an idea.

'Why would anyone put a two-year-old in a silk dress?' Morag mutters.

'Well if you have the money…' I say.

'It's an impossible fabric,' Morag says dropping the frock down into the sink and snatching her reading glasses from her face. 'I can't use any warmth on it, or it'll shrink and Flora wants her in it again tomorrow. The lassie has a wardrobe full of clothes. Can she not wear something else?'

'It's not like you to be beaten by a stain, Morag,' I say gently.

'Ignore me,' she answers, 'I'm not beaten, I'm just feeling crabbit,' and she goes back to the dress with renewed determination.

'Why?' I say and begin to slice the peaches and put them in the pie dish.

'I didn't sleep too well last night. I haven't slept that well since we had all that business with Meryl and Treasure. It goes around in my head that one of us should have seen Meryl pick her up. One of us should have stopped her.'

'She is Treasure's sister though, Morag. She's a right to take her where she wants to without asking permission some would argue. And, knowing her, she'd probably have gone anyway. She's a determined child. Like her mother.'

'And her granny,' Morag smiles ruefully at me.

'Agreed. And thank goodness for that. They both came home safely because of her quick wits.' I can't be doing with poring over the past and finding drama where there is none. Both girls came home safe and well. End of story.

'That's true. But I'm …I don't know…unsettled since the whole thing. I don't like that Meryl isn't here anymore. I've been looking after that girl since she was wee and she's no an adult yet. She belongs here. With us. Not in some flat with some guy none of us know. It's bugging me. I don't like it, and I'm not sleeping because of it.' She gives the dress a vigorous scrub. I hope that silk is strong enough to stand it.

'All of that is more than reasonable but again, Morag, there's not a lot you can do. As we've said, Meryl is a determined young woman and if things were different here, I think she'd be back but they're not. My mother was married at eighteen as were most of her generation, and I wasn't that much older and nor were you. We don't give young people these days the chance to show what they're capable of. If anyone can manage on their own, it's Meryl.'

'It's not that I think she can't manage,' Morag replies, 'Of course she can manage. Dear Lord, that girl's been managing all and sundry since she was six years old. It's that I think she should be *here*. With us. It's not the way it should be.'

'It's hard when your children leave home,' I say as I start to arrange the peach slices, not as neatly and cleverly as Morag would but they'll do.

'I dread to think how Flora must be feeling if I'm feeling like this. She's no even my flesh and blood, though she feels like it. They all do. You all do, I should say,' and she smiles at me, and I feel like if I were a different person I would go and give Morag a hug, but I am me.

'Thank you, Morag, and you are our flesh and blood,' I manage instead and hope that that is enough.

Morag smiles and nods at the dress in the sink. I think she may be shedding a tear.

'Perhaps we could text Meryl and see if she would like to meet us for lunch somewhere? Then you can see for yourself how she is? What do you say?' I try to sound cheery and bright.

'That would be grand,' Morag says quietly.

21

Flora

Tim and I have decided it will look good for the optics of the show if we increase security inside the house. There's been so much chat online about who's at risk and whether there'll be a copycat kidnapping. They did do very well in raising a lot of cash after all. We're putting together a team and we've already got one or two in place. There's room in the annexe for a couple more bodies so Milk and Shy are involved in the process, but I am thrilled to say we have made our first non-binary on air appointment: Red.

I was hoping Meryl might go more that way but, despite my encouragement, she's been happy with her gender. Shame because that would have been great for the viewing figures – imagine the reveal! OMG! Anyway, that ship has sailed apparently.

The whole LGBTQAI+ community are so supportive of The Show, and I think having a representative who's occasionally on camera will be fab. We didn't appoint Red because they were non-binary obvs. They were the best person for the job. They are ex-military and have some great experience in high end security already. They also have a law degree (imagine!) but they've chosen to travel a different path. I hold my hands up and say, 'Right On!' I could never read all that stuff a lawyer has to to prepare for a case. Boring! No, Red's the human for us!

'You're okay if occasionally you're filmed. You shouldn't be the focus but if you're living in the house it's going to be unavoidable,' Tim said at the interview. It was fascinating viewing. I was watching on a cam, but I couldn't interject which was a shame as I had a million questions.

'I'm fine with that,' Red said, 'I've watched the show. I was particularly interested in the footage where the youngest Tatton was removed by the eldest Tatton.'

'Go on,' Tim sat back obviously keen to listen.

'Four adults were in the room, the main living area which is used 55% of the time by the majority of the household. During daylight hours there is very little time where no one is in this space as it has the kitchen and a relaxation space attached.' I was impressed. Red had obviously done their homework. They pressed on. 'However, because the conversation was so compelling, all thought of the well-being of the youngest Tatton went by the by. In terms of security either conversation needs to be toned down, or we need proper protocol rigidly followed in terms of who has eyes on who at all times.'

'This is a TV show. We don't want it to be dull. I don't think we can 'tone down' conversation to help the security work better,' Tim answered mildly. 'By the way, what was the topic they were discussing?'

'Whether Ms Tatton has had, or should have, a breast augmentation.' Red maintained eye contact as they said the words. I liked that about them.

Tim cocked his head and gave this some thought. 'Well, I can see how that subject could be quite absorbing.' He shifted in his seat. 'So if you were appointed, how would you see your role developing?'

'If the focus was securing the house and the three primary Tattons, I would be looking at implementing a more formal pattern of surveillance. They would not be aware necessarily, but I think we need eyes on them at all times, one way or another. I think supplementing the team is a good start and having security in the house is an obvious way forward. I would assign personal security to all three primaries allowing full integration with their lives and needs. That's the best way to maximise success.'

'You're talking about expanding the team substantially in that case though, by at least six,' Tim sounded vexed, 'We can't have that. It would upset the balance of everything, the equilibrium. Hell, we tried introducing a third mobile camera a few years back and it just proved to be too cumbersome.'

Red stretched up in their seat and tilted their head from side to side. 'Point taken,' they said, 'In that case, you're going to need a very small team of excellent people. It's not going to be easy.'

'I thought that might be the case, and to be truthful, I find that nothing ever is,' Tim replied wearily.

'Luckily for you,' Red folded their arms, 'you've found one person for the job. I'm perfect. You should offer me the position today before I change my mind.'

'I see,' Tim looked slightly taken aback, 'Are you likely to? Change your mind that is?'

'Maybe,' they said, 'It's high profile and high stakes. One false move and everything goes tits up. And I'll be the one with everyone baying for my blood. Yep. I've seen those comments. One botch and you're unlikely ever to work again. You're right, Tim, (you don't mind if I call you that, do you?) it's a tough job but I'm willing to take it on. I love a challenge as you can see from my military service. Yes. I will take it on. Thanks for the offer.'

Red stood up and offered their hand to a rather bemused Tim who stood up too and shook it, managing a weak smile. The energy of the handshake seemed to galvanise him however.

'Okay! Okay. This is great, Red. Thanks! Thanks so much. You're going to be a real asset. We look forward to welcoming you on board.'

And the rest, as they say is history.

So today, Red is unpacking in the annexe, and we are having a party to welcome them. Nothing too fancy but I wanted to make it some kind of event. They really are going to be a fabulous addition to the *Flora Show* family.

Tim is here and I've already teased him about Red beating him to the job offer part of the interview. He totally denies it. Says he was in complete control. I heard him telling Milk he's a little bit frightened of Red though. See. I told you so.

Treasure is napping and the webcam is on in the nursery. We've got cocktails and mocktails and some gorgeous little canapés all set out in the garden in a little marquee. Shy is filming with one hand and shovelling food down his throat at the same time. Very refined!

Mum and Morag come out into the garden and Tim hands round bubbles for everyone. I've told them all today is about family, and no one is working. We all stand and chat and Marsha comes down with the baby monitor. She's in shorts which I think is a bit informal. The garden looks beautiful; she could have made an effort.

'Are you off to Alton Towers after this, Marsha?' I say warmly.

She's started chatting to Milk who's just arrived too looking a bit sleepy and dishevelled himself.

'Sorry, Flora,' she says perkily, 'What was that?'

'I said, are you off to a theme park or somewhere of that ilk after this lovely garden party?' I stare at her face then down at her scruffy flip flops.

'No, no,' she replies, 'Just thought it's hot, isn't it?'

'Well, I'll pass that on to Red, shall I? This is Marsha. She was hot so she could barely be bothered to dress herself for your welcome party!' I'm a little annoyed that my voice is so loud at the end, but the flip flops look like they should be in a charity bag not on my lawn. I pay Marsha good money; she can afford a pair of strappy sandals for goodness' sake.

'I'll just go and get changed,' Marsha mumbles and has the good manners at least to blush as she scuttles off.

'Be quick!' I pipe up as she disappears through the bi-fold doors.

'That was a little unnecessary,' my mother is at my elbow, 'She's been up most of the night with Treasure. Not that you'd know as you never made it down for breakfast this morning.'

'Thank you for the information, Mum,' I reply, 'I too had a difficult night, and was trying to catch a few hours in order to look my best for this.' My mother is one of the few people I can lie to. She rarely watches The Show so has no idea what I actually do in reality. If she checked she would see I'd been sound asleep in bed by midnight having drunk rather too much wine with Tim who had come down early for the party to talk through some other programming business and stayed over. I did indeed skip breakfast. Well, I didn't skip it, Morag brought me it in bed. Lovely.

Red appears at the doorway. They, unlike Marsha, are dressed formally. A little too formally in fact. They are in a suit. A gun metal grey three piece with a thin red silk tie. The cut of the suit is good and with their short auburn spiky hair the effect is striking but they are clearly dressed for work and not a party.

I stride across the grass towards them.

'Red! Hello! As I said, we're throwing a little party for you, to welcome you into the *Flora Show* family. Now what can I get you to drink. Now you do look a little hot. Do you want to take your jacket off perhaps? It is a party after all.'

Shy moves towards us with the cam and I know he'll be focussed on Red's responses. We want them to be a hit, to be a personality that everyone can relate to. We haven't thrown a party for any other member of staff joining the show; this is a first.

'Thanks, but no,' Red says, 'I'm sorry Ms Tatton, but as far as I'm concerned, I'm working, am I not?'

'Oh, Ms Tatton, that sounds very scary Red,' I turn round to the handheld and pull a sad clown face, 'Call me Flora, Red, everyone here does. We're family after all.'

'Okay. Yes, okay. Sorry, Flora. I'm working though. These are my contracted hours.' They look distinctly anxious.

'Don't worry about all that. We're having a party for you. Now what about a drink? Eh? Some champagne?'

'I'm sorry Ms Tatton,'

'Flora,' I interject patiently.

'Flora,' Red repeats, 'but I can't drink while I'm on duty. It's irresponsible.'

'Oh Red, you're not on duty,' I laugh trying to salvage this misery standing before me.

'Okay maybe not at the moment, but I will be later, and alcohol can affect your judgement for up to twelve hours, well it stays in your system for that long at least. By that I mean it can be traced in your blood. It can be traced in your hair up to ninety days later, but it wouldn't impair your judgement for that long.'

I stare at Red.

They stare back at me.

Tim joins us.

'They usually throw a party for you when you leave your job, don't they, Red, not when you start,' Tim says cheerily.

'I can see why,' I say.

Marsha appears in a smart tea dress. 'Just letting you know, I've got changed,' she says.

I hug her. 'You look lovely,' I say and have a swig of champagne.

Red is still standing next to me.

I grab the plate of canapés on the table next to me and offer them one. 'Can you eat some of these,' I say, 'Or will these have some kind of detrimental effect on your job?'

Red looks shifty.

'What is it?' I say.

'I follow the 5:2 diet. I'm not in an eating window at the moment,' they say.

'Surely you could manage to look like you're enjoying yourself for the sake of the party, Red,' I hiss, 'Or perhaps you need to look over your contract a little more closely.'

Again, they look shifty.

'What is it now?' I say.

'I've got a nut allergy and I'm gluten intolerant,' and they smile weakly.

'Of course you have and of course you are,' I say, 'and it was very silly of us not to check your dietary requirements.' I put down the canapés so roughly they jolt on the plate. 'Is your nut allergy life-threatening?'

Red nods apologetically.

'Morag!' I shout and Morag trots over, 'Morag, Red has a life-threatening nut allergy. I need you to deal with that new information.'

'On it,' Morag says calmly smiling at Red, 'I'm on it like a Scotch Bonnet. Don't you worry my poppet,' and deftly picks up the canapés, swiftly enlisting my mother in taking the rest of the food into the house.

'I don't think I'll do this for anyone else,' I say to Red.

'It was a nice thought,' they say weakly.

'Maybe,' I say, but I'm not sold.

'Could I perhaps have a Coke?' Red says.

'Sure,' I say, 'Marsha will get you one. I'm going for a nap. I'm hungover. I'll see you later, Red.'

And I leave them to it.

I mean, you try to do something nice ...

the.real.flora.tatton
daily contemplation: Family is not an important thing. It is everything.

Liked by **2beeornot2bee** and **6,211,577 others**

nowayback
Red is way cool #digtheirhair #sharpsuit

fuckeduphuman
Roll up for another freak show. Buddy for Meryl. Why is no one normal anymore? #nostalgic

bobbyboombastic
sending harmony across the ocean

1974999
why isn't Red packing? The threat is real #gunownersofamerica #

lilpiggywenttomarket
cute party vibes LOVE the alfresco mood #summersun #peaceout@theflorashow

cheesywotsups
Flora is so bountiful. Mi casa es tu casa. Way to welcome Red, girl #love #myheart #wishyourweremine

22

Joyce

I didn't recognise the name at first when I got the letter but that's because I knew her as Beth and now she goes by Liz. I jumped to the end of the letter to see who it was from and that's when I made the connection.

It used to be such a surprise to get a letter, a treat even; one of Robert's sons, Noah, writes to me from time to time from Australia. We made contact after Robert died. He was the one who phoned me with the news and things just kept going from there. Perhaps he felt guilty that his father had been such a poor correspondent himself, who knows? Anyway, there's something about the anticipation of a letter and the time it's taken someone to sit down and put pen to paper that is, I don't know, touching nowadays. Of course, I have no idea who any of the people are that Noah witters on about, but I have a little wallet of photos, sent over the years, kindly labelled and dated by him, and I have them sort of classified. From time to time I take them out and lay them on the table and re-order them. Like I am studying them for an historical project. It's the librarian in me I suppose.

Anyway, I digress. I was talking about Beth, not Noah. It was the name that confused me but once I thought about it properly, I remembered Beth Finnerty quite well, even though in my memory Burnley Place feels like a long, long time ago. Not Beth Finnerty now though. Liz Finnerty.

I say I used to enjoy receiving letters but since The blasted Show, there is a steady stream of 'fan mail' as Flora calls it. Most of it is forwarded from Flora's offices and so I can recognise it because of that. It goes straight in the bin unless I've got an hour to kill and then I may open one or two to gauge how much the world hates me.

Most of it is negative.

Most of the letters are from older women, like my neighbour Rita, who have had disappointing daughters or daughters who've died or daughters who never speak to them or daughters who are damaged in some way and they, 'feel they have to write and tell me how lucky' I am to have Flora. Most, if not all, would give *anything*, yes *anything*, to trade places with me and have a child like Flora who are convinced is, 'perfect'. Ultimately, they think I don't appreciate her and they want me to buck up and effuse more live on TV.

I have three words for them all.

Fuck right off.

Of course I would never say that.

My mother would be horrified.

But that's what I'm thinking as I read the rambling, poorly spelt, grammatically incorrect waffle that tumbles through my letter box.

Fuck right off the lot of you.

Amazing that anyone imagines they have the right to comment on my relationship with Flora, but I suppose she granted the whole world permission when she turned the cameras on all those years ago.

I never gave my permission though.

As far as I'm concerned, it's a diabolical liberty.

Anyway when Beth/Liz's letter arrives, it hasn't been forwarded. It's handwritten and the address is spot on. I did wonder how she'd procured it, but people have their means. The letter was well written with an ink pen no less, so I wrote back agreeing to meet Liz in one of the little tea shops in town. What could be the harm? We'd be in a public place. I wouldn't be in danger and, as a teenager, she'd hardly been a threat, a quiet little mouse of a girl. Nothing to her really.

I've never been one to manage female friends. Or male friends for that matter. I enjoy my own company and I'm not very good at chit chat. As the time comes closer to the allotted time, I find myself getting nervous. I even telephone Morag and speak to her about it. I hardly ever phone anyone; I don't like not being able to see the other person's face when I'm telling them something.

The call is ridiculously short.
Me: Morag, it's Joyce.
Morag: Joyce, hi, how are you? Everything okay?
Me: Yes. I'm fine.
There is then quite a long silence.
Morag: Are you still there Joyce?
Me: Yes, still here.
Morag: Okay, good.
Another silence.
Morag: How's the weather up there? It's spitting here.
Another silence.
Me: I'm meeting someone in a few days.
Morag: Okay. That's nice.
Me: Is it?
Morag: I don't know. You tell me.
Me: I mean, is it a good idea?
Morag: Hard to say. Do you know this person?
Me: She's a friend, no, not a friend, an acquaintance from my school days. She wrote to me.
Morag: Okay. Did you like her? When you were younger?
Me: She was alright.
Morag: Why did you agree to meet her?
Me: I don't know.
Morag: You don't have to go.
Yet another silence.

Morag: Or you could go, to see what she's like now.
Me: Okay Morag, thank you. Bye.
Morag: Bye Joyce.

I just get tongue-tied on the phone. I tried to picture what Morag's face would be telling me and I couldn't so I didn't know what to say next. So I decide to give up on the phone call. But she is right. I can go and see what Beth/Liz is like so that's what I will do.

Tim had warned me once Flora became very wealthy that all sorts of people could try to take advantage of us, and we had to be vigilant at all times. This hasn't really happened to me. I've had a few begging letters from local charities and schools and requests for sponsorship from amateur football teams and theatres, but I just write back and say, 'Come and look at my house, there's no money here.' I don't tell them that Flora spends excessive amounts of time trying to force money onto me one way or another.

Liz is sitting primly at the table in the window with a pot of tea already ordered. She is tidily dressed in a smartish pale minty green jacket with a lilac polo neck underneath. Her hair is well cut and she's wearing a little make-up but not too much. She is presentable and displaying no obvious signs of insanity which is a good starting point; however, I truly hope she is not going to jump up and envelop me in an embarrassing embrace. I hold my handbag up in front of me. Just in case. She looks up at me and registers recognition. She smiles and raises one hand. It is a pleasingly lukewarm greeting.

I venture over.

'Joyce,' she says calmly, 'How nice to see you.'

'Liz,' I nod, 'Nice to see you too,' and I sit down, and the waitress appears immediately. I order a pot of tea as well and we decide to share a fruit scone as neither of us are particularly hungry.

As the waitress beetles off Liz speaks. 'I wasn't sure whether to come,' she says, 'I'm not very good with people.'

'Really?' I say.

'Yes,' she replies stirring half a spoon of sugar into her tea, 'I felt I could manage to meet up with you as we have a bit of a head start. You,' she briefly meets my eye, 'understand my ... background.'

'Of course,' I say, and the waitress is back setting down the tea and scone and two plates and we divide the scone and I like the bottom and Liz likes the top so it seems we are well suited to share.

I stir half a spoon of sugar into my tea. 'So, are you married?' I say.

'I was,' she says, 'but I'm happier on my own. I think being in that place made me a little bit, I don't know, tougher. Or more difficult to live with. I know I was quiet in there, but I've always found it hard to trust anyone properly. I find it easier just getting on and having a quiet life. No one to worry about but myself.'

'I get that,' I say, 'I'm the same to be truthful. I was married and had my daughter, but we separated when she was young. I brought her up on my own.'

'We never had children,' Liz says, 'I couldn't face them. I worried too much that something might happen to us, and they'd end up in the care system like I had. I couldn't bear the thought. My husband didn't have much family either. I look back and I was such a worrier. Silly really. I'm more sensible now.'

I recognised what Liz was saying about that constant gnawing anxiety, often about nothing in particular, from the early years with Flora and Robert. When everything in your life changes dramatically and your life is up ended, it's hard to believe it won't happen again. I'd forgotten about it until Liz mentioned it; it took me right back. I should have been content. I had what everything around me told me would bring me happiness; a home, a husband, a child, stability even. But I never settled into it. I never felt like it was really mine to possess. Like I deserved it or that it belonged to me. There wasn't a lot of talk of anxiety or stress in those days. But I remember lying awake under thin sheets with Robert sleeping deeply and feeling utterly overwhelmed by both the futility and the responsibility of my life. Some mornings it was all I could do to drag myself out of bed though I never let it show, of course, or told anyone. And sometimes I'd look across at Robert sleeping next to me and feel like he was a complete stranger. Worse, an interloper, an imposter. I wanted him out of my life. Yes, that anxiety, that dread, it definitely contributed to Robert leaving. Well, why would you stay with a wife who didn't really like you?

'So what did you do with your life?' I say brightly, pushing all thoughts of Robert away, 'I worked in a library. I don't know if you remember how much I loved books?' I take a bite of scone and realise that this woman sitting next to me might actually understand my experiences. It's an odd sensation.

'Oh I remember. You always had your head down and were studying away. You were quite the inspiration. Truth is Joyce, without you I don't think I'd have achieved half the things I have done.' Liz smiles then, properly, not shyly but with real affection looking into my eyes.

'What do you mean?' I say.

'One of the reasons I wanted to meet you was to say thank you. I looked you up on the electoral register, I hope you don't mind Joyce, but I wanted to meet up and say you showed me I could have a different life,' and she rests her hand gently on mine, tentatively, just for a moment.

'I really don't understand,' I say, 'I don't remember doing anything.'

'Do you remember telling us all those stories over and over about your life before you were at Burnley Place? Your mum the teacher, your mum being so clever, knowing so much about all those kings and queens and battles and crusades. And you told us all those stories and you described your house and your life. Most of us had never had any kind of proper family home, not like you, so we lapped it up. And I can remember those stories as clearly as if that was my childhood. I mean they were so real to me; I could have lived that life. And when me and Patrick separated, I decided I wanted to be a teacher, like your mum, and that's what I did, I went to college, and I worked hard and I became a teacher. Not history, not got the brains for that no, but Home Ec, I love to cook and I'm good at it, though you wouldn't know to look at me, always have been skin and bone, so Cookery and now Food Technology as it's called, but I was still a teacher, like your mum and I loved my job and I loved the kids, and I truly have you to thank for it.

'Oh my goodness, I'm not used to giving such big, long speeches. This wasn't quite the way I thought it was going to go. Look I'm sorry. Tell me a bit about yourself. I'm just droning on. Normally I'm the quiet one but today you can't get two words in!' and Liz pats her cheek with the back of her palm to stem a blush which I think is very sweet.

'Liz, I can remember a little of what you say but I'm sorry, I can't remember telling you lots of stories, but then again, I think I've blocked quite a lot of those years out. I remember working hard and trying to keep out of the way. Everybody's way. I remember you though. I remember you being quiet little Beth. And I'm very pleased your life has turned out the way you wanted it to.'

I stir my tea and take a couple of sips. It's very good.

'I don't know what to say about my life,' I continue, 'It's been quite humdrum really. Like I said, I have a daughter and two granddaughters now. I see them from time to time and that suits me fine. I'm not one of these ga-ga grannies who think their grandchildren are the be-all-

and-end-all. I just hope they grow up to be respectable humans.' I bite the scone, 'Did you stay in the area your whole life Liz, or have you moved around?' Her return address is close by and so, not far from Burnley Place. I hoped she'd spread her wings a little at some point, though of course I'm still here.

'Grandchildren. Fancy. I see you now and I have to adjust my view of you because in my head, you're still a teenager. Hard to picture you with grandkids. Me and Patrick were over in Lancashire for a few years but when we split up, I moved back here. Hard for me not to come back to my roots, such as they are. I suppose there's a bit of security in familiarity, isn't there?'

'Yes, there is. I've stayed around here too. Though my ex-husband jetted off to Australia on the ten-pound pom deal years ago. Went out there and started his own business. Did very well for himself.'

'Really? You still on good terms? Does your daughter go out with the kids and visit? That's a good holiday, isn't it?' Liz finishes her scone and tea and looks for the waitress to pay the bill.

'No, he died a long time ago now. Can't think how many years. Ten or fifteen. I don't keep track.' I too look for the waitress. I was worried that Liz would drag the catch-up out, but apparently not.

'Funny,' Liz smiles, 'Patrick too, but do you know when he died, I really didn't feel much at all. Even though we'd been husband and wife for six years. He'd re-married and had three boys. Was very happy you know but it was like a stranger had died really. Oh, don't think I'm terrible Joyce, I've never told anyone that before. I went to the funeral and everything, but I could have been at anyone's. Didn't feel a thing. My marriage to him felt like it was from another life by that time. Oh, I hope I haven't shocked you. Please say I haven't.'

'Quite the opposite, Liz,' I say, 'You could be describing exactly how I felt about Robert. I mean I didn't fly to Australia for his funeral – I could have but there would have been absolutely no point because I too really felt nothing when he died. I thought it was a shame. Like I feel when a houseplant dies. I felt terrible about that; my lack of feeling if you like. The father of my child and that was my response, but I couldn't help it. How funny that you should feel the same?'

'Amazing,' Liz says a little absent-mindedly as she spots the waitress coming over and we split the bill.

'It's been lovely seeing you again, Joyce,' Liz says as we stand outside the café on the bleak and windy high street.

'And you, Liz,' and I realise I mean it. She turns to head off up towards her house. It's only a ten-minute walk she says. I'm going the opposite way. I'm taking the chance to change my books at the library which is down the other end of the high street. We wave.

I take a step or two and then turn and shout, 'Liz!' and she turns back quizzically towards me.

'We should have lunch!' I say boldly.

We set a date and I march with spring and purpose back to the library. A whole conversation with someone new who hasn't heard or seen *The Flora Show*. I know they do exist, but she is a rare find.

Perhaps I may be able to manage female friends after all.

23

Meryl

We've agreed to meet for lunch but it's a push for me to get there from college, so we make it early dinner. I choose somewhere out of the way and hope we can keep things quiet. I'm there before Granny and Morag and I choose a secluded table right at the back.

It's becoming a bit of a habit. Granny is visiting more and every time she does, we all meet up at least once. Morag brings a hamper of homemade treats to sustain me as if I am going to waste away living on my own. She's keen to do more for me despite my reassurances that I'm good and managing pretty well.

It's lovely to hear them chat on though. I miss Morag's voice. I love her accent; her voice sounds like she's sucking on a sweet and she says every letter in a word, so clearly, really sounds them out. She takes her time to speak. I love that. It's like the words are candies in her mouth and she savours the flavours of them, rolling them around on her tongue, before letting them go. When I was little, it was always her I wanted to read my bedtime story, even though I was more than capable of reading them myself by the time she was living with us. Often, I didn't listen to the tales, I just mused on how she pronounced the words as I lay against her comfortable, reliable body. She never insisted on putting an arm around me or getting too close. Morag let me come to her. She knew what I needed.

I check my phone while I wait for them.

There's nothing from Tyler.

Yesterday there was a really trashy article in one of the online mags about him. One of his so-called mates had sold a story. It was brutal. I'd tried to explain that he had to ignore all that shit; that it was just click bait, but I could see he was gutted. 'I expected him to be at my wedding,' he said, 'Mates for life. We grew up together.'

'They'll have offered him a lot of money, Ty' I said, 'And they'll have twisted his words. Don't be too hard on him.'

I said that to him, but I don't really have any friends. I've been let down over and over. Sneaky photos of private moments of me in a swimsuit or bad outfits or on shopping trips or at the cinema and leaked info about secret boyfriends or friendship dramas or parties finding their way into newspapers and celebrity mags teach you to keep your guard up. I just don't bother with all that now. I don't care what anyone thinks of me.

He said he was going to go and see Danny, the friend, and try and sort it out.

I told him not to bother.

'Hello my little pudding, how lovely you're looking today,' Morag has managed to sneak in, with Granny close behind. As they move in for efficient embraces, I am enveloped with lavender and jasmine and lemon, nice but old-fashioned. Morag has new lipstick, a sort of coral pink which looks a bit strong, and I think she's overdone the lacquer on her hair. She's a tendency to do that if the wind picks up. Better be careful if they light the candle on the table.

'You're looking better than last time we saw you,' Granny says in one of her usual back-handed compliments, 'Not so tired at least. You must be nearly at the end of term now. One more year and you'll be off to Uni. Any more thoughts about York?'

Granny is keen for me to go there as she'll be able to see me easily. 'I keep telling you Granny, I'll be living it up with 24-hour parties and sex and drugs, I won't have time to come and visit you. I may as well go to Edinburgh. It's not going to look cool is it when my flatmates are living the high life and I have to tell them I'm off to check on my aging grandmother.'

Granny bristles. 'I wasn't expecting you to check up on me,' she says, 'I was hoping to get in on some of the action. Frankly, I was expecting you to hook me up with a bit of the sex and drugs. I've been going through what you young people call a bit of a dry spell.'

She and Morag hoot with laughter as I pull a mock-shocked face. 'York hasn't got the course I want to do so you'll have to sort out your own sex and drugs I'm afraid,' I say picking up the menu, 'Let's order, I'm starving, and the service can be slow here according to the reviews.'

Morag looks appalled. 'Why are you hungry? Did you eat lunch?' She starts to rummage in her bag, 'I might have a boiling or two in here. Aha!' she says in triumph and produces a half bag of boiled sweets which she thrusts across the table at me.

'It's okay, Morag, I'm not going to faint,' I say, shaking my head and waving the sweets away, 'I'm normally hungry for someone about to eat a meal and, yes, I ate lunch. Now, look at the menus.'

There is a good deal of muttering over the choices available and the flavour pairings, but finally a decision is made, and we sit back to enjoy the anticipatory moments before the food arrives. Morag and Granny chatter on and show me pictures of Treasure who is growing and looking adorable, but I am feeling happy. Happy to be in the company of these two lovely women and away from Tyler and the cramped flat and from all the adult choices that I now crush my soul on a daily basis. I sip my tangy drink and like the tinkle of the chink of the ice against the glass and the slip of condensation under my fingertips and I am pleased to just be in the moment.

Then my phone rings.

Tyler has been arrested.

We must look like quite a surprising trio at the police station; a sullen teenager with rather too much eye make-up and two well turned-out older ladies sporting a large wicker hamper. When the desk sergeant asks who we are here to see, we all three say Tyler's name in unison. We pause and look at each other, then look back at the desk sergeant, and then we all three say it again. In unison.

He just nods and tells us to take a seat.

Tyler has been arrested for assaulting Danny. Tyler found Danny in a pub, and they got in a fight. They both got arrested. That's all we know.

Granny phoned Flora on the way over.

I didn't stop her.

Flora is sending a solicitor.

I'm not stopping her.

I know that makes me a hypocrite.

We sit and wait in silence, Granny with her bag on her lap and Morag with the hamper on hers.

I'm still starving but it seems unreasonable to break open the hamper and start tucking into it in a police station. It's not Glyndebourne.

Eventually Granny turns to me and says quietly, 'I've made contact with a friend from my past, we were at school together but she's younger than me by a few years.'

'That's nice,' I say.

'She's called Liz and she's quite a shy person but we're getting on quite well. We like similar things. We've been out for lunch a couple of times, and we went to the cinema last week too. Saw the new Judi Dench film.'

'Lovely,' I say and put my hand on my knee to stop it jiggling so much.

'When I knew her when we were young, she called herself Beth, but now she calls herself Liz. I thought I could call myself Joy instead of Joyce but then I thought that wouldn't really suit me.' Granny looks at her hands over her bag.

'No, maybe not,' I say.

We sit in silence for a while longer.

A spikily thin woman marches into the station. Her heels ring out into the silence. She is dressed in a stylish pinstripe trouser suit with a green carnation in the buttonhole. I can't work out if this is a joke or not. Her short blonde hair is slicked back, and she has no make-up but is very tanned. She looks like a villain from a Marvel film.

'I'm Helenka Goralski. I'm here for Tyler Bayliss,' she says.

We all stand up.

'Yes Ms Goralski, of course, just one moment, and I'll take you through,' the desk sergeant replies.

'Ms Goralski,' I say and she turns to me and it's hard not to cower a little in the fullness of her glare and authority. 'I'm Meryl Tatton, Tyler's girlfriend. I'm Flora's daughter.'

'Of course, Meryl. Lovely to meet you. We'll have this sorted out in no time.'

The door next to the desk opens and Helenka Goralski disappears.

We sit back down.

It's barely half an hour before a rather sorry and battered Tyler appears through the door with the impressive Ms Goralski.

She is all business and Tyler is all apology and thanks. She will have none of it and marches off into the night having offered a curt goodbye to us all.

Tyler is free to go. He will face no charges. There will be no repercussions. We shuffle out of the police station and hail a cab and all four of us sit in silence as we make our way back to the flat and try not to look at the bruises on Tyler's face.

Once inside, Morag and Granny set to in the kitchen making coffee and bringing food from the hamper to revive us all. There is peanut brittle and white chocolate cookies and homemade Scottish tablet, and the sugar is just what we all need.

Tyler and I sit on the bed, with Granny at the foot of it on the ottoman that Tyler decided was a must-have, and Morag manages astride the exercise bike. I am embarrassed.

Embarrassed to the point of despair.

I see the flat through their eyes as I watch them both taking in all the details and evidence of Flora's money and the effect it is having on sweet, sweet Tyler who sits with his head in his hands unable to look at any of us.

They finish the coffee and wash the cups and Morag calls an Uber and I walk them down the stairs thanking them for everything and hugging them both hard on the dandelion marked path that leads to my front door.

I go back upstairs, and Tyler is in the shower. I stand outside the door.

I can hear him crying.

24

Flora

Don't get me wrong, I like the boy. I always have. In theory.

But when the police start getting involved, it's hard not to take the view that someone might need to step in. To give her a nudge. Or to give him a push.

I mean I can't have my daughter involved with a con.

This isn't *Eastenders*.

We have to have some standards here.

Of course the real issue we have is the Romeo and Juliet syndrome. Force them apart and you push them together. This has been Shy and Milk's view from the start.

'She's like you, Flo,' Shy says, 'She sees what she wants and she takes it. Nobody can tell her what to do.'

I have nipped over to the annexe which I try not to do as the fans know it's off limits. We have Tara here doing Bedtime Baby Yoga with Treasure and Marsha though so I can take ten minutes. I can go and join for the pranayama and put Treasure down for the night.

'I agree,' Milk joins in, 'You forbid her from seeing this boy and she will choose him over you every day of the week. Just to spite you. Even if she doesn't think he's awesome.'

'Totally,' Shy says, 'You have to let it play out. Let him make the mistakes. Which he will.'

'Yea,' Milk adds, 'Or better yet, ditch her, and she'll come running back to you, all broken-hearted.'

'Woah, harsh, Milk,' Shy stops him, 'We don't want li'l Meryl to suffer. We want her to decide he's no good for her. We want him to show he's not worthy.'

'Okay, yeah,' Milk gets excited, 'what about a honeytrap? Set him up with another girl. A fine young girl?'

'Hang on boys, I think you're getting a bit carried away here. We are not exploiting any young women to break up my daughter's relationship. Okay? But I agree, I can't force Meryl to stop seeing him. I have to do what I can to look supportive but hope that she sees he's not for her.'

'So how are you going to do that?'

'I'm going to do everything I can to make him a better man.'

Both men look at me askance.

'What're you talking about?' Shy says.

'Well,' I explain, 'If I give him all the opportunities he thinks he wants and then he fucks it up anyway, he'll have no one to blame but himself. I mean maybe he is a great guy and he'll come good ... If he does then it's the greatest love story ever told, but if not, I'm in the clear and Meryl can't blame me either.'

'So you're going to bail him out?' Milk sounds surprised.

'I'm going to provide him with an excellent brief. Like I say, everything he thinks he needs. We'll see what Meryl makes of it all once he's 'free' and where they go from there.'

'Who do you have in mind?' Milk is checking his phone. A decision has been made and his mind has moved on.

'Helenka. Call her Shy, will you? Or call Tim and ask him to. I'm exhausted. I'm going to back to check on the yoga.'

'Okay, will do,' Shy answers.

Milk and I head back over to the house.

Later, in my room, I see Morag and Mum come back on the feed. Helenka has already text me.

I text Meryl and ask her and Tyler to lunch at the weekend.

She agrees. With a thumbs up emoji. No words.

It's ten months since she last set foot in the house.

I tell myself I will not make a big deal out of it.

25

Joyce

Liz and I have taken a day trip to Harrogate. She has driven. I don't know why I never learned to drive. I suppose I always lived near to where I worked so I didn't feel the necessity. I like the train too. Flora provides me with cars now. Insists on it. It's nice to be driving with Liz, sitting up front and chatting as we speed over the timeless moors which are looking particularly beautiful against a brooding sky.

'Shall we have tea at *Betty's*?' I ask Liz, 'My treat? After we've been round the gardens?' We're going to the RHS garden at Harlow Carr. We discovered we're both keen gardeners and Liz said she visits regularly. I've only been a couple times so I jumped at the chance. It really is incredible how many things we have in common, and I remark on this in the car.

'Perhaps it's because of Burnley Place,' Liz says, 'All our interests have their roots in never having a proper family.'

'I did have a proper family, Liz,' I correct her, 'For most of my childhood.'

'Yes, of course,' Liz puts her hand to her face and looks away, 'Sorry, I forget that you were one of the lucky ones.'

'I wouldn't say that,' I argue, 'I had my perfect life snatched away from me, remember? At least you never knew what you were missing.'

'So because I'd never had it, I didn't miss it, you mean. That's a stretch. That's like saying someone born without hands isn't going to miss them because they've never had them. Or someone who is deaf will never miss music because they've never heard it. Or miss hearing the sound of their children's voices because they can communicate through sign language.' A tension wire of anger is unmistakably taut in her voice.

I turn away to the dull and lifeless ribbons of green and grey undulating past my window. Clouds are in front of the sun. I feel desolate. Lost at not knowing what to say to retrieve the situation. Flora agrees with everyone; it's her first response to everything and I find it extremely irritating. The world loves her unconditionally though.

'You're right, Liz,' I say, 'It's not a competition. We were both equally deprived. Denied in different ways. I'm sorry. I didn't mean to upset you.' It's funny, I have always found it very hard to apologise, but not to Liz. I want her to be my friend. I want her to like me.

'That's okay, Joyce,' she says easily and, thankfully, her open and cheery expression returns to her face. She accepts my apology without complications as she always does, and the drive continues in restored good humour.

'You're a very easy person to get along with,' she says after a minute or two, as if she is reading my mind.

'I was just thinking the same!' I say and we laugh a little.

A couple of days later Liz phones to cancel our planned visit to Hadrian's Wall. I told her at Harlow Carr that my mother loved the Romans and we got to talking and we hatched a plan to head off to Vindolanda. Liz had never been, and she got quite excited about it. We had had several trips over there when I was a girl; Dad and I marvelled at how Mum could bring the dusty stone ruins to life with vivid tales of the centurion's lives and tiny details of day to day living all those years ago. I told Liz quite a few bits and pieces in the car on the way back and, by the time we were home, she was thrilled at the thought of seeing the site in person.

'One of the things I love about being older,' she says, 'is that I feel I'm catching up on all the things I missed out on when I was young. Not really paying attention at school, you know and not going on all the trips.'

When she phones, she is clearly disappointed. 'The car's packed up and it's going to be a big bill. It'll have to wait until after payday I'm afraid, Joyce.'

I have to confess I have got out of the habit of budgeting and paydays as Flora pays money into an account to top up my library pension. I try to limit what goes in but it's all I could do to stop her buying me a completely unsuitable new house. We have argued and argued and in the end, I gave up and I accept that the sum goes in.

'Please don't be offended, Liz, but why don't I loan you the money for the car? It wouldn't be any bother to me,' I say impetuously, 'I mean, I'd like to help, we don't have to go to Vindolanda.'

'Absolutely not Joyce. I've never borrowed a penny in my life. That way lies madness. I have to be straight, or I couldn't sleep at night. But thank you for the offer,' she replies curtly. I can hear from her voice that she hasn't liked me saying it though. I said I'm not good on the phone. I should never have brought it up.

'I'm exactly the same Liz,' I rush on, 'Forget I said a word. I should have thought before I said anything. I don't know what came over me. I apologise. We can wait a couple of weeks. Vindolanda has been there for 2000 years, I don't think it's going anywhere,' and I hoped I hadn't crossed a line with this reserved and proud woman who I realised I respected very deeply.

There is a silence on the other end.

I wait.

I hear Liz take a deep breath, like she is making a decision, and, to my surprise, I involuntarily cross my fingers, even though I am not in the least bit superstitious.

'I agree,' she says calmly, 'Vindolanda can wait. We'll rethink in a few weeks. Now I meant to ask, did you see *Eastenders* last night? What a shocker that was.'

I smile to myself, and we chat happily over our joint guilty pleasure of tuning in to life in the square. I do not know why I watch it, but I do and I have done for years. And so, miraculously, does Liz. We wonder whether it's the routine; having a fixed point in the day to sit down and visit the same people. Though we both agree they are all generally very irritating.

Anyway, after that call, I resolve I must be careful not to offer Liz money again. I don't want to jeopardise our friendship over something so trivial.

26

Meryl

It's like watching a super-fast-forward social experiment except I'm in the middle of it and my boyfriend is the main subject. As the flat is full to bursting and he's battered his friend and got arrested, Tyler is now finding 'creative' ways to fill his time and spend the money. He started by talking about buying properties and began dressing up like some geek and meeting with estate agents all over town and taking endless phone calls about different places that he thought would be 'sound investments'. Then he found out just having access to a bank account funded by Flora Tatton was not enough to secure any kind of mortgage.

Today he's moved onto business ideas. 'I could own my own club. A chain of clubs. Like internationally. Like in Ibiza and shit. That would be peng. And they could be really cool and open at ten in the morning.'

'Who wants to go to a club at ten in the morning Tyler,' I asked without much interest, I was trying to finish a maths paper for college.

'Doesn't matter. That's what gives it the USP, baby.'

'USP?' I say not looking up from my calculator.

'Unique Selling Point. You got to have something like that. Like my club opens at ten in the morning. Or we have cage fighters. Or caged tigers. Or it's in a cage.' He was pacing around what little space there was in the flat.

'Seems like a lot of cage-based USPs there,' I say.

'I'm just rolling with the idea is all,' he says, 'You got to have some reason everyone wants to come to *your* club.'

'What about good tunes and cheap drinks?' I say, 'Anyway you don't really like clubs, Tyler, you say they're dingy and tacky and every night you spend in one never lives up to the hype.'

He stops still and I feel him staring at me. 'I have *never* in my life said that. I love to club. I love to club. I *love* to club. My soul is made for the club. The hub of the club is a rubadubdub. The nub of the club is a rubadubdub Don't you diss me and the club. We are tight. I love clubbing. I'm gonna call my club the Rubadubdub.'

'Hmmm.' I say, 'Just I've never been to a club with you is all I'm saying and again, lots of club-based language there Ty. Are you okay?'

He plant-faces onto the bed, bouncing my work around me and I scrabble to stop him squashing it. He says something I can't make out into the mattress.

'Didn't hear that,' I say wearily.

Without lifting it, he turns his head to me.

'I'm high,' he says.

'You amaze me,' I say flatly.

'You mad?' he says.

'Why should I be? It's your life,' I say, and I gather my stuff and squeeze it into my rucksack. 'I'm heading back to college to finish this. I'll see you in a bit.'

When I get back, he's getting ready to go out.

'I've had a brilliant idea,' he says as he zips up his jeans, 'Me and Tee have hired that warehouse down the end of the industrial estate. I'm not going to own a club. I'm going to run a rave! We're going to check it out now. Tee's going to DJ and we're posting on TikTok about it. Should make a mint. See you later.'

And he's gone.

I don't see him again for three days when he rolls up in the same clothes, grinning and starving and telling me how lit the whole vibe was and how they have another one planned next weekend, only this time they're going to go to Bristol to do it.

I don't bother to ask why Bristol.

I have end of year exams to worry about which will count towards my predicted grades for Uni. I block Tyler's escapades out of my head. When I picture him getting arrested again or ODing on something dangerous or lying in the twisted metal of a car crash or getting beaten up by a group of menacing thugs because Flora has given him the means to escape from the little box we were happy in before, I shut my mind against it all. I can't be responsible for him. I have to think about myself.

27

Flora

Meryl cancelled the lunch date saying she has exams to revise for. I can't say I revised for a single exam in my life, but we are very different my daughter and I. She did, to her credit, rearrange however and we are expecting her today.

I told myself not to go overboard but let's just say I know how Jacob felt when the prodigal son came home. Okay I don't literally have a fatted calf to kill but I'd wield the knife myself if I did. I cannot wait to see her.

People think it must be hard to live your life with all these cameras but in lots of ways I find them a blessing. I saw practically every moment of Meryl's childhood once we moved in here. And I have it all to look back on, good and bad. I can see her playing in the garden, dressing up, digging in the sand pit, making cupcakes with Morag, riding on Milk and Shy's shoulders round and round the garden. I can re-live it all, anytime I want to. I can see all the tantrums and rejected food and clothes and late for schools and arguments too, but I love those as well. I have every single moment.

These last few months I've lost her. I don't know what she's been up to. I mean I know she was seeing Tyler before and she was round at his place and that was fine, but she always came home. I always saw her come through the door and up the stairs and into her room and that was all I needed.

Now I have nothing.
And I hate it.

So. Today I need to build bridges and bring her back. I hear that Tyler has not learnt from his first misdemeanour so I'm hoping that she may be open to some suggestions I have.

It is exhausting all of this.

I may have a little nap before lunch just to revive me, so I am at my best for her arrival.

It's Red who wakes me up. I can't believe I've overslept, and Meryl is expected in less than half an hour.

'Tia has been here for an hour. We didn't want to disturb you though. You were sleeping so soundly,' Red says as they open the blinds and obviously do a check of the perimeters.

'I won't bother with a shower, send her up and she can do my hair now. I haven't decided on my outfit either.' I try to pull myself out of the heaviness of sleep and stretch and yawn on the edge of the bed.

'From what I can tell from the clothes Meryl left behind, her favourite colour is black,' Red says unhelpfully.

'It's fucking June, Red. It's 24 degrees outside. I'm not wearing black.' I walk into the bathroom and run cool water in the basin. I can't believe how deeply asleep I was. Like I was drugged. I rub my shoulder too. It's aching. I must have slept on it funny. Great! Another reason to be grumpy on this important day.

Milk arrives with the handheld followed by Tia who air kisses me and then starts to fuss over my hair.

'I haven't even had time to wash my face,' I snap and Tia backs off. I can hear the comments in my head –

```
Flora's nerves are really showing
today #bigday
     She  needs  to  keep  it  together
#dontblowit
```

'Tia, be a doll and look for something for me to wear would you, maybe the new Tracy Reese. I want to wear something joyful and bright.'

'Great choice, Flora, perfect vibe.' Tia disappears into the walk-in wardrobe and I plunge my hands into the clear water and watch my fingers tremble. I know Milk will have got this.

```
She cant stop shaking. She scared
of that girl.
    Meryl   for   the   win  #tellyomama
#gogirl
```

'I bet she can't wait to see you, even if she doesn't tell you,' Milk says quietly as I dry my face. I squeeze his arm as I move past to the dressing area.

'Early arrival! I repeat, early arrival!' Red blares out from next to the window overlooking the drive.

'What?' I say, irritated. The whole security jargon is wearing a little thin.

'Meryl's here,' they say sheepishly. They had wanted code names for all three of us, like the cougar, the hawk and the lamb but I drew the line. We aren't the First Family for goodness' sake.

'Bloody hell!' I snatch the dress from Tia, 'Well fucking turn around the lot of you,' I say and peel off my pyjamas showing my tits, not for the first time, to the world, and step into the dress.

I march to the dressing table. 'You'd better be quick, Tia. She could be in and out before I get downstairs!' and Tia sets to on my mop with impressive alacrity.

Five minutes later I glide into the kitchen. Meryl is sitting at the kitchen counter with a bag of crisps, chatting to Morag as if she's never left.

She doesn't bother to get up to come over and hug me. But then again, she never liked to hug.

She also doesn't break her conversation to acknowledge me.

`#whosthebossnow?`

I wait. The smile frozen on my face.

Because I have stopped by the door, moving in further looks weak. Like a clockwork toy, stop start stop start. I don't know what to do.

Meryl carries on speaking. I know she has seen me. My dress is lime green and orange for Christ's sake.

'Meryl!' I bark and Morag, back to me at the hob, startles. 'Sorry Morag, I didn't mean to make you jump, I was just … I just wanted to …' I walk over to my daughter, 'How are you, darling?' I say as if I am a real mother talking to a real daughter.

Meryl looks at me, 'I'm good,' and she offers me the bag of crisps, 'Want a crisp? Morag says lunch is going to be half an hour and I'm famished.'

Morag turns round and we happily roll our eyes at each other.

'How have your exams been?' I say plonking myself down on a barstool.

'Not bad. I've worked, so hopefully they'll be okay.' She says all this through a mouthful of crisps; I resist the temptation to comment.

Morag passes a glass of white wine across the counter to me. I look at it. 'Do you know, Morag, I think I'll just have some sparkling water. I can't seem to face the thought of wine; must be because I've just woken up.' I smile at Meryl, 'Shall we go and sit outside? We've laid the table under the canopy so we can eat out there too.'

'No,' says Meryl, 'Let's keep Morag company until it's ready. In fact, is there anything I can do? And when is my sister going to wake up? It's unbelievable I arrive at midday and half the household is sound asleep.' Her impersonation of my mother is spot on, and Morag and I both enjoy it.

'I wish your Granny was here,' Morag says, 'Have you heard from her lately?'

'Yes!' Meryl is remarkably animated, 'I got a post card from her. She's gone on holiday with her friend Liz! I've never known Granny go on holiday. They've only gone down to Bath for a few days to visit the spa and look at the Roman ruins she says, but I was surprised.'

Morag turns round from the oven, her glasses fogged from the steam, she takes them off and wipes them on her apron, 'Yes!' she says, 'I was surprised too but they seem to be having a lovely time. Staying in a small hotel behind the Royal Crescent she said. Lovely people she said and a very good breakfast.'

'Perhaps we should ask Liz to come down here,' I suggest. 'I don't think I've ever known Mum get on with anyone apart from you Morag. It would be nice to get to know her.'

Red clears their throat ostentatiously in the background.

We all turn to look at them.

'Oh come on Red,' I say, 'It can't be that big a threat, an old woman from Yorkshire. They were in the same children's home for goodness' sake.'

'I'll do a background check,' Red says rocking on their heels.

'No you will not,' I say, 'Mum is a very sensible person. Besides, she might not agree.'

I turn back and hear Red huff.

After what I am told is a delicious lunch, kept light and fun by Milk and Shy and Morag and Treasure and not too focussed on how difficult Meryl finds me, I finally feel I have to mention Tyler.

'So why didn't you bring Tyler?' I say as I pour her coffee and pass a box of macarons around the table.

I can see her guard go up. 'He was busy,' she says quietly.

Shy is filming and moves the camera onto Treasure and Marsha who are on the swing set further down the garden. I know, and Meryl knows, that if things get more interesting, he'll pan back. That's what he's paid to do.

'Was that with his new party party party people business?' I say.

'You do know he is an undesirable, right?' Red jumps in.

'Excuse me? Who the fuck asked your opinion? I mean, do I even know you?' Meryl turns to glare at them. Red was not comfortable sitting and eating lunch with us but instead remained 'vigilant and alert at all times' standing just out of shot. Sometimes I think they think they are in an action movie. Sometimes, they are a teensy bit of a ball ache.

'Red!' I say in a tone that any of the longer serving members of my team would understand to mean, 'Shut the fuck up!'

Instead, Red moves closer to Meryl and then sits down next to her, 'I'm Red, pleased to meet you,' they say straight into her face, 'Let me elaborate. In security terms, your boyfriend slash partner slash significant other – I'm unfamiliar with the term you use for him – aka Tyler Bayliss, is an undesirable. He is volatile, drifting rather than gainfully employed, easily persuaded into reckless behaviours, has a history of drug use and has had a very unstable upbringing. Just one of these factors would be a cause for concern but the combination of all five of them makes it my priority to eradicate him from *The Flora Show* parameters.'

'Your priority?' Meryl repeats incredulously.

'Yes ma'am,' Red replies.

'To eradicate him? Who uses words like that? This isn't Nazi Germany. He's my boyfriend. He's a person. A human being. Like you. You don't get to make decisions like that. I do. Not that I would ever use the term eradicate. Do you understand that?'

'No ma'am,' Red says.

'Why do you keep calling me ma'am? Are you American? Is there something wrong with you? Call me Meryl. That's my name.'

'Yes, Meryl,' they say.

Meryl stares at Red for a little longer but realising they have nothing further to add, turns to me.

'What do you think about this, Mum?' she says.

If only I hadn't hesitated. I shouldn't have. I didn't really want to take Red's side; they were speaking out of turn and had no right to hi-jack the lunch with their half-baked ideas of who my daughter should be dating. I should have said that. I should have fired them really.

But I hesitated.

That was all Meryl needed.

She was gone in less than a minute.

Red held up their hands as if to say good riddance to bad rubbish, as if they'd done me a favour.

I would have really got into it but the whole thing upset me so much I went and puked instead.

Defeated, I crawled back into bed.

#betterlucknexttimebabe

28

Joyce

The trip to Bath was surprisingly successful. Liz was an easy companion and the hotel was clean and efficient.

Before we went I determined we had to finally have a discussion about Flora.

Liz has heard of her but had no real idea of the extent of her notoriety or the difficulties which that presented to me. As it is summer, it is easy enough for me to wear large sunglasses and a sunhat of some sort and there have been no incidents, but if Liz and I are to continue to see each other, there will be something or rather someone who spoils that unblemished record.

We were sitting in the tea shop in which we were first reunited when I filled her in on what could be the reality of my day-to-day.

'So, you mean complete strangers just come up and ask for your autograph or want you to tell them private information about Flora or the grandkids?' she said.

'Yes, that's right. Mostly they want selfies and they demand that I smile, which as you know I'm reluctant to do at the best of times,' I answered picking at the tea cake in front of me. I had no appetite for it. I had been sick with worry at how this was going to affect my friendship with Liz. Would she think me a terrible fraud for not having divulged anything thus far?

'That's a blooming cheek if you ask me,' she responded with a pleasing outrage as colour rose in her cheeks. 'It sounds like you need a bodyguard, Joyce Tatton!'

'Oh, it's not as bad as all that,' I shook my head, 'It's just that I have to avoid certain places and situations.'

'Go on,' Liz frowned with concern.

'Well I would feel very uncomfortable in a busy pub for example or a popular restaurant. You're more likely to get a lot of fans there. Sometimes if one spots you, they kind of magnetise to each other and gravitate towards you. Then it's very hard to repel them.' I looked at the tea cake.

'Good grief,' said Liz, 'Mind you,' she added, 'I can't stand pubs. I hate the smell of beer. It's somehow so…masculine. I'd much rather settle for a cup of coffee any day,' and she smiled sympathetically.

'The thing is,' I said, 'nobody bothers much about me around here. I'm a bit of a fixture and fitting. Or possibly a standing joke. I've been so gruff and grumpy with everyone for so many years that no one tries to find anything out. I haven't been away on holiday for ages. It never really appealed anyway. I like being at home.'

'I understand,' Liz said but she looked a little crestfallen.

'No, no,' I said quickly, 'You misunderstand me. I *want* to go away with you. It's just I think it's only fair to tell you what you're letting yourself in for.'

She raised her eyebrows, 'Hordes of Flora fans beating down our doors? Is that what you're saying?'

'Don't tease me,' I said, 'Everything might be fine, or we might get some harassment. The issue is that I find that if you don't give people what they want, they're nasty. Vile sometimes.'

'Oh I see,' Liz looked a little uneasy about this, but I pressed on.

'I've been sworn at, and spat at, and one woman tried to thump me. She missed but it was close. Like I say, you need to know.'

'Oh Joyce, you poor thing,' and she rested her hand on mine for the second time in that café. 'Listen,' she said, 'We really don't have to go. It was only an idea. It was just my newfound interest in the Romans really, after Vindolanda. Let's just leave it, shall we?'

'No Liz, I'm not saying that. I want to. Heck I should be able to spend a couple of days in Bath surely to goodness. Let's try it and see how it works out. Nothing ventured, eh?'

'Only if you're sure, I'm happy either way,' and I truly thought she meant it.

So we packed our bags and aside from a couple of cheery shouts from across the street, there was nothing of note. When the first cry of 'Oy, you're Flora's mum!' rang out though, Liz hooked her arm in mine, and I felt immediately protected.

'Come on,' she said, 'Let's get out of here,' and we did.

It was nice to feel like I didn't have to face the world on my own all the time. She was at my side. Looking out for me. And I was looking out for her.

Then Flora phoned and asked us both to go down and stay at the house. 'I want to meet this mystery friend of yours, Mum,' she said, 'You can't keep her from us forever.

So now here we are sitting in the back of another embarrassingly big car, steaming down the motorway. There's an expanse of cream leather between us and I almost can't bear to look at Liz. I hope she's okay and not too nervous. I have the strangest impulse to reach across and squeeze her hand, but she is staring out of the window.

'You must be Morag,' Liz says easily offering a hand to shake, 'I've heard so many good things about you.'

'Come in, come in and let me make you some tea, or coffee? Which would you prefer?' Morag is smiling and smiling, and I am wringing my hands. The cameras are on Liz, and everything is about to change.

'Tea would be lovely, with half a sugar, just to take the edge off the bitterness, please and thank you,' Liz says.

'Oh goodness,' says Morag in surprise, 'Just the same as Joyce. Now there's a coincidence,' and she turns to attend to the tea.

'Is Flora around?' I ask weakly.

'She's just been having a wee rest. She'll be down momentarily. She can't seem to shift a tummy bug that Treasure picked up at nursery.' Morag produces homemade flapjacks, soft and golden and obviously freshly baked. 'Red's gone up to wake her.'

'Okay,' I say.

'This is a beautiful room,' Liz smiles, 'I could just about fit my whole house in here.' We all have a little laugh, but I realise that though Liz has been to my house I've never been to hers. She really is a very private person and I like that about her. She was quiet in the car on the way down and she said she was troubled with car sickness from time to time, that was why she preferred to drive herself. At one point, she sat up front with Michael and I had a little doze. She seems a bit brighter now anyway.

Flora arrives with Red and Milk in tow. She is sporting an apple green dress; it is very light and summery.

'Hello Mother,' she says with pretend formality. She cannot help but show-off in front of guests. She strides towards me. 'How was your journey?' she says, grasping me by both shoulders as if she might shake me, and looking deeply into my eyes.

'It was perfectly acceptable,' I say, 'That is a very pretty dress, but you shouldn't wear that colour. It gives you the most terrible pallor. You look like you have jaundice. Now say hello to my friend Liz,' and I shrug her hands off me.

'Thank you, mother. Your fashion critique is duly noted. I have been a little under the weather tbh. Perhaps I should go and put some more slap on.' She moves towards Liz as if she is the Queen receiving guests. 'And you must be Liz,' she says in the voice she uses that she thinks is charming and whimsical, offering her hand, and for a terrible moment I think Liz will either kiss it or worse, curtsy.

Thankfully, she does neither.

'Hello Flora,' Liz says in a completely relaxed and normal tone, 'Yes, I'm Liz. And I'm lucky enough to be your mum's friend.'

Morag catches my eye and winks.

'I gather you don't really watch The Show?' Flora says, still all smiles.

'No, I can't say I was familiar with it until your mother explained who you were. I don't really like reality TV. In fact, I don't watch much TV at all. I like to read, and I enjoy the outdoors more, I suppose.' Liz is perfectly happy to honestly share her answer with Flora. She is unapologetic. I want to cheer.

'Okay. I get that,' says Flora, 'Can I have some ginger beer, Morag. I still have terrible indigestion.'

'In fact,' Liz continues, 'perhaps you could explain to me why you think people do watch The Show? It's a very odd idea from what Joyce tells me.'

'Have you seen *The Truman Show*, Liz' Flora says taking her drink from Morag and moving over to the comfy chairs.

'Yes, I have. A few years ago now but I enjoyed it,' Liz says, joining her.

'Well it's the same principle. I share everything with the world. My whole life is available for all to watch. I love *The Truman Show*. It's my favourite film. I wanted to be Truman when I first saw it. So I created *The Flora Show*.' She relaxes back into the comfort of the deep cushions happy with her answer.

Liz looks confused. 'I don't understand,' she says slowly, 'The whole point of *The Truman Show* is that it is a lie. He is not a True Man, he is a False Man. Nothing about him is real; that's the central theme of the film, isn't it? The world is fake. It's morally appalling.'

A shadow of irritation crosses Flora's face. 'Yes, ultimately that's true but that's because Truman wasn't given the choice to be in it whereas I am a willing participant. I *choose* to be here. This is my dream. To live my life on TV 24 hours a day 365 days a year for the rest of my life.'

'So none of this is fake, like *The Truman Show*,' Liz says.

'Absolutely not,' Flora says, 'This is my life, uncut, unedited in real time as it happens.'

Suddenly Red is standing in front of Liz, legs astride and hands on hips. 'What are you planning?' they say.

'I'm sorry?' Liz says.

'Perps usually clarify this sort of intel before carrying out some sort of attack or strike. I need to search you. Stand up.' Liz stares up at them, open-mouthed.

'Flora!' I say.

'Red, calm down. We're just talking,' Flora says.

'Sounds like a threat level increase to me,' Red says.

'Stand down, Red,' Flora says firmly.

'I'm sorry,' Liz says, 'I don't know what came over me. I'm normally very quiet. I don't know why I would say all of that. Please ignore me and I apologise if I've offended you. You must know my background. I'm not used to this sort of social situation.' She gulps at her tea and blinks up at Red. 'You have a lovely home,' she says to Flora and then she looks balefully over at me as she sets her teacup down. 'That's what I should have said, shouldn't I?' and I stretch across and squeeze her hand.

29

Meryl

I like the smell of books. Old books, new books. Any books. It's a shame that eBooks came along. Maybe someone will invent an eReader that replicates the smell of books. That would be cool. I'm spending more and more time in the library. That's why I'm thinking about books. It's an ugly building. Low ceilings, painted cinder block walls, metal shelves and the section I sit in is Computer Science and so none of the books are even that interesting. To me that is. There's a slim view of the river and a slice of its green bank through the arrow slit window designed presumably to limit student distraction. No one comes over here; presumably, you can find everything online for computer science.

My life feels like I'm running up a down escalator or paddling against a fast-flowing river or standing under a never-ending waterfall of tiny irritations and difficulties constantly bumping and knocking against me that aren't of my making. I feel itchy in my skin, like it is too tight or a bad fit and I want to peel it off and set it aside and breathe in peace without it. Just for a little while.

I want a break from my life.

I am throwing myself into my A levels. There are only days left until we finish for the summer and that is the end of Year 12. At the edge of the river, I can see my peers lounging in the safety of numbers in bleached clothes and dark glasses, sinking into the cool grass and warm weather, their thoughts already stretching into summer plans of parties and holidays and fun, fun, fun.

I, on the other hand, am already powering through the summer work set by my tutors and have requested more from those who are still replying to emails. I have completed my UCAS application, and I have worked ahead through most of next term's psychology modules. Anything to keep my brain busy and rattling around the simple black and white of college work rather than all the complicated shades of grey that are my life with Tyler.

I had a favourite book of Greek mythology when I was little. There were gorgeous, detailed coloured pencil drawings of all the gods and creatures and I would pore over the stories and lose myself in the battling harshness of the world for hours and hours. I am currently Odysseus in the Strait of Messina. There was a picture of him in his ship with the monster Scylla on the cliffs and the whirlpool Charybdis in the sea. Scylla, a six-headed devil, who had begun life as a beautiful nymph, could reach down and snap the head from a passing sailor without a second thought, if they sailed too close. On the other side was Charybdis, a swirling mass of water in my book with a manic pair of watery eyes, a whirlpool that could swallow a ship whole should it edge too close to her to keep away from Scylla.

The treacherous passage between the two engendered the phrase 'between a rock and a hard place' and that is where I find myself today. Yes, I am sitting in a gloomy corner of a college library but in reality, I am steering my ship between the terrifying and all-powerful devil that is my mother and the 24-hour whirlpool of emotions that Tyler has become. If I can just hold steady perhaps I can find a way through and sail into calmer waters away from the impossibility of the situation I've landed in. Odysseus did it. I'm smart. I can work out a way I tell myself, though I'm not completely convinced.

I watch those carefree teenagers on the grass who would probably trade places with me without a second thought. Who, when I pass them in the corridors or push through them to sit down in class, try to meet my eye, either eager to be my friends, or with disdain because they think I'm so up myself.

If only they knew the reality of my life.

At the moment I truly understand the phrase out of the frying pan and into the fire. Yep. I can't stand the heat and all exits are blocked from the kitchen. Not many options open to me at the moment, no siree.

The fire is roaring and I'm in need of a fire extinguisher.

No question.

30

Flora

I get a call from my friend Talia. I say friend, we've done a couple of TV magazine shows together over the years. She's into holistic therapies and wellness but she's incredibly bright. Went to Harvard or Yale or somewhere like that to do her MD. Now she's a TV doctor. Incredibly beautiful too. Thousands of followers. Hundreds of thousands.

'You should go and get a proper check-up, hun,' she says.

'I'm okay,' I say, 'I've been overdoing it at the gym, and I had that bug and I just need a bit of a boost. Maybe a vitamin shot or something.'

'Go and get a full work up, Flora or I'm coming over. Don't make me do that,' she jokes, 'I can make the appointment for you. I know you're busy.'

'We're all busy, babe. I'll get to it, I promise. I'll go and make myself a super green smoothie, okay? That'll pick me up.' I yawn but the thought of the smoothie makes me want to heave. I shudder.

'I'm going to check in with you tomorrow,' she says and rings off.

Ten minutes later she rings back.

'I've made an appointment for you with Anya. She'll see you tonight at 6.30. I'll pick you up just after 5.'

My stomach lurches.

Anya is my oncologist.

We haven't seen each other since my post-treatment six-month check-up.

I fumble a goodbye and head to the annexe.

Shy follows with the handheld. 'Go and see what Morag's up to,' I say lightly, 'Just have to check on something real quick.

I head into the living area and Milk is playing on the X-box. He glances round expecting to see Shy. He pauses the game, throws down the control and vaults over the back of the sofa in one move to envelop me in his arms.

'Hey,' he says quietly, 'Is it Meryl?'

I shake my head against his t-shirt.

'Your ma?'

Another shake.

We stand there for a while in silence.

'Is it back?' he says eventually in barely more than a whisper.

I stand completely still and let him hold me.

31

Joyce

Liz stays just the one night and then Michael drives her home in the morning. This has all been agreed. I am staying on to spend some time with Flora and Treasure and, dare I say it, most importantly, Morag. I'm hoping we'll see Meryl too, but Morag tells me she is working obsessively hard at the moment. This fills my heart with joy.

It's raspberry time and there are still strawberries too, so Morag and I have a most satisfying day in the kitchen making preserves to see everyone through the winter. I prefer marmalade myself; jam is too sweet. Liz is the same, but I love to make it and I adore the smell of the hot bubbling fruit filling the room. Morag is planning to make a couple of summer puddings too, so we go outside and strip the blackcurrant and redcurrant bushes. She always heaps far too much sugar in them to my mind but I'm sure everyone else will approve.

'The kitchen garden really is a credit to you Morag,' I say as we walk back through the burgeoning vegetables. There are wigwams of beans and trellises of peas and lush green potatoes in neat rows on top of rich piles of earth. The lettuce is crisp and hard, and the carrot tops are vibrant and feathery and the tomatoes are getting heavy and starting to blush in the sun. 'You put in so much work. They're so lucky to have you,' I say as I stoop to pull an isolated puny weed.

'I love to be out here and most of it just ticks along. But you know who enjoys working here as well?' She pauses to snap open a pod of peas and runs a few into her mouth with an earthy thumb and offers me the rest. They are sweet, crisp and fresh. 'That Red. They love it here. Knowledgeable too. We're a great team. They're happy to do a lot of the heavy lifting that I'm finding more difficult now I'm not so spry as well. Lovely young person they are. Lovely way with them.'

'Super to have a bit of help,' I say, 'You've not got much slug damage this year,' I note.

'Been too dry,' Morag answers, 'We're on a hosepipe ban. Bit of rain and they'll all come out and run riot. They're just biding their time. That's another thing Red's happy to do. Happy to lug around the watering can. Often find them out here after their shift or first thing in the morning just topping up the salad bed or giving the tomatoes a wee drink. It's a great help.'

'I'm sure it is,' I say.

We head back to the kitchen with our bounty. 'Shall we have a cuppa before we make a start,' Morag says, 'I think we deserve it. Or maybe some lemonade?'

'Sounds perfect,' I say and am more than happy to sit down for a moment or two. The lemonade is sharp and cold, and I suddenly remember my mother making it one summer. I recollect all the squeezed out half peels on the kitchen counter and all the pips. So many lemons for a few small glasses. 'In some countries,' my mother said, 'It's hot enough for oranges and lemons to grow on trees in your back garden and you step out of the door and simply pick them from the branches. Imagine that!' She had flashed her eyes and taken a drink of the extravagant concoction. My father had rolled his eyes at me. She was always asking us to 'Imagine that!' She had one foot in the past her whole life, imagining so many different times and places. I think my father found it tiresome. I thought it was magical.

My eyes swim with tears.

'You okay?' says Morag.

'Just a bit sharp,' I say swallowing and blinking the tears away. What a sentimental fool I'm becoming. I need to have a stern word with myself!

Morag settles in the chair opposite me.

'So hen, tell me about Liz. She seemed awful nice,' and I tell Morag everything I can remember about Beth from the past and Liz from the present.

Morag listens attentively.

'What did you think about her, Morag?' I ask.

'It doesn't matter what I think Joyce, she's your friend. But I thought she was nice. She liked what you liked.'

I felt like she wanted to say more.

'Go on,' I say.

'Oh it's nothing,' she says, 'What do I know.'

'No, please, Morag. Say what you need to say.'

'It's just that … well when you're at school there are some lassies who are scared to have their own opinions and ideas and things they like. It's like they think if they say what they really feel or show who they really are, no one will like them. Do you know what I mean?'

'Go on,' I say again.

'I get the feeling that Liz is like that. She says what you want to hear. I thought she was nice, but I don't know if she was genuine.'

I say nothing. I look at my lemonade and then out of the window.

'Oh dear. I didn't want to offend you, Joyce. It's just how I found her is all.'

'Yes. I understand,' I say tetchily, 'You thought she was nice. You said that three times. Personally, I can't think of a more offensive word.'

'I wouldn't want to see you get hurt …' she trails off.

'I'm quite capable of looking after myself, thank you. This lemonade has far too much sugar in it. I think I'm going to go and have a bit of a lie down. Since you're so concerned for my welfare all of a sudden, I'm going to go and stretch out. I don't want to overdo things.' I stride out of the kitchen resisting the temptation to throw my glass in the sink en route.

What a cheek! Liz was here barely twenty-four hours. How can Morag have judged her and found her lacking in that short time? I am tempted to text Michael and have him come and pick me up in the morning, but I tell myself to calm down. I am not an impetuous person.

I sit on the sofa in the guest suite. Does Liz agree with everything I say? Am I being taken for a fool?

I pick up my book on the Roman Emperor Trajan and decide I should never have bothered with female friends at all. It's all too much hassle.

32

Meryl

When I get home Tyler has been sick in the laundry hamper. I prefer this to when I got home last time and about fifteen of his 'mates' were crashed out in the flat. There is no sign of him.

I stuff everything from the hamper into the washer and make myself some instant noodles.

I sit on the bed and wait.

He will be back, and we are going to have to make a decision.

Then I realise that the exercise bike has gone and so has the rowing machine. The rug is missing and the pictures, including the signed movie still from *Die Hard* that he said he was going to take to his grave. I go back into the kitchen. Half his gadgets are missing too. There is space in the cupboards. I mean they're still stuffed but they're not rammed like they were before.

I go back to my noodles.

I approach this logically. He surely can't owe money; he can access the account and get as much as he needs. Is he swapping the stuff for drugs to cover how much he's spending? Seems like a stretch. Has he got a needy friend that he's given everything to? If that were the case, why not just give them cash? What good is a picture of a grimy Bruce Willis to anyone?

It doesn't make much sense. Why are half the gadgets missing and not all of them? Has he had some sort of epiphany and realised he never eats paninis and, therefore, doesn't need a panini press? If that were the case, he never cooks rice either and the rice maker is still there.

I switch on the TV and wait.

I don't have to wait long.

He's grinning and exhilarated when he bursts through the door. An epiphany seems to be the right call. He jumps on the bed and grabs my hands. It's the first time he's touched me in days, weeks maybe months, it's hard to tell.

'Mare! You're here! Thank God! I've got so much to tell you,' and he moves in closer with a sense of urgency that is intriguing.

I'm pretty sure he's going to say he's joined
a cult. Or found Jesus.

'First I have to say I am so so sorry I do not know what the hell I have been doing but that is going to change. Correction!' he holds up his index finger like Willy Wonka, 'That *has* changed! I know what I am doing. I have been blind but now I can see.'

So, it is God that he's found.

'It was all the money. All the stuff. It drove me crazy. It polluted my brain. And I can see that now and I know what I have to do but first I have to show you something, so I want you to come downstairs.'

He jumps off the bed and opens the door expectantly. 'Come on!' he says.

I slide off the bottom of the bed and put on my shoes. I dread to think what we're going to look at. Is he going to have a horse tethered in the garden? A string quartet set up ready to play? A party bus raring to go? It could be anything. I feel like I could step out of the front door into some kind of weird, animated film made of tattered bits of paper and scribbled characters and fly off into outer space with him in a rocket made of tin foil and sweetie wrappers. Nothing feels real or substantial even though he takes my hand, and it is warm and dry in mine and he is definitely there and not some kind of hologram or illusion.

He flings the front door open.

'Ta da!' he says, and I look at the custard yellow beaten up old camper van parked at the end of the path.

The tinfoil rocket suddenly seems preferable,

'What's this?' I say quietly.

'It's our new home!' he says triumphantly.

I turn around and walk quickly back upstairs to the flat. He trots behind me like an obedient dog. 'What's wrong? Don't you love it? It's got everything inside. A double bed and a little kitchen and even a teeny shower. It's sic, Mare. We can go anywhere we want to. Anywhere!'

I turn and face him as we get back inside. I open my mouth to speak but words will not come out.

I sit down on the bed.

'I'm taking all this shit to the charity shop. That's what I've been doing today. I came home last night, so wrecked and I thought something has to change. And I'd seen this ad for the van, and it was like a sign.'

He sits down next to me, and his voice quietens. 'I don't want to do any of this shit, this running around trying to figure out what I'm supposed to do with all this money. I want to get away. I want to travel. I want to see the world. That's what we need to do. So that's what we're going to do. We're leaving. Just getting in the van and going. There's nothing tying us here. We're young and free and we can do whatever we want to do. So we're out of here, baby. We're hitting the road. Give me one day to get rid of this junk and then we're gone, baby, we're gone!' and he picks up my hand and turns it over and kisses my palm, showing me more tenderness than he has for days or weeks or months.

I shake my head.

'What are you talking about Tyler?' I say, 'I can't come with you?'

'Why not Mare?' he says, 'You can dye your hair, or cut it or wear contacts or something. You can't hide from the world forever. We've got to make our own way and we are going to make our own way in our little love mobile.' He bends down and kisses my shoulder.

'It's nothing to do with hiding Tyler or not making my own way, I've got A levels next year,' I say.

He snorts. 'You don't need those with all the money that's coming to you some day. Let's blow off a little steam. Have some fun. We can go anywhere. *Do* anything, baby.'

'Stop calling me fucking *baby*,' I say and push him away from me. 'I can't believe you have no idea how important my exams are to me.'

He raises his hands, backing off, 'Look I'm sorry, I know they're important, but you could do them later, yeah?'

'I don't want to do them later; I want to do them now. While I'm young. I want to go to Uni. I want to get a good job and I want to have a normal life that doesn't revolve around how many clicks and likes I can accumulate.'

'What're you talking about?' Tyler slows right down, slumps and sags where he sits.

'My whole life,' I say, 'I've watched Flora have to … be on her best behaviour every single minute of the day. I've seen the price she's had to pay for the fame and success that she's achieved. She doesn't *know* anything; she just knows how to be on TV. That's okay for her but it's not okay for me. I can't stand the … shifting sands of it all. I hate the sense of having to keep your head above water the whole time, of having to think of the next great idea, of waiting to see whether what you've come up will work, fucking hell I hate the whole … prostitution of your life. Because that's what it feels like. Selling every scrap of yourself to please faceless people whose only delight is to sit in judgement of everything you say and do.

'I can't have that anymore or live like that and I don't want any part of it. I want to support myself with my brain in an ordinary way in normal working hours and have real people around me who don't care that I'm Flora fucking Tatton's daughter.

'So, no Tyler, I will not be getting into that heap of junk with you and going to God knows where, and if you had been paying any attention to me at all, you would know that I would never ever, *ever* do that.'

I grab my suitcase from under the bed and start to hurl my clothes into it.

Eventually Tyler says, 'Where are you going?'

'I don't know,' I say, 'but I'm not staying here because this isn't working. I don't care whether you're going or not.'

My phone pings.

It's Flora.

33

Flora

One of the best things about private health care is that there is very little waiting time for results. One of the worst things about private health care is that there is very little waiting time for results. I would have liked a little longer in the Not Knowing Limbo. In the Kidding Myself Everything's Okay Dreamworld that I had been floating around in for I don't know how long. But as soon as you're through the doors and they're drawing your blood and you're in a CT scanner and having an MRI, there's no more denial. It's only a matter of time, a very short time, before you hear the words, and you have to work out how you're going to deal with it all again this time.

When I finished my treatment last time I kind of made a conscious decision to put it all behind me. Yes, the chemo had aged me about twenty years physically; yes, my hair was thinner and, a different colour; yes, I had gone into early menopause but I didn't want any more babies, did I. No. I just wanted to forget about the nausea and exhaustion and bleeding gums and mouth ulcers and bone aches and inability to drag myself upstairs and the brain fog and tears and high temps and terror of anyone with a cold or cough and the steroid injections in my stomach and all the endless tablets for every different side effect. I just wanted to forget.

I was done with cancer.
I had had my treatment.
Next!

Time to move on.

I honestly didn't think it would come back.

My survival rate was high. That was what Anya told me, but it was triple negative which is aggressive. It's called triple negative because unlike most breast cancers there's no progesterone or oestrogen receptors in the cancer cells. If there are, you can get more treatment options and take stuff to stop it coming back. There's also something called HER2 protein which can be there in the cells and used for treatment and as a prophylactic afterwards. But if you've got none of these as well, you're triple negative and, double whammy, the cancer is usually fast growing. Woohoo! I do remember Anya explaining all this to me, but I know I didn't fully take in the implications.

Now I'm sitting here waiting for the results of the barrage of tests they've completed, I remember her saying that there was a high chance of a recurrence in the first two years.

I haven't got to the two-year mark yet.

I don't think I really took in what that meant.

I thought if I suffered through all the treatment, I'd be okay. They told me there would be no choice with the chemo and radiotherapy; I had to have it to survive. They also recommended a lumpectomy instead of mastectomy in case of recurrence. 'It's easier to deal with a recurrence in breast tissue rather than your chest wall,' someone said.' Again, I didn't think they were saying there would be a recurrence.

As I trawl through my memories, recurrence features a lot. But it felt like they were talking about someone else's body. Not mine.

No. Not my incredibly reliable body which had allowed me to refurbish most of an old farmhouse in France pretty much single-handed without too many aches and pains.

No. Not my incredible body which had grown and produced two beautiful children, which had managed two uncomplicated and fairly natural childbirths all on its own.

No. Not my incredible body which knew when it needed to eat, to sleep, to drink to regulate itself to stay in good shape; which had always managed my periods without any particular pain or problems; which kept my skin free of spots throughout puberty and beyond; which had fought off infections and illness quickly and efficiently throughout my life giving me an outstanding school attendance record and the reputation of a hale and hearty warrior who could keep going while all around her flagged.

Until that is my body failed to fight off cancer. Or my body turned on itself and began to mutate and replicate in a way that it shouldn't. Tiny cells multiplying in a higgledy piggledy way that couldn't be stopped. And at an alarming rate.

I thought science and modern medicine had my back but I was wrong. My body having always been my most trusted friend was now also my most mortal enemy.

What the hell was going on in there?

As Talia and I wait in Anya's tasteful and expansive waiting room, I ran through my symptoms.

Fatigue, nausea and sometimes vomiting, shoulder and some back pain, did I have headaches? Or was that my imagination? And how much of this was attributable to what was going on with Meryl or the general stress of The Show?

I tut with irritation at the whole situation.

'You okay?' Talia says, 'Shall I get you some water?' I shake my head and look over to Shy and Milk.

'Not long now,' I say brightly into the handheld.

I'd text Meryl and asked her to come to the clinic. If there was bad news, I wanted her to know before the Gen Pub, or at least at the same time, but I, as I have said so many times before, have made the commitment. We've agreed Milk will sit next to me in the office and Shy will film.

Meryl hasn't replied to my text.

'I'm not going to waste your time, Flora,' Anya says, 'The news isn't good.'

I grab for Milk's hand but stay focused on Anya.

'There's at least one mass on your liver and several areas on your lungs that are a cause for concern. We want to run a bone scan tomorrow and biopsy your liver. I'm sorry my darling but I think tomorrow we'll be confirming that you have metastatic breast cancer that has spread to at least one other part of your body. I'm so sorry.'

I look at my hands.

'Shit,' I say quietly.

I am surprisingly furious.

Milk cocoons my hands with his and I feel Shy gently touch my shoulder.

I look up at Anya and my heart is pounding. 'Okay,' I say, 'so what does this mean, what's the likely outcome? What's the fucking prognosis, as they say?'

'We'll know more tomorrow once we've biopsied,' she says calmly.

'Don't give me that. I'm sure you know plenty now. Tell me what you know now. Best guess. You're a fucking expert. Tell me what you know.' I feel my cheeks flush.

Talia leans towards me and puts her hand on my forearm, 'Babe ...' she says.

'Don't fucking 'babe' me,' I say, 'Did you hear what she just said? I want to know what's going on. Just tell me.'

Anya looks, breathes out and says nothing.

'JUST FUCKING TELL ME!' I shout.

'Best case, you'll be dead within a year. More likely six months. It could be less. The primary tumour in your liver is sizable and inoperable and there is more than one. The type of cancer you have is aggressive. The biopsy will probably confirm it's grade 3. I'm going to recommend treatments to contain and halt the growth but there are few guarantees, and there are side effects. I'm pretty certain it's in your lungs too. If it's travelled to two areas, it could already be elsewhere, your bones, your brain. Like I say, we'll know more tomorrow. I'm sorry, Flora.' She keeps looking straight at me. I respect that.

'Thank you for your candour,' I say, and I find the information, the certainty strangely calming.

I stand up. 'Good,' I say, 'I feel better now I have more idea what's going on. I hate being in the dark.'

Milk stands too. He is holding back tears.

'No,' I say to him.

'I'm going to admit you, Flora,' Anya says, 'You're not in a good way, my love. You need fluids and a transfusion. You blood count is way down. That okay?'

'Really?' I say, genuinely surprised, 'I feel okay.'

'Do you though?' Anya says, 'I don't think you can, not looking at your blood work. We need to take care of you for a few days.'

A nurse arrives with a wheelchair.

'That's a bit excessive,' I laugh, 'It's not a great look for TV.'

'In you pop, Ms Tatton,' the nurse says, 'We don't want to take any chances.'

As she wheels me to my room, I think about how out of puff I was climbing the stairs to Anya's consulting, how breathless generally I've been the last few weeks and how nice it is not to have to walk.

'I could get used to this,' I say cheerily to the handheld over my shoulder and give a salute.

the.real.flora.tatton
daily contemplation: Never be an option

Liked by **kinky_boots** and **11,708,235 others**

nowayback
You are a warrior. So much love

fuckeduphuman
Flora will kick the shit out of the big C #ifanyonecanshecan #inittowinit

bobbyboombastic
sending love across the ocean

1974999
get a second opinion – don't trust big pharma. Was she even a real doctor? Kwak kwak

lilpiggywenttomarket
freeze your eggs flora. Clone yourself. #weneedtheflorashow

cheesywotsups
you and your beautiful little family are my whole world. take my heart. Fight Flora.#youcandoitflo

34

Joyce

'Did you know she was going there?' Morag says, as she paces around the kitchen. All thought of our falling out over Liz is forgotten as we watch the footage currently screening on The Show.

Marsha has Treasure jiggling on her knee who is sleepy, and I wish Marsha would put her to bed but I suppose it's like any of those important moments in TV history; the whole household gathers around waiting to see how the event will play out. No one dares move away in case they miss anything.

'I thought she was going to some dinner, or some screening,' Marsha says for the umpteenth time, 'I mean I never see her diary really. Apart from the shared calendar and I've checked that. It's not in there,' and she waves her phone at us again as she has already and then checks it again as if it will explain how she has been left out of the loop of this crucial piece of information.

'Marsha,' I snap, 'She's entitled to some privacy, isn't she? Obviously, she didn't want everyone to know. Goodness knows it's completely impossible to keep anything private in this madhouse.'

Marsha's lip trembles and Morag glares at me.

'I'm sorry, Marsha. I'm a little on edge. I am her mother after all, and she chose not to tell me either,' I say, trying to soften my tone.

'Of course,' Marsha says, 'I just hope she's okay. That's all. She's not been great though, has she Morag? You told her to go the doctor, didn't you?'

We've also heard this about twenty times. I feel about ready to burst but I too do not want to leave the room in case I miss anything.

'Why don't you put Treasure down,' Morag says gently, 'Then you can properly concentrate. It won't take a minute. Put the TV on in the nursery so you don't miss anything as soon as you get up there. What about that, pet? We could be waiting long enough.'

'Yes, that's a good idea,' Marsha says, and we kiss little Treasure and I'm sure we're all trying not to think horrible thoughts about her future so it is better for all concerned that she is out of the room.

Morag brings over tumblers of whisky and we settle together in the calm and quiet. The camera is panning around the waiting room. They have been in there for what seems like an age. This is the longest period of time I have ever paid attention to The Show. I refused to watch the birth of my granddaughter – I found it vulgar and attention seeking – but this, well, this is something else.

Flora looks ill. There's no doubt. Shadows under her eyes and a greenish tinge to her skin, she's sallow. No colour in her cheeks. She looks like she did when she was going through the chemo; like her blood is thinned, like she is drained. And she's bony too. We know she's not had her usual appetite, but we've put that down to this wretched bug...

'I should have insisted she go to the doctor. I'm her mother,' I say to Morag.

'She never does anything anyone tells her, hen. No point starting with should haves now. It's what we do from this point on that matters.' Morag sounds upset. And no wonder, a second mother to Flora. A better mother some would say.

They're in the office and we sit up and lean forward. Morag turns the sound up.

As I hear those horrific words, 'you'll be dead within a year,' I drop the whisky and the tumbler smashes on the slate floor. Neither of us even look at it. We are transfixed on the TV. I feel giddy, sick and a cold settles over me like I've never felt before.

When I was a very little girl we went abroad just once, down to the south of Spain and it was supposed to be a beach holiday of summer sun and buckets and spades and lazing by the sea, but my mother grew restless, and we hired a car and she drove us into the hills and we walked out of the blistering sun into a thickly walled stone church. In my memory it was vast. Perhaps it was a cathedral; I have no one to ask the location and there are no photos to check. It was baking hot and airless outside in the Spanish square and we stepped into this building, and I could not understand how instantly cold it was in there. I laid my hand against one wall in the darkest corner and the stone was cold, damp almost. The sun was beating down outside but, out of its glare, I was chilled in my thin T-shirt and flimsy shorts. My mother said it was a relief to be out of the sun for a moment or two, but I thought the cold was strange and unnatural, like I was in a different country.

That is how I feel in this moment. My daughter will die, and I am stepping into a different dark world, an unnatural world, out of the sun; a cold place that the sun cannot reach. That chill seeps right through me and settles in my bones.

'We need Meryl,' Morag says through her tears, 'She should be here.'

I can't find any words so I just nod.

35

Meryl

After I leave Tyler's – funny that, in my head I always think of it as Tyler's not ours – my first thought is to go to the library. How sad is that? The only place I can think of to go to is a brutalist building in a crummy concrete college which is going to be half-dead by now. I check my phone. The library closes in half an hour.

I head for a hotel. I always carry a wig for emergencies. It just makes things easier. My hair is blonde and this one is dark. It's good quality. Proper hair, a bit creepy really. It does change what I look like though. I put on my sunglasses and a cap too and I get some cash so I can tip generously.

It's a good hotel. One of those country club type ones at the edge of town. Loads of grounds and spa treatments and golf and shit.

I adopt a persona. I cannot be sulky Meryl Tatton or someone will clock me no question so I am all smiles and upright posture. I turn into my mother. I tip the doorman and valet an excessive amount; they'll keep their mouths shut hopefully and I swan into the lobby as if this is what I do every week of the year.

I beam at the receptionist and take the most expensive suite marching ahead of the bell boy and my cases with just my handbag over my arm. I arch a haughty eyebrow at a couple of young guys in sharp suits who call for me to hold the lift. I don't.

My character doesn't even travel in the same lift as the bell boy and the luggage trolley.

I dole out another enormous tip once my suitcases have been stowed - I refuse the offer of the unpacking service - and wait for the door to close. I tear the wig off and throw my sunglasses onto the smooth linen of the gargantuan bed.

Realising I am starving, (noodles are not enough to keep body and soul together Morag would say) I order a Caesar salad and fries from room service and get some tonic water from the mini bar. I open a tub of salted cashew nuts and start on those while I'm waiting. I realise the receptionist didn't bother to check any ID. Amazing how far a bit of confidence can get you.

I turn off my phone.

My plan is to eat, run a deep bath and then to sleep. I have nowhere to go and nowhere to be so I will stay here until I work out what I want to do next.

36

Flora

I dream that I'm surfing with Treasure. We're riding wave after wave on an azure blue sea. She is standing rock steady at the front of the board in a tiny wet suit, her long, blond curls blowing as we follow the flow of the water. I laugh along with her joyous giggling, and I feel the wind and spray of water against my body. I am strong and powerful, and she is my future. I look to my left at a perfect white sand beach, and it is completely empty, smooth and flat and deserted. No one cares what we are doing. No one is watching. I look to my right and a shark is swimming with us. It glides effortlessly below the water. It has always been there.

'Treasure,' I call, and she turns round and she is perhaps seven or eight.

'It's time for me to go now,' I say.

Treasure nods and turns away from me to watch the view ahead of her, her golden hair lifting in the wind.

I look down at the shark. Its nose is parallel with me now and it slowly opens its mouth as we rush along.

Once it is fully open and I can see all the little rows of razor-sharp teeth, I jump in.

I wake up.

Milk and Shy are still here even though I told them to take it in turns. Shy is napping and Milk has the handheld doing a shot out of the window. If I'm going to be here for a couple of days, they have to pace themselves.

I shut my eyes again for a moment more to myself. I check in on my body.

Nope. I still don't feel like I'm dying. I've got no pain and I subtly push and squeeze around the place and there aren't that many niggles that feel life-threatening.

Could Anya have it wrong? I ponder over the ratings for a switcheroo of a misdiagnosis. Unlikely though.

She'd never have said all that stuff if she wasn't sure; I know that in my heart.

I open my eyes and turn away from Milk reaching for my phone from the nightstand.

Meryl still hasn't even read my messages.

I just don't get that girl. No doubt she's going to be mad with me again for this. I tried to get her here though. I tried to warn her. There's nothing more I could have done.

That's not really true I suppose. I could have sent someone physically to her. But I didn't. Hey ho.

The messages have been pouring in. Too many to read. And they've had to start refusing flowers and gift baskets. They're diverting them to other places instead, nursing homes, homeless shelters and the like. It's an outpouring of love is how they're reporting it on the news.

Yes, my diagnosis on the news.

I really wish Meryl would look at her bloody phone.

I've sent Red home too. I thought they were going to collapse. Breaking down and crying so loudly in a most unprofessional way. The hospital has security; I told them to take a few days.

So the plan is to get all the tests done and then it's going to be more chemo to shrink the liver tumour. It's for prolonging life rather than to cure and for pain management from what I can gather. Anya is already talking about managing my treatment from home, calling in hospice support and so on. It's not even been 24 hours. I mean, let's give this a shot at least. Let's look at all the options first; I've got a two-year-old at home who kind of needs a mummy.

That's my main problem.

I don't want them to be orphans.

It's just not a great look.

I mean, they'll be provided for but they need a tribe and our tribe is small I realise.

I don't want them to think I've let them down.

Milk moves round and I automatically run my fingers move my hair and manage a smile, 'Good morning, my lovelies,' I say, 'How are we all? I've just had the most beautiful dream.'

I glance down at my phone again.

Still nothing.

37

Joyce

When we get to Tyler's flat it's obvious they've moved out. It is quite hard not to panic. We've brought Red with us too, I'm not sure why, perhaps from a fundamental need to all stick together, to look after each other and they seemed like they were at a loose end this morning.

'I'll see what I can find out,' they say and wander off up the street, tapping their mobile phone.

'Where can the pair of them have gone?' Morag says.

'They can't have got kicked out,' I say, 'I can't believe Meryl wouldn't let us know what's going on.'

'She'll be eighteen soon and she's always been old for her age. She's often been the adult in her relationship with Flora frankly, she won't have thought it was necessary to keep us informed. Won't have crossed her mind,' Morag answers glumly.

'I don't see there's any point hanging around here. We'd be better off at home in case she comes back.' I look around at the rundown houses and rubbish gathered in the doorways, the scratched bus shelter and the over-flowing dog waste bin. I don't want to be here a minute longer than I have to be.

'Let's wait and see what Red comes up with,' Morag says and nods in the direction of Red who is heading back towards us purposefully.

'Any news?' I say.

'They've moved out,' they say.

'We'd gathered that,' I say tetchily.

'Tyler has possibly left the country and Meryl's whereabouts are unknown,' Red continues ignoring my tone.

'Left the country? Is he in trouble?' Morag says alarmed.

'No, he's in a camper van,' Red replies.

'But not with Meryl,' I press them.

'No, apparently not. Not according to my source. She left separately. They 'split up',' and Red does little air quotes around split up.

'Well that's good news, isn't it?' I say to Morag, 'I mean not about the splitting up necessarily but that she's still in the country.' I turn back to Red, 'Now, can you find out where Meryl has gone? Or which friends she may be staying with perhaps?'

'Negative,' Red says.

'Why's that?' I say, perplexed.

'Already asked,' they say.

'I think you've done really well so far, Red,' Morag says encouragingly, 'We can work with what you've told us.'

'I agree but couldn't you find out where Meryl is?' I persist, 'It didn't take long for you to find out all that other stuff.'

Red shuffles about a bit. 'It's not that straightforward,' they say.

'How so?' Morag asks.

'Well I just went in the greasy spoon round the corner and one of Tyler's mates was in there and he told me everything I've just told you.'

'I see,' Morag nods.

'Home then,' I say.

'Yep,' I agree, and we all bundle back into the car no further forward in getting to Meryl and telling her about Flora face to face than we were at the start of the day.

38

Meryl

I knew I shouldn't have gone down to breakfast. I should have ordered room service, but I was getting a bit of cabin fever even though the suite was way bigger than Tyler's flat. It was the monotony of those matte mushroom walls somehow. They were depressing.

I knew the waitress recognised me and then I saw her with her phone, and I just legged it.

It was only a matter of time before there were fans and cameras, so I packed and paid up. 'I'm so sorry by the way,' the receptionist said as I was leaving.

As I drive off down the long gravel driveway, I think Tyler has some cheek leaking our breakup to the press. I fucking walked away. How dare he re-write the narrative? No surprise though, this has happened to me before. Guys who were supposed to be crazy about me turning into total douches once I dumped them just in case I said anything publicly about them. I thought Tyler knew me better than that.

I formulate a plan.

I'm going home but I'm going to move into the annexe where there's no cameras plus an exit that can't be filmed. I can come and go as I please. I have one year to go and then I am out of there for good and nothing is going to stop me. I've spoken to a tutor at college about applying for schools in the US; as far I'm concerned the further away the better.

I drive far too fast spurred on by my fury at Ty; the look of pity on that receptionist's face is burned into my brain. She can't have been much older than me. I don't need her feeling sorry for me; I ditched that loser. I consider turning the car around and telling her. I imagine screaming it in her face and then smashing her simpering smile onto the plush oak counter and the sound echoing around the cavernous lobby.

I'm enjoying the fantasy a little too much, and it takes me a moment to register the blue lights behind me.

'Fuck,' I say as I pull over.

'In a bit of a hurry, are we?' the police officer says as I wind down the window. I try to smile apologetically and I know this can go one of two ways. If he's a fan, we could be here for hours and I could get let off, or if he's not and he recognises me anyway it could take hours because he may want to lecture me on how celebrities shouldn't think that that they are above the law.

Either way I don't hold out much hope that I'm going to get away very quickly. I am a captive audience one way or another and he holds all the power.

'Is this your car?' he says.

'Yes,' I say. He hasn't looked at me properly yet.

'Very nice, very nice. Any idea how fast you were going, miss?' he says.

'Not really,' I say, 'I'm guessing too fast.'

'Too fast, yes, indiddly deedy. Too fast. Do you have your driving license with you, miss?'

I reach for my bag and get my license. Here is the moment of truth.

He looks at the license and looks at me.

I pull off my wig and give him an ironic smile.

His whole demeanour changes.

'Where are you going to Meryl,' he says completely seriously.

'I'm on my way home,' I say.

'Understood,' he says with a nod. He looks down at the license and takes a deep breath in. 'Are you okay to drive?'

'Yes,' I say slowly, 'I think so.'

'Look,' he says, 'I can come along with you, hang back, discreet you know, make sure you don't get bothered. It's up to you.'

'No. It's okay,' I shake my head, 'I'm okay.'

'Good,' he says, and he sounds ... proud. 'You always were a strong girl. On your way then, but stick to the limit, okay?'

I nod.

He reaches in his pocket, pulls out a card and gives it to me. 'You need anything Meryl, you call me, okay? Anytime.' And then he hands back my license and I watch in my wing mirror as he walks back to the patrol car and start to talk on the radio.

I start my car and move off.

What the hell has Tyler said? And to who?

39

Flora

'We want to do a lumbar puncture Flora, get some spinal fluid. It's going to be uncomfortable at best, painful at worst. I want as full a picture as possible before we decide on all the treatments,' Anya says.

I've had the blood transfusion and my breathing is better. Anya said my platelet count was dangerously low. She keeps saying it's remarkable I was managing as much as I was.

I keep telling her I don't feel that bad.

She just tilts her head as if to say, 'Just you wait.'

She was like that last time. She realistically managed my expectations. I wonder how much she's going to be involved this time. I thought she was a boob woman. Are livers and lungs her jam too? Or do I see someone different for all of these?

I haven't said anything properly to camera yet. Tim is coming soon and it's going to be hard to do any planning here. On WhatsApp we've agreed a blackout on camera re my death, my passing, my demise, my croaking, the moment when I shuffle of this mortal coil, the moment when I turn my toes up, for when I kick the bucket, bite the dust, give up the ghost, for when I finally and forever check out. Yes, we're not talking about it until Meryl knows and we can all talk about it off air but it's already going around in my head.

Of course it is.

I can't think about anything else.

In lots of ways, I'd much rather skip all the difficult procedures and pointless therapies which aren't really going to do any good and just get on with it.

I mean realistically what am I going to do in six months?

Milk would say I'm being selfish, but the six months are for the living not for the dying. They're to give them time to get used to the fact that I'm hanging up my dancing shoes.

'Get your affairs in order,' is what they say in old films when they're telling someone they're not long for this earth. Seems like a bit of a cheek to me. I don't want to be bothered with anything like that frankly; I'm not worrying about whether my council tax is paid up. No. I'm turning a thought or two to the next life and I'm thinking about how I'm going to be leaving this one.

It's all very serious I have to say.

Not many punchlines.

40

Joyce

We're ringing round all the hotels when Meryl comes through the door. Morag and I cannot help but enfold her with the hugs that Meryl and I both normally hate. Thankfully, today she patiently accepts them and because she does, I have to conclude she must know.

'Thank goodness you're home,' Morag says.

'It's certainly easier than trying to track you down,' I say. 'We've been at it for ages and hotels are very loathe to give out information about their guests,'

'Quite right too,' Meryl says and the suitcases in the hall are at least a positive sign that she's here to stay.

'So how are you?' Morag says and she presses her lips together to hold back tears.

'I don't want to talk about it really,' Meryl says.

'Okay,' Morag says, 'That's fine. We've been so worried though. Would you like something to eat? Can I make you a sandwich?'

'No, no, I'm okay, really. I had some breakfast at the hotel actually.' Meryl nods and sits down on the sofa tucking her feet up under her.

'So you were at a hotel? That's what we thought,' I say.

'It really is unbelievable,' Meryl shakes her head and looks a bit angry.

'It is, darling, it is, but there's nothing we can do about it now.'

'Is it in the papers or a magazine? I can't believe it got out like that,' Meryl says.

'Oh it's everywhere,' I say, 'It was on the news last night.' I go and sit next to her but not too close. 'I think they're reporting it internationally too of course. So shocking.'

'You're kidding!' Meryl looks appalled.

Morag comes over with a tray of coffee and biscuits which she sets down in front of us. 'It's not that surprising, hen,' she says, 'The Show's watched by millions all over the world.'

'I know,' Meryl says, 'but I really didn't think they'd be that interested.'

She picks up a biscuit and bites into it.

I look at her more closely. There's no sign of crying or fatigue. Morag and I look at each other.

'What do you think we're talking about Meryl?' I say tentatively.

'Me and Tyler breaking up,' she says, 'The receptionist in the hotel said she was really sorry for me and some cop let me off for speeding on the way over here. He's blabbed to someone, right? Made out it's my fault or he's dumped me. It's so lame. I'm gonna kill him the next time I see him.'

'Where's your phone?' Morag says carefully.

'Dunno, in my bag.' She takes another biscuit. 'Good batch, Morag,' she says through the mouthful. 'I'm going to move into the annexe by the way. There's no cameras in there. I decided on my way over. Red can have my room. They can be closer to Flora that way.'

'Great idea, let's go and have a look at it now,' Morag says, and we leave the coffee to get cold and all head over there. 'I can run up some different blinds and we can freshen it up with a coat of paint, I'm sure. We can move over some of your furniture too so it feels like your place. That would work, wouldn't it?' Morag keeps up the chatter as we cross the courtyard and get off camera.

Red is sitting in the living area reading a book. They look up, surprised at our entrance.

'Scram,' Morag says, 'please,' she adds and smiles and Red trots out with their book.

I turn to face Meryl; I know it falls to me to tell her.

'Meryl, there's been some news. That's why we've been trying to get hold of you. Come and sit down darling,' I say.

We make it to the safety of the sofa.

'It's Flora,' I say, 'She's in hospital.'

Meryl says nothing. She's frowning.

'The cancer's back,' I say, 'The news isn't good, I don't think she's going to beat it this time. I'm sorry sweetheart.'

'She's in hospital?' Meryl repeats.

'Yes,' Morag answers, 'We've been trying to phone you, we've been texting. We didn't want you to find out on the TV.'

'Mum wanted you to be at the clinic,' I say, 'She really did.'

'It's back? It feels like she only just finished her treatment. I thought she was better,' she says almost inaudibly.

'We all did,' Morag says.

'Okay,' Meryl says, 'I'm going to my room.'

She pulls her hood up over her head and runs back across the courtyard into the main house.

Morag and I sit and look at each other across the space that Meryl has left between us.

41

Meryl

So the three of us will become two. And sooner rather than later it seems. I watch Mum on the drive from my bedroom window when she comes home; she looks like a rag doll, limp and knocked about with a stitched-on face that's grinning from ear to ear even though there's fuck all to be happy about.

She's says she's feeling better since the transfusion but they're starting chemo at the end of the week and I've seen what that did to her last time. She was little more than a zombie by the end of it. If anything is going to be sorted out, it's going to have to be soon before she's slipping and sliding in and out of the necessary drug-induced sleep-walking life that was her day to day when we all went through this before.

I've emailed my UCAS application.

It was the first thing I did when I got up to my room after Granny and Morag told me.

It felt like some kind of statement of intent.

Stupid really because I know I will never be able to leave Treasure and go to Uni.

Maybe there's a way I can do both.

Maybe.

I spoke to Mum on the phone in hospital – or rather I listened to her ramble on and on. I barely said anything. I think they had her on something as she was all over the place, but I let her apologise and I apologised too and I meant it; I'm not going to argue with her now.

Tim's in the car with them. I'm relieved. I'm hoping we can have the last few months in peace together without all the cameras. I know that's unlikely to happen, but this is a game-changer surely? You have to retire from your job if you're told you have a terminal illness, don't you? And it is just a job. A crazy, wild, insane, irrational, unique one, but it is just a job.

There's a knock on my door. It's Shy. 'We're having a programming meeting in the annexe in twenty minutes. Can you make that?'

'Sure,' I say.

I switch on *The Flora Show* and see the Coming Up feed trailing a bit from Morag on cancer busting smoothies in fifteen minutes and Treasure's swimming lesson in the pool at the same time. Both will be popular. They really don't want anyone to notice the gap.

I brush my teeth and hair. I remember Mum's sense of smell went all to hell last time. I freshen up my make-up and run down the main stairs. I check in on Morag and Granny in a happy and positive way in the kitchen. They are busy sorting through mounds of vegetables that look like they're fresh from the garden.

I scoot through the courtyard and across to the annexe. I will be early, but I don't want anything being decided without me; that would be typically manipulative of all concerned.

Mum is lying on the sofa with a flannel across her forehead and her eyes closed.

It is utterly still and silent.

Tim puts a finger to his lips to stop me speaking and I stagger to a stop.

Mum's eyes flick open.

She sees me, throws away the flannel and pivots quickly to sitting with a manic smile on her face. 'Meryl, darling, how lovely, you're here. Come and give me a hug.'

I do as I'm told but there is something odd about hugging someone when you know their bones are riddled with cancer - you don't want to touch them. You don't want to hurt them or break them. Mum said on the phone that her bone scan looked like someone had thrown a handful of soot over her skeleton; so so many black spots and patches. I'm finding it hard to shake that picture.

I sit down next to her. 'Do you want something to drink, darling? Tim tell Milk to bring the drinks through now,' and Tim disappears to the annexe kitchen.

'I'm good, Mum,' I say, 'You look pretty ill though.'

'I know,' she says, 'Sorry, can't seem to manage to hide it at the moment. It's like it's been given a name and now it wants to reveal itself. Do you know what I mean?'

'Yes,' I say, 'Sort of.'

'While I was pretending I was okay, well not pretending, just hoping really, or not really facing up to things in a sensible way, it was all more manageable but, I don't know Meryl, since Anya told me, now it's got the full run of me, it's like I can't get ahead of it. I'm sore and sleepy and I can't think straight. But,' she smiles, 'I am *so* pleased to be home and,' she grasps my hand, 'I am *so* pleased that you're here too.'

'Me too, Mum,' I say.

Milk and Tim come in with a jug of juice and glasses. Milk pours it out and sits down. Tim remains standing in front of the monster flat screen. Shy comes down the stairs and perches on the back of the sofa behind Milk. Tim says, 'Let's get started.'

'We should wait for Mother,' Mum says mock-seriously.

'That journey has wiped you out. You need to get to bed. Let's make a start at least. Joyce won't be long,' Tim insists but Granny appears through the door.

'Sorry,' she says and slips onto the sofa the other side of Mum, 'Have I missed anything?'

'Just about to get going,' Milk says.

'We are gathered here today to join together,' Mum intones and starts to giggle, 'Oh you all look so miserable. Come on cheer up, I'm not dead yet!'

'Flora!' Granny interjects.

'Well really,' Mum carries on, 'I can't spend my last few months looking at all of this misery. If you continue like this, I'm ringing the girls and we're jetting off to Ibiza.' She fist pumps the air but stops as it is clearly incredibly painful. 'Fuck,' she says to herself, closing her eyes against what is evidently agony.

Tim tries to take charge. 'Okay everyone. We need to make some decisions in the light of recent events,' he says.

'Yes,' Mum says, 'In the light of me being diagnosed with terminal cancer.' She raises her glass, 'Cheers!' and has a swig. 'We could do with some vodka in this, Milk,' she says.

'Flora, for heaven's sake,' Granny says.

'Indeed,' Tim ignores Mum but raises his glass too in a slightly absent-minded way. 'We need to decide about what is going to happen to The Show. We need to decide on the practicalities. Sooner rather than later.'

'Yep!' Mum says, 'Clock is ticking!'

'There's nothing to decide is there?' I say, 'The Show's over. This is the end. We finish filming. Have a farewell party, a finale or something and then cease transmission. Let Mum have her final few years in peace.'

'Oh darling, it's months, weeks maybe. Let's not kid ourselves,' Mum says. I knew this but I couldn't quite bear to say the words. Or think of that as a reality.

'Okay, even more reason then, to quit it now. As Tim said sooner rather than later.' I say looking to Tim for affirmation. He looks down at his shoes.

'Milk, Shy?' I say, 'What do you think?' They shrug and look dubious.

'I agree with Meryl,' Granny chimes in, 'You can't be going through all the treatment and what have you live on air, it's ... it's ... distasteful. Who would want to watch it?' She finishes. I know this argument will hold no sway with this TV-centric crowd.

I can't believe they're seriously considering this.

'What are you actually proposing, Flora?' I say, looking at her directly.

She smiles at me and then up at Tim.

'I have to think of my fans,' she says to me.

I blink.

'What are you saying?' I say, 'I want you to say the words. Go on say the words.'

Tim folds his arms and I feel like Milk and Shy are collectively holding their breath.

'I want it to be live,' she says slowly.

'What?' I say quietly, 'You want *what* to be live?' My heart is racing.

'I want my death to be shown live on TV,' she says.

I look at her.

I have no words.

'I gave birth live on TV,' she says.

I have no idea how to respond.

'This completes the circle,' she says.

I just look at her. My mother.

'It could be beautiful, Meryl,' she says, 'People are so afraid of death, and they don't need to be. People die every day. It's part of life. Do you know how many people got in touch with me during and after my cancer treatment to say thank you. To say thank you for showing them the truth of what they or their loved ones would be facing? Thousands Meryl. Thousands and thousands. They needed to see the reality of my life. They needed to see what I went through, and don't you see Meryl, this is the completion of the circle. I can show people the final journey to my death. I can de-mystify it. It will be there for everyone to see in their living rooms all over the world and it will be beautiful. Or maybe it won't. Maybe it will be painful or difficult or violent or brutal, but it will be *real*. It will be reality, Meryl. People need to see reality and I want to show it to them.

'I made the commitment to share my life and in so making that commitment I didn't realise it, but I chose to share my death. I knew it as soon as I heard the words that I was going to die.

'I know this is a shock Meryl, but you'll have time to adjust. You will. It's the right thing to do. I promise.'

She reaches for my hand, but I snatch it away.

'You're a monster,' I say, 'This isn't just about you, you know. In fact, you have the easy part. You get to step out of all this and leave all of us behind to pick up the shit. You want to *die* on television. I've never heard of anything so sick and twisted.'

I turn to Shy and Milk and Tim, 'I don't know why I was invited here; you've made your decision anyway. You should be ashamed of yourselves allowing this, but I think I've said that to you once before.'

I stand up, 'I don't know if I can stay here for this,' I say, 'I don't think you should put me through it. I think it's cruel and unnatural and not what a daughter should have to witness. I'm going now.'

Granny stands up. 'I agree with everything Meryl has said. The cancer must be in your brain, Flora. This is utter madness.'

As we cross the courtyard together Granny says, 'Don't disappear again Meryl, we'll work this out.'

But I don't see how we can.

42

Flora

We settle into some sort of routine and things are looking pretty chipper. Amazingly the tumour in my liver is responding to the chemo which isn't yet quite as drastic as I feared it would be. Yes, there are mountains of tablets, and I am being constantly monitored but there is still some sort of living to be had in my dying.

The weather is favouring us and, though I have to be careful of the sun, Treasure and I are spending hours on the grass under the big oak tree at the end of the lawn. We have piles of cushions and blankets, and the effect is like a Bedouin tent crossed with Toy Town but I love it and so does Treasure who drags more and more of her toys out from the nursery every day.

It's odd but I don't remember actually playing with Meryl when she was this age. I think she got on with things herself. I mean I might have sat with her while she stacked some bricks or scribbled on some paper, but I don't remember real playing.

Treasure and I have whole worlds we are diving into. She is a mean coffee shop owner and often won't serve me what I ask for or snatches back what I am given if I don't have the right response to what I receive. 'Ooh this pastry is so light and delicious,' I say.

Snatched back by her chubby little paw.

'No! It's burnt! I cooked it too long. It's horrible,' she growls.

'You're right it's horrible. Can I have one that isn't burnt?'

'No sorry, we've sold out. Big bus of frogs came and bought everything half an hour ago.' She splays her hands in despair.

'Oh drat. I'll see you tomorrow.'

'Okay see you tomorrow. But,' warning finger pointed at me, 'I'm not making any promises. You get what you're given and eat it ALL UP!'

It's always a gamble with that coffee shop I must say. Then we have the hairdressers where we take it in turns to do each other's hair. Mostly she puts about a million tiny hair clips in my wig.

I hate wearing my wigs but I bring them out for our hairdressers' game and Treasure loves brushing them. Sometimes if I'm reading her a story, she'll sit with one across her lap and stroke it and suck her thumb.

I'm hoping she won't remember any of this. But then of course every second is being filmed. She'll have the option to watch and re-watch it all once she's older.

As a hairdresser, she's much more benign.

She bases her character on Tia. 'I told him he was just too much, and he had to *give me some space*,' she tells me as she attaches another clip.

'Good plan,' I say with total commitment to my role.

'I ain't going to be told where *I can go* and who *I can see*,' she tuts and puts her hands on her hips.

'Yaass queen,' I say, 'You go girl,' and we high five and Treasure falls forward onto one of the cushions and pulls up her knees and giggles and giggles and I think this is my favourite sound in the world.

Our other firm favourite is 'What do we love/what do we hate?' For this we have giant out-sized sunglasses, parasols and fans and we are very, very posh. We walk around the garden very slowly, sometimes we are pushed, Treasure in her buggy and me in my wheelchair and we pronounce on things we see or things that pop into our heads.

'The sun!' Treasure points to the sky.

'Oh we LOVE the sun,' we say, and we flap our fans and hide our faces and look at each other behind them as if we just told each other a big secret.

'Waking up in the morning!' I shout.

'Oh we HATE waking up in the morning,' we cry, and we flap our fans.

'Shy!' Treasure points at Shy who is filming us, and he pretends to be scared at what we will say.

'Oh we LOVE Shy,' we pronounce and Treasure chortles as she fans herself.

'Wearing knickers!' I yell.

'Oh we HATE wearing knickers,' we bellow at the top of our refined voices.

And so it goes on, day after day, as the long hot dry spell continues and Marsha sits and reads steamy romances and suns herself on the terrace by the house and I only go inside to nap if I can't get comfortable, or for an infusion but we are out there for hours and hours and it puts me in mind of the early days in France when Meryl and I were waiting to start on the house. Except this time, we're waiting for an ending.

43

Joyce

It feels like we are living on our nerves. I did not bring enough clothes to see me through and I am anxious to get home at least for a few days, just to have a break from the cameras and the intensity of everything.

I still cannot fathom why Flora is still filming. She has enough savings to last the girls several normal lifetimes from what I can gather so why does she have to put us all through this extra anxiety? Because that is what it is.

During the normal course of events, we would be able to speak freely and behave spontaneously. As it is, I can see Morag is frequently overcome with emotion and yet is having to stopper up anything she is feeling because it is simultaneously broadcast across the nation and beyond.

Red, who has only been with us a matter of months, is particularly brittle. For someone who has served in the military, they are really not coping well.

Morag and I have discussed this and Morag decides to tackle this with them, hoping to help.

Having all just eaten a light supper, Flora has gone to bed early and we are all sitting out in the evening sun on the terrace. Meryl is not with us and I can't tell if that's a blessing or a regret; these days there is no telling how she will behave. Neither Shy nor Milk has the handheld; it's been a gruelling day for both of them, another round of tests and scans up in London and they are worn out. They've agreed to let the house cams do the work for half an hour.

'You don't speak much about your military service, Red, do you?' Morag starts.

'No,' they answer, 'I don't like to dwell.'

'That's a good philosophy,' Morag says.

'I agree,' I say, 'I can't bear raking over the past for no good purpose.'

Red stares at me. 'I think what I did had a good purpose, Joyce,' they say.

'You misunderstand me, Red,' I say, 'I'm talking about the analysis of the past having no purpose rather than what happened. I like to look to the future. Obviously, I'm talking about the past from a personal point of view. I love the analysis of history. And by that, I mean events of social or political importance not the minutiae of people's lives.' I smile at them.

'Oh yes,' Red says, 'I see what you mean. Sorry. I'm naturally a bit defensive about all of that. People can be a bit funny about the armed forces, but we all need them.'

I see Milk and Shy exchange looks.

'Absolutely,' I say.

'So what are you thinking of doing once … The Show finishes, Red,' Morag says.

'I guess I'll look for another high-end gig like this. Shouldn't be a problem. Flora said she'd set me up. She's got the contacts, right?' Their eyes fill with tears.

'She surely has,' Morag says, 'Come on now, don't get all upset. We're all here with you, aren't we?'

But they were off, tears running down their cheeks as we'd witnessed just about every day since Flora's diagnosis.

Morag put her hand on Red's. 'You feel things very deeply, pet, don't you?' and Red nodded and wiped their tears away with a napkin.

'Have you always been this way? Since you were a wee girl?' Morag was looking at Red, so sweet and kind and I don't even think she thought about what she was saying.

Red just stood up, 'Excuse me,' they said and left the terrace, walking back through the house.

Morag looked dumbfounded.

'Well, that was very odd,' she said, 'Right enough, they don't talk about their childhood. I shouldn't have asked. Maybe a bit too personal but I thought we were all getting a bit closer.'

'You shouldn't have said that, Morag,' Milk says.

'I was only trying to help,' Morag answers, 'I hate to see them so upset all the time and, to be frank, it's not good for Meryl, or any of us. I've known Flora as long as the lot of you, excepting you Joyce, obviously, and I'm no in tears at the drop of a hat. They've got to toughen up a little. How are they going to cope at the end? I was only trying to see if there was any pattern or any way we could help, that was all.' She glares at Milk annoyed at the accusation.

'Not that,' he says, 'You shouldn't have said about them being a girl.'

Morag starts and sits back in her chair.

'Did I?' she says. She looks to me, 'Did I, Joyce? I didn't mean to. I was only thinking about them as a child. I wasn't meaning to say anything to upset them further, oh God. What have I done?'

'They're sensible, Morag,' I say, 'Anyone could make that mistake. I'm sure it's not a big deal. I don't see that any real harm has been done, and I look at Shy and Milk to help me calm Morag down.

'I need to go and apologise. I'd hate to think I'd upset them even more. Oh no, how stupid. Stupid, old woman,' and she knocks her hand against her head in frustration.

'Just leave them,' Shy says, 'I'm sure they'll be okay.'

'If they were okay, they wouldn't have left, would they?' Morag says but she stays seated at the table, nibbling on her thumb nail, deciding what to do.

Milk checks his phone. 'Looks like you've missed your chance anyway. They've just left according to the gate cam. Obviously needed a bit of space.'

'Oh that's even worse,' Morag says forlornly.

'I'm sure they'll be fine when they get back. You can have a chat and set everything straight,' I say.

I can tell from Morag's face that she's not convinced.

the.real.flora.tatton
daily contemplation: Be just what you want to be not what others want to see.

Liked by **frankenswine** and **8,699,722 others**

nowayback
transhater transphobe transwar #moraghastogo

fuckeduphuman
Red we love you. Don't listen to the haters. You are the bomb

bobbyboombastic
sending support across the ocean

1974999
Why does she get to comment on Red's gender? Keep your nose out lady. Why're you all up their bizniz #moragout

lilpiggywenttomarket
nonbi love here all da way #wedigdafloshow

cheesywotsups
typical baby booma shit. don't give airtime to this #moragisnomore #nomoremorag

44

Meryl

'This is getting out of hand' I say, 'You're not thinking straight.'
   She won't accept that even though I'm pretty certain there must be brain mets from the way she's acting so completely crazy.

'Morag never even came to apologise,' was how Red started but then when they watched the footage back and saw how totally contrite Morag was and how she was advised by Milk not to go and how she couldn't apologise because Red left straight away, they began to see things in a different way.

The thing is that Red and Morag are really close. They're out in the kitchen garden together all the bloody time and Red will do anything for her and vice versa.

When Granny pointed out to Red how emotionally difficult a time it was for everyone and how easy it was to misstep and use the wrong word, Red backed down. Morag was so apologetic and so was Red.

'I'm so used to being under attack,' they said, 'And I felt like you all had accepted me for who I am and then when you said that it was, I dunno, a shock. Like that's what you really want to say, like that's what you think.'

'Not at all,' Morag said, 'I get who you are and I thank you for opening up the world for me and helping me understand it better. What I said, I said with no malice or intent. You're my friend and I care for you. I would never ever want to hurt you. It was a lesson learned. You have to continue to help me to be better at this. You can teach an old dog new tricks, Red, you can!'

They had hugged and cried, and in any other world that would have been an end to it.

Online though there was a head of steam building up that Flora felt she could not ignore.

We are in the annexe again with Tim.

I am pissed off that he has been summoned. He's like the Grim Reaper, only turns up when there's bad news on the cards. Flora hides behind him. It's pathetic.

'What are you saying you want to happen?' I say, 'They're happy together. They've made up. It's water under the bridge. There's no beef.'

'That's not strictly true,' Tim says, 'There were complaints and it's caused a lot of controversy. We can't, I'm afraid, be seen to do nothing.'

'Well issue a statement then or something,' I say, 'Do what the politicians do when they've had affairs and they appear at their houses with their wives to show they're forgiven. That used to be enough. And Morag has been forgiven. Red understands. It was a slip of the tongue for God's sake.'

'I have to think of the fans,' Flora says.

'Yes, okay, but this Show has a finite date now Mum, it's not going to last forever. You don't need them to like you like you used to.' I realise I'm putting off hearing what I know she's going to say.

'Darling,' she stretches her bony, emaciated hand towards mine. It's bruised dark indigo from the IVs on the back and looks like the hand of a 70-year-old. 'Sometimes we have to make difficult decisions,' she says.

'Morag's been with us since I was six,' I say, 'Every day, twenty-four hours a day more or less, seven days a week.'

'I know,' she says.

'She's cooked our Christmas dinners, our birthday cakes. She's made us soup when we were sick. I've spent more time with her than I have my own grandmother.'

'I know,' she says.

'I've spent more time with her than I've spent with you,' I say to her.

'Too far, Meryl,' Tim says.

'No,' I say, 'This is too fucking far.'

I stand up.

'I will never forgive you if you do this,' I say and I leave the dark of the annexe and step into the brightness of the courtyard unable to see because of the tears that are blinding me.

45

Flora

When you're cancelled you have to be careful because it's catching. It's a bit like the McCarthy witch hunts in the 1950s. Friends giving up friends as supposed communists in order to spare themselves a life in the cultural wilderness.

I don't want to see Morag go but the comments are raining down on me and they are becoming the story rather than The Show and I can't have that. Bless her, she says she understands. Of course I'll see her right and she's reached the time of life where she deserves to take it easy though I'm not sure where she's chosen to go or what she'll actually do.

I have other things to worry about, like the fact that the tumour in my liver has started growing again, with alarming alacrity and his friends are growing too.

Yes, I'll miss Morag but not for long, because I don't think I've got very long left to miss anything.

the.real.flora.tatton
daily contemplation: Unless you love yourself you can't love anybody. Be selfish.

Liked by **missfits** and **4,555,767 others**

nowayback
best choice ever. freedom wins out. #youarethebestflo

fuckeduphuman
watch your back mOrAg

bobbyboombastic
sending encouragement across the ocean

1974999
Why does she get to live her life with no consequences? Attack attack attack #revengeforRed

lilpiggywenttomarket
nonbi love rules da day #floshowshowsusdaway

cheesywotsups
BOOM! And she is gone! No more gender toxicity #moragisnomore #Redrules

46

Joyce

I get a text from Rita – Lord knows how she got my number and to my horror someone has started a shrine outside my house. Probably her, the psycho. I tell Flora I have to head home for a few days and call Michael to arrange a car. I'm hopeful the Red/ Morag issue will resolve in its own way and I'm speeding up the motorway within the hour.

As I'm shovelling the flowers and candles into the wheelie bin with Rita scowling from her bedroom window, I make a mental note to change my number but then think I must text Liz and see if she's free. With everything that's been going on, we've hardly exchanged two words over the last few weeks.

I give everything a quick dust and hoover and water the houseplants which are in desperate need, and I feel so happy to be home. I know there are a few spots at Flora's where the cameras can't pick you up, but when you're there long-term the wretched thing is that you forget about them and your guard drops. It is nice to be able to completely relax and not to have to worry at all.

Rita had made a terrible fuss on my arrival. She had a hideous bouquet prepared to thrust at me as I stepped out of the car, and she blubbed and blubbed to the point where I wanted to slap her. 'Is she your child?' I wanted to say, 'Are you on the brink of losing one of your last living relatives?' 'Do you wake up in the night in a cold sweat unable to imagine how you will get through the reality of the death of your daughter?' I want to scream at her.

Of course, I say nothing but accept the flowers as frostily as I can and practically beat her back with them as I retreat into the house. Hopefully my clearing of the shrine will have annoyed her enough to give me a wide berth for a least the next twenty-four hours.

My phone pings and Liz tells me she is free tonight. Could she come round to me? She's a bit under the weather and can't face going out anywhere in public.

I reply, 'Of course,' and have a root through the freezer for a few of the luxury ready meal dishes I keep on hand for when I'm feeling lazy. I will heat these up and open a bottle of wine and we can relax together and catch up on what's gone on.

When I open the door to Liz, I am shocked by the change in her appearance. In the few weeks since I last saw her, she's clearly lost weight as the clothes she's wearing are hanging off her, and, I hate to say it, she looks terrible. Despite more make-up she appears haggard and skeletal, like the flesh on her face has lost all its tone or plumpness.

I try not to show my reaction. 'Come in, Liz,' I say, 'How lovely to see you,' and I hug her. She flinches as I touch her as if it's painful and it's then that I notice that she also using a slender walking stick.

'It's lovely to see you too, Joyce,' she says, with some effort, 'I've missed you.'

We go through to the kitchen where the wine is open and breathing as Morag has shown me to do. I've opened some crisps and nuts and, as I go to pour a glass for Liz, she says, 'Do you have something soft, Joyce? I can't face a glass of wine tonight. Sorry.'

'Of course,' I say and go to my cupboards which, I'm ashamed to say, are bare. I turn back to Liz. 'I'm so sorry, Liz, I've only tap water to offer you. I could nip around to the shop. Get some coke or elderflower?'

'Water is just fine,' she replies with a wan smile.

'I feel terrible,' I say as I hand her the glass.

'Really, don't,' she says, 'This is perfect. Just what I needed,' and she takes a tiny sip.

We go through to the living room with the crisps and nuts, but she doesn't touch them and she says how sorry she is about Flora. She says she read about it all in the newspaper and that I must be feeling terrible about everything.

We chat a little about my plans to go back down south and she asks how Meryl and Treasure are, and it is all very nice but it's like she's sitting on the edge of her seat. Or like she metaphorically hasn't taken her coat off. She's different. She's not relaxed.

When I dish out the food and she manages a forkful or two, then pushes the plate away, I decide enough is enough.

'Liz, what's wrong, are you ill or unhappy?' I say.

'I'm fine Joyce, really,' she says.

'Well that's a bare-faced lie if ever I heard one,' I say and she manages a little laugh.

'Look,' I say, 'You can tell me. I'm your friend, aren't I?'

Suddenly she looks terribly upset.

'I didn't want to burden you Joyce with everything you're going through with Flora,' and her bottom lip trembles.

'Burden me with what?' I say.

'Oh Joyce,' Liz cries out, 'I'm ill, I'm really ill. I found out just after you left. I'm so sorry to have to tell you. I thought if I put on enough make-up I could keep it from you,' and I think she's going to cry but she doesn't.

'Liz, no!' I say, 'What on earth has happened?'

'It's just not fair,' she says, 'It's pancreatic cancer. Practically no chance of survival. Not on the NHS anyway. It's advanced. I'm sorry Joyce. I wasn't going to tell you until after Flora …'

She trails off.

I can't believe it. So I am to lose my daughter and the first friend I have made in years and years.

It really is better just to be on your own then you never have to experience loss. You spare yourself the terrible agony I am feeling as I look at my dear friend sitting across from me at the table.

'Oh Liz,' I say, 'this is too cruel.'

She nods her head and fumbles for a hanky which she puts to her mouth.

'I'm sorry about the wine and the food,' she says, 'I can't face much now. That was my first symptom, feeling sick. Plus a bit of pain.'

'What are the chances?' I say, pouring myself another glass of wine, 'Both you and Flora. So unlucky,' and I'm talking about myself as well as them.

'I'm sorry, Joyce, I really think I'm going to have to go. I'm exhausted,' Liz says and she gets up from the table.

'Of course,' I say, 'but I'd like to see you tomorrow. Will you be up to that?'

'Yes, I should think so,' she says and we go to the door.

'Don't give up!' I say as she walks off down the drive and then I hate myself for it. The number of ridiculous messages Flora has had of that ilk. Of course you don't want to give up but there comes a point where you have to face facts.

I truly hope I haven't offended Liz.

I close the door and hear my phone ringing.

It's Morag.

'I've been cancelled,' she says matter of factly, 'Can I come and stay?'

'Sure,' I say, 'I'll wait up for you.'

47

Meryl

I haven't looked at the joint account that Flora set up since Tyler left. Why would I? I'm back at home. I'm being fed. I'm trying not to buy anything. Frankly, I could probably last the next year or longer without buying anything else. Flora has given me back my credit card, unasked for on my part. I'm not using it. Hence I'm not checking the bank account.

A statement arrives though. I'd changed the address obviously when I moved out of Tyler's, and Mum's office have now removed him from the account, I think.

When I open it, I don't see it straight away.

Shows how much money was slushing through it and how little attention I was paying.

There's a transfer.

A sizable transfer on the day we broke up.

Tyler took £500k and put it into another account.

In terms of how much money Flora has that's small potatoes as the saying goes, but I try to work out how I feel about it. Is it theft? The account was in his name so the money technically is his, so I guess not. Was it morally his? Well, that's a more complicated question.

I think my main take away from it is, that it means I'll never see Tyler again.

He won't come back because he will feel deep shame at what he's done. There's a part of me, a small piece of me, that was hoping that maybe Tyler might be a part of bringing up Treasure because I know that's going to fall to me. And I don't want to do it on my own.

When I see the transfer, I know that he's not in my future or Treasure's. And that makes me sad.

I'm not going to say anything about the money though I'm pretty sure Flora will already know.

48

Flora

I've been considering donating all my money to charity and, as a result, I'm being bombarded with begging letters. Well, begging emails and texts, though I am getting some letters. One of the celeb mags did a piece on it as click bait and, even though it wasn't true, I kind of ran with it. I thought about what I'll leave behind. What is my legacy?

    I met with my lawyers. They arrived at the house and we sat on the cushions with Treasure and they accepted Duplo bricks as bars of soap and pretended to be sailing across the bubble bath ocean (another game), and we talked about setting up some scholarship programmes or funding a library, even though I don't read, and I signed papers for a trust fund for Treasure and making the house over to Meryl once she's twenty-one on the proviso that Treasure lives in it until she too is twenty-one and we looked at the second draft of my Last Will and Testament and I asked them how much money do my kids actually need? How much could I give away?

    We talked about The Show. What is going to happen to the royalties from the re-runs. Will there be re-runs? Once I'm dead, will anyone have any interest at all?

    'You know the network already want you to sign an option for Treasure?' one of the lawyers says, 'She's a great looking kid and she's clearly got some imagination. She could be another Shirley Temple with those curls.'

I look at my little girl as she trots around handing everyone a hairclip. 'What a dream!' I say, 'I wanted to be Shirley Temple when I was little.'

'You've done a hell of a lot better than she did,' another suit says and there is sycophantic laughter.

'Have I indeed?' I say, 'Well she got breast cancer too at 44 you know but, unlike me, she managed to live to 85. I've achieved quite a lot, you're right, but I'm not going to match that, am I?'

That seemed to put a bit of a damper on things.

'I'm tired,' I say, 'Tired of you,' is what I want to say but I don't, 'Can we pick this up next time? And can we all put our heads together about the charity angle? I think I want to pursue that.'

They all nod and bow and scrape and wander off across the grass and leave Treasure and me to snuggle down under a blanket and I pull her hair through my fingers and listen to her breathing and think about Shirley Temple tap tap tapping away when I was a little girl. My liver is so swollen it is bulging out of my side now. I have achieved a lot, but it all seems fairly futile in the face of this.

the.real.flora.tatton
daily contemplation: Grow for you. Show up for you. Get better for you.

Liked by **oxfam101** and **6,434,105 others**

nowayback
give your money to greenpeace #savethewhale

fuckeduphuman
I have a great idea for a start up Flora. Have DMd you

bobbyboombastic
sending wisdom from across the ocean

1974999
Why does she want to give her money away to charities? They're all a con - bigtime #charitybeginsathome

lilpiggywenttomarket
LOVE to see Treasure Show for real. Would watch that all day #floshowtreshshowwaytogo

cheesywotsups
Treazz is one sic kid. She gonna be so cute #starinthemaking #likemamalikedaughta

49

Joyce

I get Morag settled in the largest of the back bedrooms. She is remarkably calm and sanguine about the whole affair. I am livid on her behalf and have half a mind not to go back. If it weren't for Meryl, I wouldn't .

'I just boxed everything up and put it into storage,' Morag says as she wheels in two modest suitcases. 'Once I work out what I'm going to do or where I'm going to be, I'll get it all out again. Amazing how much stuff I'd accumulated in some ways but also a little frightening how little I have. I'm sixty and I don't own a property, Joyce. I've not really given my future any proper consideration.'

'Surely it's not permanent,' I say as I make us a pot of tea. It's after two in the morning but we're both wide awake.

'Of course it is, you silly besom,' she replies, 'In a few months at the most, there's going to be no Show to go back to, is there?'

'Oh yes, you're right,' I say, 'I hadn't thought of it like that.

'I can't believe I didn't think about my retirement; I just thought it would go on forever. Flora kept saying that and I just thought The Show would outlive me.' She opens the packet of chocolate digestives I've plonked on the table.

I pour the tea and bring over the cups.

'Frankly, I never for one second considered that I'd get cancelled,' and she dunks the biscuit in her tea.

We look at each other and she starts to laugh and so do I; big belly laughs at the absurdity of harmless little Morag being singled out as some malignant force for evil.

Eventually, we calm down.

'You'll just have to move in here,' I say, 'There's plenty of room.'

'Okay,' she says and reaches for another biscuit.

Later in bed I think about poor Liz. I haven't told Morag about her; she has enough on her plate. I just wish there was something I could do for her. It's going to be very difficult for me to split my time between Flora and Liz and, obviously, Flora is my priority though after her treatment of Morag it's hard for me to feel so generous towards her. I know this is only a temporary feeling though.

My hope is that as Morag is at a loose end, she will be able to provide some support to Liz. I know they didn't get off on the right foot, but things are different now for both of them.

I turn over in bed and it feels strangely comforting to have someone else under my roof. I'm surprised I feel like this.

I hope Morag decides to stay.

50

Meryl

Mum is determined to stay at home until the end and I respect that. I just wish it wasn't such an international event. Yesterday she spiked a fever and today Anya has come down to check on her.

She has a hospital bed in her room now and, more often than not, Shy or Milk or Red are carrying her up and downstairs. She's as slight as a child. We have a team of nurses on hand, and she's employed what she terms 'a dashing young doctor' called Yves who's done a couple of years with *Médecins Sans Frontiers* and is between jobs. He's all olive skin and strong jaw line but he is on it and, despite my best efforts, I'm warming to him. He's doing regular to camera updates on her health. His English is excellent and the way Shy and Milk light him or frame him against one of the terracotta walls or under the green of the wisteria, I can't believe anyone is listening to a word he's actually saying. He doesn't wear a white coat but favours sage green linen shirts with sleeves rolled up, or a crisp white T-shirt the better to show his gleaming even teeth. He has his stethoscope on him at all times though, slung around his neck or folded into his shorts' pocket. It's a visual reminder that, despite his devastating good looks, he really is a doctor. He's going to make some money once this is all over. No doubt.

Yes, so Yves had called Anya and obviously everyone knows all of this because it's all televised.

We've had an encampment at the perimeter since the diagnosis. Morag said it was like Greenham Common and I looked that up and there are similarities though the end goal is a little different.

When Morag was here, she was baking batches of sausage rolls and brownies and sending those down to keep everyone's spirits up. I dread to think what the sanitation's like even though we've had portable loos and shower facilities installed. The council have been very accommodating, though I'm not sure how the neighbours feel about it. At least they know it's short term.

So, Anya's arrival has sparked a little bit of hysteria at the camp; rumour has got around that this is it. The end is nigh.

I guess if you've been camping out for days, maybe weeks, waiting for an event to happen you want a ringside seat.

'We've got a problem,' Milk whispers to me in Mum's room, and indicates I should step out of the consultation with Anya.

'Can't it wait?' I say irritably. Mum is not looking good and there is some discussion about moving her onto a morphine driver. I've read up on this and knew she'd be in and out of consciousness once we hit this stage. I want to be part of the discussion.

'Nope,' Milk says.

Once in the hall, Milk shows me the gate cam on his phone, 'It's the storming of the Bastille,' he says.

'What the fuck?' I reply.

The raggle taggle group are heading down the drive with cries of, 'We just want to say goodbye,' 'We have a the right to see her one last time,' and 'She wants us to be there too.'

There weren't enough guards at the gate to stop them coming through. Not once they'd made their minds up. This was just the sort of madness I'd worried about.

'We need to phone the police,' I say.

'Already done,' Milk replies.

Yves steps out to join us. 'What's the plan?' he says, 'I've just had a text from Tim.'

'The house can be locked down in some way surely?' I say.

'Did you see the storming of the Capitol Building?' Milk says nervously.

Red appears at the top of the stairs. They turn and looks at the cam pointed at us. They jump up and athletically snatch it off the wall and disconnect the feed connector, leaving it dangling mid-air. It's impressive. I know Milk, with his love for the technology wants to protest but he bites it back.

'I'm moving Flora to the annexe,' they say as they stride purposefully towards us.

'Are you sure that's a good idea?' Milk says looking from Red to Yves.

'We have a security breach and the mob don't know the layout over there. We move Flora stat and set up a visual of a replacement Flora leaving here and going to hospital. Marsha's prepped to go.'

'Is it safe to move Mum?' I say to Yves.

'Is it safe to have a hundred people in the house trying to get a piece of her?' Red says, 'Now let's go!'

We follow Red into the bedroom and Yves goes to Flora, whips out his stethoscope and listens to her chest for about five seconds. 'You need to be admitted,' he says, 'We're taking you, now.'

Anya looks affronted to say the least.

'No time for an ambulance, Yves?' I say.

'Quicker by car,' he says as he and Red untuck Flora and Red gently but quickly scoops her up. Yves unhooks her IV and they leave the bedroom.

'Walk with me,' I say to a startled Anya.

'There's a security breach,' I say once we're in the hall with no cameras. 'We're taking her to the annexe. There's no cams there. I'll explain once we get there. Hurry.'

We head down the stairs and there is thumping and banging on the front door. A lot of thumping. And shouting. It's frightening.

I've lost sight of Red and Mum and Yves; they are moving fast.

We're through and out into the courtyard, locking the kitchen door behind us, and we can hear the noise of the crowd at the front of the house. There's a loud crack of glass. A window is broken. They will be in the house in no time.

Milk appears out of the annexe with Mum, limp in his arms, she looks totally unconscious. 'I'll see you soon,' he says to me, and Yves is behind him.

'Mum!' I run to her and grab her limp hand and she squeezes back with such strength. I look closer and of course it's Marsha. I was told the plan two minutes ago but the fear has disorientated me.

I keep going towards the annexe with Anya as I hear fists beating at the upstairs windows. I look up and the rioters are in my room. Angry faces crowd at the window yelling noiselessly at Milk and 'Mum' as they disappear into Michael's waiting car.

I know they'll be down and into here in no time.

As we run the last few steps inside, I hear sirens in the far distance and hope that Red's plan has bought us enough time.

Red is standing by the window to the courtyard and Mum is lying on the sofa with Anya monitoring her; Treasure is busily working on a puzzle on the floor by her feet. The blinds are down and Shy is standing shell-shocked having just woken up. 'What the hell is happening?' he says.

Red puts their finger to their mouth to silence him. Mum has her eyes closed and is wincing with pain. We have nothing here to help her.

'We just have to wait for the all clear, Mum,' I say, 'It won't be long now.'

This takes longer than expected.

A few of the fans can't believe their luck at actually being 'on set' and chain themselves to Flora's bed in what they call a peaceful protest, though what they're protesting is unclear. The right to invade someone's home and privacy I suppose. There has been rampant looting also and some superficial damage to deal with. Once the police are happy there is no immediate danger the security team and housekeeping start the clear up.

Red and I go back into the house.

It's quite impressive how much of a mess they've made. Or how much they've 'smashed and grabbed'. The detective in charge has told Red there is a pile of confiscated items in the drive that have been taken from all those arrested.

We go out to inspect.

They've had a go at everything from taking the art off the walls to nicking every last teaspoon from the kitchen. It's like a swarm of man-sized, deranged locusts have ravaged every corner of our house; anything and everything that could be snatched and grabbed has been.

When we go upstairs, they've stripped Mum's room, her medication is gone, her bedding, her make-up and toiletries and there's even a whole sheet of wallpaper ripped from the wall. It's utter madness.

A few days ago, I had driven down to the camp and taken a few cases of bottled water and some beers and boxes of crisps and fruit. I've been trying to keep up the support that Morag had started. Everyone was so grateful and reasonable. As I unloaded the stuff from the boot there was an easy sense of the community as different items were passed around the group. No one grasped or jostled, no one demanded anything and, whilst I wasn't there to be thanked or made a fuss of, a woman called Sky brought me over a dream catcher she'd made and said to take it back if I wanted to. 'It'll help Flora sleep, she needs to sleep at this time,' she said gently. It was a lovely object, delicate, carefully made, the colour of wheat.

'Thank you,' I said, 'I'm sure she'll appreciate that.'

There were more well-wishers, not pushy or pestering, just concerned human beings.

I can't believe it's the same group of people who've ransacked our home.

'Pack mentality,' Red says, 'Give a person permission to behave badly and nine times out of ten they'll do it.'

'I don't believe that, Red' I say.

'Why do you think the Nazis were so successful?' they say, and they bend down and pick up the trampled dream catcher from the bedroom floor.

51

Flora

I am so sleepy. I feel like it is all I can do to keep my eyes open for twenty minutes at a time and then I just drift back into sleep again. And that is a blessed relief because I cannot say that being awake is a barrel of laughs at the moment. My pain is not good. My liver is no longer just sore, it is sometimes really, really bad. But we don't want to talk about that, and I try not to show the reality of it too much because it's just not great for The Show.

I have found a solution for my charity drive. I think about those shitty kidnappers all those months ago and how everyone was so desperate to help and so we set up a series of instant donations via The Show and people can donate to Cancer Research or the NSPCC or the Samaritans or Doctors without Borders. That one's doing rather well because of Yves – he's gone down really well, certainly has a delightful bedside manner. I'm hedging my bets with the afterlife too. We have the option to donate to all the major faiths and there are daily prayers available on the website to download depending on your bag. I figure I may as well tap into all the help I can get and if I do a little good with him or her upstairs perhaps there may be some reward once the final curtain falls.

It's funny. I think people are watching me suffer but are feeling a bit guilty about it so their handing over of the cash to charity is somehow assuaging their guilt. Meryl keeps saying it's sick how everyone is still watching but they've all lived with me in their lives for so long, how can they stop watching now?

I am having a lovely dream where I am sitting cross-legged in the school hall for assembly. Remember how we did that? Lining up and marching in and sitting down in rows and all of us listening in more or less silence to the teachers or adults who came to talk to us? Such well-behaved children we all were. And I am sitting with Heidi and Pam and Lou and Netta and there is a magician talking to us. Well, he is performing for us. Not speaking. And he does lots of clever tricks, the old-fashioned ones with cards and doves and rabbits out of his top hat and we are laughing and laughing, and he is performing another and another and another. And I look down at my knees and they are bouncing with excitement because the magician is so, so brilliant and this is the longest assembly we've ever had but all the teachers are laughing too, and they don't care because the magician is so completely fantastic.

And then the magician does a deep bow and speaks to us for the first time. 'For my next trick, I need an assistant,' and every single one of us puts up our hands. We stretch our arms up out of their shoulder sockets and we all cry out, 'Me! Me! Pick ME!' and even the teachers have their arms up. Even the crotchety old teachers whose mouths are set into permanent frowns and who never leave their desks and never want to talk to us. They have their hands up, their arms straight and true, desperate to be picked by the clever magician in front of us.

He spreads his arms wide and bows his head and we all know that means he wants us to put our hands down and to let him think. So we do. And it is so quiet in the hall, you could have heard a tiny ant trot across the parquet floor going about its busy business.

We wait and wait and then all of a sudden, the magician looks up and his eyes fix on me and he points straight at me. 'Flora Tatton,' he booms, 'Will you be my assistant?' and everyone in the hall claps and cheers and his pointed finger becomes an open palm and he steps towards me, and I step towards him and I take his hand.

He leads me to the back of the hall, and he draws back a swishy red curtain.

On a gold podium there is a wooden box.

'And now,' he says, 'I will saw this beautiful and spectacular little girl in half!' and the hall erupts into more cheers as I mount the steps to the box and climb in.

My head and feet are sticking out like they are supposed to, and I chuckle and laugh as he spins the box around and around on the podium.

We come to a stop, and he raises a glinting silver saw above his head, then leans in close to me and says, 'This really won't hurt for long,' and I am suddenly terrified as I watch the teeth of the saw snarl and grind through the wood of the box. I see more of the saw disappear and I wriggle and wriggle to try to get away from the sharp metal teeth, but I am held fast by the box.

The magician is sweating with his efforts. He pauses and wipes his brow with a never-ending handkerchief that the audience finds hilarious. 'Stop!' I say, 'Stop!' but no one can hear me.

There is more cutting. The blade is going to be upon me at any second.

He stops again.

'Boy, this is thirsty work,' the magician says and takes off his top hat to remove a cold glass of water from inside it, 'Cheers!' he says and just before he drinks, a large drop of sweat from the end of his bulbous nose splashes into the water.

I can see the inside of his mouth, his teeth his glugging tongue, through the bottom of the glass. I try to scream but no noise comes out.

The magician leers down towards me, his lips wet from the water, his brow slick with sweat, 'Why are you complaining?' he says, 'You always said you wanted a career in Showbusiness!' and he sets to again.

I feel the blade, sharp and deep on my right-hand side. I writhe and writhe and wait for the box to fill with my blood. The pain is terrible.

'Why don't you sing us a song?' the magician bellows in my face.

I wake up and the pain in my side is astonishing.

Yves is there. I vomit. I try to speak. I try to speak. I try to speak. I vomit.

He pushes something into the IV.

I am crying.

He holds my hand.

I give up trying to speak.

52

Joyce

I meet Liz in our old café, late the next morning. I've left Morag to unpack and head off to the shops. She is 'black affronted,' by my lack of provisions and wants to stock up. I am more than happy to let her crack on.

Liz arrives later than we had arranged, very unlike her, and from my window seat I can see her limping slowly down the street. A little way away from the café she stops for a breather as if she may not make it all the way. I shake my head at the deterioration in her in such a few short weeks, but then I have watched Flora decline just as rapidly. Cancer just ravages the body, sapping strength and vitality and leaving nothing behind.

'So sorry I'm late,' Liz says as she reaches the table, and she clutches the back of the empty chair to get her breath back.

'It's no trouble, Liz,' I say, 'but I think you would be better to get a taxi home. Why didn't you drive?'

'I'm trying to keep walking a little. My oncologist says exercise is good and I can't manage anything else.'

'But this is ridiculous,' I say, 'You look half-dead!' and then I put my hand up to my mouth in a pointless gesture to stop the words that have already left it. 'Oh Liz, I'm so sorry. What a dreadful thing to say.'

She laughs a little. 'It's okay, Joyce, you have a point!' and she heaves herself into the chair and picks up the menu. 'What are we having?' she says brightly.

'Whatever you fancy,' I say, 'My treat.'

I see a look of repulsion creep across her face as she takes in the options available, and she carefully places the menu back on the table. 'I'll just have a mineral water, I think Joyce.'

The waitress comes over and I order a tea and hope the smell won't be too strong for her. We chat about the weather a little and our drinks arrive. She barely touches the water.

'Tell me about the treatment, Liz. Flora responded quite well to her chemo at first. She had it to shrink the tumour in her liver and there was talk of immunotherapy I think as well but she wasn't a suitable candidate for that apparently,' I say.

'It's all pretty hopeless, I'm afraid. I'm under the palliative care team now. When they diagnosed me, they had a meeting and came up with a plan and, whilst there's a slim chance that surgery might help, they're not willing to take the risk on the NHS. So I'm just on pain management.' Liz takes a sip of her water.

'What do you mean they're not prepared to take the risk?' I say.

'There's some radical surgery that could be performed but we don't do it in the UK. I'd have to travel to France probably or Germany. I've looked online. I had a zoom meeting with a consultant, he was great, but the reality, the expense was way beyond what I could realistically raise. I looked at re-mortgaging and selling the car, but I was still nowhere near. So that's that.'

'So you're saying they do this procedure abroad but not here, that's crazy! The NHS are supposed to be world leaders!' I am furious on her behalf.

'You don't understand Joyce, it's a question of risk really. In an ideal world it could be offered to everyone but the cancer I have is rare and the procedure I need is even more so. There just aren't that many specialists who offer it. And there aren't any guarantees anyway.'

'But there's a chance it could work?' I say.

'A chance, yes but only a small one,' she smiles at me, 'It's okay, Joyce, I've come to terms with it. My number's up as they say and there's nothing I can do about it. I just have to get on with it.'

I find it hard not to cry but Liz is being brave so I take a deep breath. 'So how long do they think you have?' I say, 'If you don't mind sharing that with me…'

'Weeks rather than months, I'm afraid. It's aggressive,' she says.

'Just like Flora,' I say shaking my head.

'I'm so sorry, Joyce,' she says, 'If this is too much for you to cope with I would quite understand. Flora is your daughter and she's your priority.'

I lay my hand on hers. 'I want to help Liz,' I say, determinedly, 'I really do. I'll be here as much as I can. I don't want you to be alone,' and her eyes fill with tears.

'How much is the surgery?' I say.

'It's not important,' Liz says.

'I'm interested,' I say.

'It's a lot,' Liz says, her voice resigned, defeated.

'How much?' I persist.

'Around £300,000,' she says.

I sit back in my chair. 'That is a lot,' I say, 'I'm not surprised it's not available on the NHS.'

'It's actually not too bad cost-wise, apparently,' she says, 'but yes, it makes sense.'

'What if …' I start to say but Liz puts up her hand.

'If you're going to suggest what I think you are Joyce, then please don't.' She looks out of the window. 'Like I said, there are no guarantees, it might only buy me a few years. Look at Flora, less than two years and her cancer was back. No, it's an enormous sum and if the NHS doesn't think it's worth the investment, then I'm going with them.'

I draw breath to speak but she interrupts me, 'Plus think of the recovery and the risks. Look at the state I'm in now. It's not a viable alternative. Now drink your tea and let's not think any more about what could have been,' and she takes another tiny sip of water.

53

Meryl

Treasure is sleeping in my bed. I don't mean when I am in it, I mean even when I am not in it. Every time she is put to bed in her own bed, she climbs out and toddles through at some point and climbs into my bed. The first few times she made herself a pillow wall to stop herself falling out (she has a bed guard); now we've got her another bed guard to put on my bed.

I don't mind her being in my bed. She's not a wriggler and she doesn't hog the bed or the covers.

What I mind about it is, I don't know how I'm going to break this habit.

I don't know how to be a mother.

It's getting towards the end of August and soon it'll be the start of term again. I'm pleased I did all that work in July; it's not going to matter that I miss the first couple of weeks. I don't think it's going to be longer than a couple of weeks.

Mum organised an End-of-Life Dula, Cara, before she checked out consciously and she's been here a lot. She's pretty cool to be honest, not like the birth Dula Jan. She was annoying as fuck.

Cara says there's a pattern that pretty much everyone follows when they're dying, and that death can be beautiful. She says that because Mum is sleeping so much at the moment, she's getting towards the end.

I think it's the drugs she's on. I don't know how she could do anything other than sleep.

Cara says if she wasn't ready to die, she'd be fighting the pain more. She says her body is shutting down and she is getting ready to slip away. She says when it is close to the time there will some time of lucidity and that is when she will say her goodbyes to us.

She tells us to go and talk to her all the time.

I am trying this at the moment.

We are alone.

She is asleep.

It looks like she is deeply asleep.

'Why are you dying Mum? I'm a bit pissed off about it. I mean you set all this stuff up and then you just check out. It's not cool. I'm seventeen and I don't want to be a mum and there's no one else to look after Treasure unless I set up another *Flora Show* and have her be like Truman in it. God, you would *love* that wouldn't you? Well, I'm not going to, okay? I'll look after her, I guess.

'And why did you send Morag away? What difference would it have made if some people had switched off? You hurt me and you hurt Granny, but most importantly you hurt Morag. And she loved you. Again, not cool!

'I'm supposed to be sitting here saying lots of soppy things to you, aren't I? Instead, I'm telling you off. But you infuriate me, Mum. All the time.

'Treasure's sleeping in my bed. She knows there's something going on. I don't mind. I'm just telling you. And Tyler took a load of money. From the account. Like £500k. You should never have set that account up. You broke us up with that money. But that was probably your plan, wasn't it? He was okay, Mum. He was a good boy and you made him something else. I'm quite mad at you about that too. I'm really not sure that this is what Cara had in mind. I'm really not sure this is doing either of us any good.'

Of course, I don't say any of this out loud. The cameras would pick it all up, wouldn't they? But I think it all. It clarifies things for me. I look at Mum sleeping and she looks younger, smoother, peaceful. The light is a mauve grey through the window, and I realise I have sat through the night with her and that is the first light of dawn in the sky. I must have dozed in the chair and not woken up when Yves came in to top up the driver. I let go of Mum's hand and tuck it under the blanket and go back to my room and cuddle in next to Treasure's safe little body.

the.real.flora.tatton
daily contemplation: A disco ball is hundreds of pieces of broken glass put together to produce a magic ball of light. You aren't broken. You're a disco ball.

Liked by **heartofgold** and **9,007,633 others**

nowayback
meryl showing her love. My heart is breaking for you #staystronggirl

fuckeduphuman
FINALLY some emotion from the weirdo

bobbyboombastic
sending hope from across the ocean

1974999
Why does she get to be there at the death bed after the way she has behaved? We're onto you #baddaughterpayback

lilpiggywenttomarket
blood is thicker than water #floshowrulesdawaves

cheesywotsups
Treash is one sneaky kid. She gonna be a handful #boundaries #toddlertaming

54

Flora

I am grappling with a snake. A long, thick, muscular snake with bright jade eyes and a darting forked tongue. I hold it by the neck to keep its milky fangs from striking me, but my arms are weak and its head is getting closer. My mind drifts and I wonder where a snake's neck ends and its body begins. If you were to fit a snake for a tie, where would you place it? Under its chin I suppose would be the logical place, but then that would just accentuate that oh so long body.

It must be the same problem for a giraffe. Plus, you'd require the most enormous length of tie for a giraffe apart from anything else, unless you stuck to a dickie bow. I think a dickie bow would work well, that would balance out their cute little horns.

Sensing the weakness in my lapse in concentration, the snake veers towards me and the jaws gape wide.

I wake up.

Marsha is walking Treasure around my room and *The Good Ship Lollipop* is playing for me. I asked for it. I listen to the words. A dream land built of beautiful candies; a child's delight. I look at my room with its beautiful colours and lovely things, the names of which escape me as I lie here, but I know I loved them when I chose them. Loved them so much more than the adequate bedroom of my childhood.

I have fashioned a perfect world here in this house. A world of harmony and delight and nothing bad has happened here and everyone has had a perfect life. Flora

World. How lucky we have been to sail to these shores and bask in the sunshine I've created.

I look away from Marsha and Treasure who have sat down on the floor and are playing with a doll, I think.

In the chair on the other side of the bed, sits my father.

We smile at each other. He visits me quite a lot. He's in a dark overcoat, dark suit, dark lace-up shoes. The sort of clothes I remember him wearing. His legs are crossed and there's a conker brown felt trilby on his knee, trimmed with a black ribbon. I love that hat, but I know he never wore one like that. I know that my mind is kidding me with this detail. I see his face though. All the detail of his face that has been lost for so many years. He has my eyes, the same greenish blue with thick, short lashes and he has Meryl's mouth, a beautiful full top lip, a slight overbite. He is tanned from his living in Australia. His hands, that stroke and smooth the hat from time to time, are strong and capable. I am pleased, so very pleased, he is my father.

He draws the cuff back on his sleeve and looks at his wristwatch and I can hear its precise and tiny mechanism tick tick ticking. He looks at the watch and he looks at me.

Soon I know that I will have to go with him.

55

Joyce

When I get home I find Morag up to her elbows in dough. The kitchen smells incredible and there are already several pies cooling at the open window and a tray of blondies on the table. She doesn't bother to stop pummelling the bread but looks up at me with a hearty smile.

'Are we expecting company?' I say.

'Some people eat when they're blue,' she says, 'Some people drink. But I,' and she punches the dough,' bake! You'll be pleased of that when you tuck in at teatime.'

'I will,' I say, pulling out a chair and sitting down. There are dishes in the sink, and I could don a pinny and offer to help but I've too much on my mind. I need to talk to Morag properly.

'So how was Liz?' she says stretching and kneading with concentration.

'No better than yesterday obviously. She told me a few more details though. The surgery she could have but not on the NHS, that sort of thing. It's a terrible situation, Morag.'

'Tell me more,' Morag says.

By the time I've got through the whole story Morag has finished with the dough and put it to prove. She sits down opposite me.

'So you're saying you offered her the money and she refused?' she says.

'Not even that,' I say, 'I started to raise it as a possibility, and she wouldn't even let me finish the sentence. She's just given up. It's a damn shame.'

I tell Morag about the time her car broke down and we had to postpone our trip and I offered to pay for the repair. 'It was only going to be a loan; I wasn't being all flashy or anything but she was offended I even offered.'

'I suppose you haven't known her that long …' Morag says.

'I've known her my whole life and here we are both of us more or less on our own because of the start we had in life. Why shouldn't I offer to help her?' I sound affronted.

'I'm going to make us tea,' Morag says and puts a blondie onto a plate for me.

'What do you mean because of the start you had both had?' she says as she fills the kettle.

'It doesn't take more than a bit of cod-psychology to realise that you're affected by not being brought up by your parents,' I say, 'Burnley House wasn't a terrible place, not by any stretch, but it wasn't a proper home with a proper family. Liz and I both know we have … trust issues. Look at us! Same pattern in our lives practically – short marriage, divorce and then nothing and no one. I mean I have Flora but even that hasn't been a rip-roaring success, has it?'

'Flora has turned out fine, Joyce,' Morag says sternly.

'Oh I know that but we're not … I mean I wasn't a good mother. I didn't take to it naturally. I struggled to … connect with her. From when she was a baby. It wasn't straightforward like it is for some women.'

'I'm not sure it's simple for anyone, hen' she says, 'but I get what you're saying.

She brings the tea over and we wait for it to brew.

'So she wouldn't take the money, eh?' Morag says.

I take a bite of blondie and shake my head. 'Damn that is good,' I say.

'I always do my best work when I'm at my bleakest,' she says proudly.

She pours the tea. 'Get your laptop,' she says, 'I think we should do a bit of research into this surgery. See what we can find out.'

'I'm finishing this blondie before I go anywhere,' I say, 'Priorities!' and Morag laughs.

'There's a surgeon here who performs your own liver transplant,' Morag says, looking at her iPad, 'Removes the liver, holds it in some kind of icy stasis, removes the tumours and then reinserts it, like they do in a transplant. Why doesn't Flora have that? She could afford anything God knows.'

'Too many tumours,' I reply, 'She had a consultation with him remember? But her liver was riddled. They hoped that maybe the chemo would shrink everything enough, but it never happened. The tumours stopped responding and just started growing again, faster than before. I'm not surprised you don't remember, there were so many consultations.'

I move over and sit next to Morag. 'This must be what she was talking about, it's about the right price and it fits with her description. It's for pancreatic cancer and not offered as standard in the UK.' I'm on a radical and experimental cancer treatment website. There are some incredible cancer stories here; I am feeling there could be a chance for Liz.

'What are you thinking?' Morag says.

'I'm thinking I can't save Flora, but I could save Liz. Is that ridiculous?' I look at Morag, shoulder to shoulder with me. Her opinion counts on this.

'She might say no, Joyce. And that's her choice, isn't it? You said so yourself, she's very proud. If she refuses, you have to respect that. And she already has today. In some ways, if you don't offer, you'll save yourself that.'

'But in other ways, if I don't offer, I'll never know,' I answer.

'I agree,' she says, 'Let's get our coats.'

'Are you coming too?' I say.

'Surely,' Morag says, 'I wouldn't miss this for the world. It's got the potential to be better than *The Flora Show.*'

I tut and roll my eyes, but I am glad she's coming with me.

At the front door I realise I can't remember Liz's address. 'I've never been to her house,' I say, 'but I do know her street and I'm sure her car will be on the drive. Shall we just go and try anyway, it's only a ten-minute walk away.' I'm excited and I can't stand the thought of not putting our plan into action.

'Why not,' says Morag, 'She's likely home anyway given her current state. Even though it's Saturday night.'

It's a beautiful evening, a warm wind and a clear sky. I feel hopeful and we're at the road in no time. I spot Liz's car at the far end, and we march up towards it. The house is bigger than I thought, a semi, but then she is a teacher so why shouldn't she have a nice property.

There are lights on, so it looks like she's not in bed. I ring the bell and stand back expectantly.

It's a while before we hear noise behind the door. Eventually, an unshaven and bleary-eyed youngish man stands before us, bare-chested and in filthy pyjama bottoms. 'Yeah?' he says rudely jutting his chin at us as if we are most definitely not welcome.

'Hello,' I say, 'we're looking for Liz Finnerty, I think I may have got the wrong house but that's her car so…'

He's rubbing his eyes and only half listening, 'Liz you want, yeah? Yeah, she lives here. She's not in though.'

'Oh, I see,' I say.

'She's down The Dog,' he says and points his finger vaguely to the end of the street.

'The Dog and Duck?' I say, 'The pub along from the café on the high street?'

'Yeah,' he says, and he unceremoniously shuts the door.

'I don't understand,' I say to Morag, 'She hates pubs. She told me.'

'Maybe there's a function on in there,' Morag says.

We walk back down the drive to the pavement.

'So,' says Morag, 'Is it home you want to go or are we off to The Dog?'

'I think,' I say, 'we're off to The Dog.' And we set off in silence.

56

Meryl

Cara says we should write down our thoughts and feelings and memories as they come to us and read them to Flora. We should write down our thoughts and feelings about each other too if there's anything that we're finding helpful or difficult about each other's behaviour. She's provided a broad necked teal green vase in the kitchen for us to drop little messages into and the plan is to sit and read them at the end of every day with the smell of a burning candle or sometimes incense. It's supposed to bring us together as a community and to help us to heal after Flora has died.

Cara is very keen on using the words death and dying and dead. She is very keen to face what is happening head on, not in a brutal way, just in a direct way.

I'm with her on that.

I hate the term 'passing away' or 'passed'. It's as if you have floated away ephemerally, glided through a wall or drifted off on the breeze. From what I can gather so far death is no picnic. Cara keeps saying it can be beautiful but there's not much evidence of that so far. There's been a lot of pain and indignity for the person who's dying and a lot of misery and hanging around for those of us who are living with the imminent death.

That's the other thing. When is it going to happen? I feel guilty if I read a book or check my phone and watch a dog in sunglasses and a party hat play the piano. I feel bad if the food we're eating tastes good – generally is doesn't as we're all mucking in and trying our hand at feeding each other – and I want to eat more of it. I don't want my mother to be dead, but I want this stage of her life to be over.

We are trying the comments in the vase. Treasure is sleeping in my bed and Yves has just topped up the pain meds so Mum is settled.

Cara is sitting cross-legged on the rug in front of the wood burner in the kitchen. Milk is filming. Shy and Marsha are sitting very close together on the sofa (I'm pretty sure they're fucking) with Red next to them, and Yves and I are on the chairs. Ted and Nial the technicians are squashed onto the sofa too and Sonja and Yetta, the nurses are sitting on the bar stools. Han, the other nurse is upstairs with Mum; they said they did rock, paper, scissors as to who missed the session.

'Okay let's see what's in the vase tonight,' Cara says brightly and upturns the messages onto the rug. '*I like how Shy whistles when he chops the veggies*, That's a good start,' and she grins.

There are smiles all round. 'What can I say, I'm a happy guy,' Shy says.

'*I wish we could all sit and pray together for Flora*. Okay that's a little more out there. We can't impose our own personal beliefs on the whole community. We've already talked about this.'

'I don't think it could hurt,' Sonja says, 'All healing comes from God. You could all do to open your hearts to him. For Flora's sake,' and she tuts loudly.

'No judgement here please,' Cara reminds us all gently. She does have a soothing voice and such smooth skin too, like I say it's hard to be irritated by her.

She picks up another message. '*I like that Meryl is taking more interest in Treasure*,' she reads.

They all smile and nod in agreement. 'I was always interested in Treasure,' I say, 'She's my sister. Obviously I'm interested in her. What kind of a comment is that?'

'Okay Meryl, we hear your reaction and we acknowledge that you haven't been given the opportunity to realise your relationship with Treasure in the way that you would wish so far.'

'I didn't say that. I did not say that. She's my kid sister. I am interested in Treasure a perfectly normal amount. God! I never said anything about what I wanted to do or not do with her.'

'My apologies Meryl, I shouldn't have put words in your mouth, I overstepped. Let's move on.' She picks up the next message. *'I wish Meryl would stop complaining about her mum. She is lucky to have her.'* Cara says and carefully lays the message on the rug.

I cross my arms. 'I'm not complaining about her.' I say, 'How can I be complaining about her, she's lying in bed all day semi-comatose, what's there to complain about? Our relationship is the best it's been for years.'

'You see that's what's I'm talking about,' Marsha says, 'It's those little digs, you can't say anything nice about her, can you? It's upsetting when she's the way she is. It's disrespectful.'

'That would make her laugh,' I stare at Marsha, 'She would agree with me. She would hate us all to be sitting here so po-faced and miserable. She'd be saying crack open the gin, put on some music, live a little. She's not dead yet, Marsha.'

'Okay, thank you Meryl. I think you have both heard each other's points of view here,' and Cara looks at both of us to check we're not going to keep going. Marsha adjusts herself so she's turned away from me. Snotty cow! First point of order, once Mum snuffs it, is to sack her.

'What have we here?' Cara says her voice all warmth and reconciliation, *'Meryl puts too much garlic in the food when she makes it. Did her boyfriend like garlic? I think it's too much.'*

'You've got to be kidding me?' I say, 'Let's re-name the jar, Complaints about Meryl, shall we? Anyone have any comments about my dress sense? Perhaps I swear too much? Hmmm? Or talk too loudly? What about that? Here let me see, Cara what else have we got?' and I reach down and snatch the pile of messages from the floor, '*Meryl's music is too loud sometimes. It must disturb Flora,*' I read loudly, '*Sometimes Meryl doesn't clear away her plates after she has eaten, everyone else does, Meryl can say mean things which she thinks are jokes but I don't think they are funny, Why doesn't Meryl say anything when she is in the room with Flora, she comes across as heartless and uncaring.*'

There are more but I stop reading. It's pretty dispiriting to note they're not all written in the same hand either. It appears quite a few of them are pretty pissed off with me.

Cara looks dejected. 'I was hoping you would write caring and supportive things about each other,' she says, 'This process is about growing and healing and nurturing. I've never seen the vase used to … well … to bully someone.'

She stands up and comes over to me. 'I'm so sorry to have put you through this Meryl. You are the most vulnerable person here and I realise now no one understands that,' and she bends down and hugs me and holds me.

Against my better judgement, I burst into noisy, uncontrollable tears.

57

Flora

'What is it like to be dead?' I say to my father who is sitting on the edge of my bed.
'You'll find out soon enough,' he says.
'Is there a god?' I say.
'You'll have to wait and see?' he says.
'Can I come back as a ghost? I say.
'That depends,' he says.
'What on?' I say.
'Many things,' he says.
'Like what?' I say.
'You'll find out,' he says.
'You're not very good on concrete detail, are you?' I say.
'That's because I'm not really here,' he says.
'Fair enough,' I say.
He sits and looks at me for a while.
'Did you watch my Show in Australia?' I say.
'No,' he says.
'Why not?' I say.
'Because you remind me too much of your mother and she was the love of my life,' he says.
'Is that true?' I say.
'Of course not!' he says, and we laugh together at the thought of my mother being the love of anyone's life. My father takes out a meticulously ironed large white hankie and wipes his eyes. He puts it back in his trouser pocket and says, 'No, the truth is we couldn't wait to be

shot of each other and I couldn't wait to be rid of dreary old England with its drizzle and misery.'

'But what about me? You left me behind. Why didn't you take me with you?' I say.

'You were a girl. I needed boys. I had boys down under,' he says.

'I understand,' I say.

'I knew you would, he says.

'But I'm an international superstar,' I say, 'You backed the wrong horse.'

'True,' he says, 'but you're going to be dead soon.'

'Aren't we all?' I say and we laugh.

58

Joyce

It's a busy night in The Dog and Duck and, as music pumps out of the upstairs window and the raucous hubbub of chatter and laughter blasts through the open door, I pause for thought as to whether I want to venture into this uncharted territory.

It's a long time since I've been in a pub on a Saturday night.

Morag has sensed my trepidation. 'It's okay, I'm right here with you, hen. If we can't see her, we'll just get out and head home, okay?'

I nod and we step into the prattling ruddy faces and the crush of people and push our way through as politely as we can searching for Liz. 'I thought pubs were in decline,' Morag yells in my ear as she hangs on my arm behind me. She's right; there's no evidence of this here. The bar is full, heaving, with all sorts making merry, making the most of it.

A burly man lurches in front of me clearly three sheets to the wind. He staggers unsteadily, 'Sorry ladies,' he sways, 'Just off for a piss,' and he rolls past us.

Morag laughs. 'Lovely,' I say and press on around the end of the bar.

It is quieter there. Maybe this is what is used to be called the snug end.

I hear her before I see her.

'And she says, 'I don't want you to be alone,' and I think that's the key, Rick, because she's alone, isn't she? If we just wait a little longer, she's going to realise that once I'm gone, she's going to be left with no one.'

I put my hand on Morag's arm to stop her. We are unseen at this point, hidden by the curve of the bar, but I can see her skinny leg at a table just past the turn.

I take a step back.

'If you think so Betty but it's risky, isn't it?' A man's voice replies and Morag and I look at each other.

'Not really. She's blind at the moment, isn't she? Her daughter's dying, Rick. The only thing is we need her to make the decision soon I reckon, before she goes back down south.'

'Why do you think that?' the man's voice says.

'Well what if she has a change of heart and decides to stay down there with that freak of a granddaughter, eh? I mean she's never going to manage that little un on her own is she. No. I was catching up on The Show this afternoon and all hell was breaking loose. The lot of them were turning on her. Setting her straight. Calling out her spoilt brat shenanigans. About bloody time too. Hope Flora has left all her money to charity, it'd serve that silly bitch right.'

I felt Morag surge forward, but my arm held her fast. We needed to hear it all.

'Why didn't you just let her give you the money at lunchtime, pet?' the man whines, 'I don't get it.'

'No, you wouldn't, would you. It's like reeling in a fish, you tug them in and then you let them out. That's the game, Ricky boy. You need to make sure the hook is fast. Secure. If I'd jumped on the money, she'd have suspected something or that nosy Jock bitch would have. You heard what she said about coincidences. didn't you? She's clever that one, not gullible like Joyce.

'No, if I'd agreed to the money then we'd be on a hiding to nothing, but you see, she'll be on the phone offering it tomorrow. I guarantee it.'

'You're like some criminal mastermind. It's brilliant. Cannot wait to be spending that moolah, and cannot wait to get ourselves out of this shithole,' the man says, 'Do you want another drink, love? A half maybe?'

'Make it a pint,' Liz says.

Morag pulls me back into the main bar.

Her face is flushed and furious.

'What's your plan?' she says.

'I don't know,' I say, 'I'm open to suggestions.'

'I'm for bottling her,' Morag says her fists clenched.

'Sounds good,' I agree, 'but shall we try something a little less messy.'

'Okay,' Morag is disappointed.

'Let's go home,' I say.

I text Liz and arrange to meet her in the café the next morning. I tell her that I'm heading back down south but I have important news.

She's not late this time though she is maintaining her part of terminally ill patient extremely well.

Morag and I have ordered coffee and she has water again and we cut straight to the chase. I tell her excitedly about looking into the cancer treatment and say that as I cannot save my daughter, I would be honoured if she would give me the chance to save her.

'But I told you Joyce there are no guarantees,' she says, 'It's difficult surgery and look at the state of me.

'Well there is your answer, Joyce,' Morag says, 'I told Joyce not to get her hopes up,' she says to Liz, 'We respect your decision and now we must be getting back as Michael will be waiting with the car,' and we stand up to leave.

'Just a minute,' Liz says, ' Perhaps I am being too hasty,' and we sit back down. 'Perhaps I do deserve a chance. I mean even a small chance is better than none, right? Oh Joyce, if you believe in me maybe I should try the surgery.'

'It really is your choice,' I say, 'if you feel you have the strength to go through with it.'

'Oh but it's so much money,' she looks down at her hands and Morag rolls her eyes at me, 'I couldn't possibly take it from you. I'd never be able to pay it back. Never.'

'Again,' Morag says, 'If that's your final decision we have to respect that and we understand that it's a lot to take from a friend, a good friend.' She stands, 'Michael will be waiting Joyce,' she says.

A look of irritation flashes across Liz's face. It is there and gone in a moment. If we hadn't been in the pub last night, I could have passed it off as a stab of pain or such like, but I knew what was really going on.

She reaches across the table to me and lays her hand on mine. It is all I can do not to bat it away and slap her double-crossing face. I breathe deeply and force myself to look at her.

'I'd like to accept,' she says, 'If you're happy with the arrangement then so am I. Thank you so much. I shall make all the appointments and I'll keep you posted as to how everything is going. Joyce, you may just have saved my life.' And she dabs at her eyes with her hanky but there are no tears.

I reach down for my handbag and take out my cheque book.

Liz looks a little taken aback.

'Can you not do a bank transfer,' she says?

'Not for that amount,' I say, as I complete the details, 'Not without contacting the bank directly and today is Sunday, after all. You can pay this in online and it will have cleared in a couple of days.'

'Of course,' she says but she's not really listening, she's just mesmerised at the number of zeros I'm writing on the paper I'm about to hand her. I tear it off and give it to her.

She cannot take her eyes off it.

'We really have to be going, Joyce,' Morag says, and we move away from the table. Liz has barely managed a goodbye.

At the door, I turn and say to her, 'Oh Liz, give my love to Rick, won't you?' and she smiles and says,

'Yes of course.' Then the smile dissolves on her face and she looks about her, panic replacing the absolute satisfaction she was enjoying a moment ago.

The two plain clothes police officers sitting at the table next to us stand up and move towards her. She cowers beneath them.

'You fucking bitch!' she screams, and we step out onto the high street.

59

Meryl

'I don't care what you all say I want my Granny and I want Morag. My mum is dying and this is horrible and I need them here with me,' I shout.

Flora is definitely worse and I have already sent Michael to get them both though I haven't told Tim this. He is here a lot now. He is unshaven and miserable. He mooches about and spends a lot of time sitting on the floor of Mum's room. I guess he doesn't know what he's going to do with his life once this is all over, but with the money he's banked, he doesn't have to do anything.

'She made a decision. It's what she wanted,' Tim whines.

'She didn't make a decision, the public made a decision, the cameras made a decision based on one stupid little incident. I need Morag. I need her here. She would know what to say. She knows me. She knows all of us.' If he keeps arguing, I am going to start smashing stuff.

'I'm going to have to check with the board,' he says listlessly.

'No you're not,' I say, 'because it's happening.' I turn to the camera nearest me. 'You can't take everything away from me in the name of fucking television. It's child abuse. I need my Morag. I need my Granny. They are coming and all you haters can just switch off if you want to. We all love Morag here even Red, especially Red, and we want her here so she is coming back. We are humans and we need each other. I can't go through this without her.'

My throat aches with misery. Yves comes and puts an arm around me. 'It's okay,' he says, 'You need to calm down now.'

'You're right,' Tim says, looking at the barely breathing pile of bones that is my mother, 'What does it matter. It's all over. It's all going to be over soon, yes?' he says to Yves.

'Yes,' says Yves, 'Very soon.'

Tim and I nap on the floor and in the chair through the night. Sonja and Han and Yves move in and out and Cara softly sings or reads beautiful ancient poetry. I wonder what Flora would have made of this. She'd probably have rather had the latest celebrity gossip, but Tim loves it and alternates between weeping into his sleeve and what can only be described as manically grinning with joy. It feels like days since Mum has managed anything more than a few minutes of consciousness, but I don't know whether this is accurate. I have no idea of the day or date. We are cocooned by our journey, hand in hand with death.

Around three in the morning, Granny and Morag arrive. They have had a hellish journey. A motorway pileup, north and south bound delays that have driven them to despair. Granny was beside herself that she wouldn't get here in time, but Flora is still with us. We huddle away from the bed and talk in whispers, and Shy brings more chairs and Cara embraces them both and smooths their hair and brings them chamomile tea.

Flora stirs and turns over. She peers towards us, and we move as one to the bed. She manages to stretch one spindly arm as if she is Sleeping Beauty waking from her hundred years nap. 'I think I'm hungry,' she says with confidence.

'What do you want, darling?' Morag says going closer.

'Some of your split pea soup, please,' she says, and she pulls Morag to her with her arm and plants a kiss on her cheek. 'Thank you, my sweet,' she says.

'Coming right up. I brought some with me,' Morag says and dashes out, choking back tears.

'What time is it?' Flora says, 'It's so dark in here, shall we have a little light on?' Tim moves to her bedside lamp and turns it up a little brighter.

'That's better! Hello Tim! It's been a long time since you were in my bedroom, you saucy devil,' she says with a wink.

'Not really, Flora,' he says, 'We're basically living in here at the moment.'

'I meant in the biblical sense,' she says, and she winks again.

'Oh good lord,' Granny says, 'I think I'll go and help Morag with the soup.'

'I'm sorry to disappoint you, Tim darling,' Flora says, and she takes hold of his hand with both of hers.

'You're never a disappointment to me, Flora,' Tim says gamely but I can tell he doesn't quite know what to do with himself.

'I mean I just don't think I'm up to a shag at the moment,' and to my horror she goes to pull down her nightie to flash her skinny boob at him. Luckily, Cara interjects and stops her.

'Okay Flora, let's keep you covered up, eh? We don't want you to get chilly now, do we?' and she mouths a 'sorry,' at Tim.

'I'm just trying to explain, that's all,' she says, closing her eyes, 'But you're right whoever you are.' She's quiet for a moment or two and I wonder if she's going to go back to sleep. It must be the drugs that are making her so weird, surely.

I move towards the bed. I'm aware, acutely aware that this could very well be what Cara has referred to as her final moments of lucidity. This could be my last chance to speak to her, to say anything I need to say, to ask her anything I need to ask. She hasn't asked for food for weeks it feels like. She hasn't really been aware of her surroundings. There's a change for sure. It's unrealistic to expect that she's getting better. I think I have to accept that we are finally moving towards the end.

I take her hand in mine. It so slender, bird boned and thin skinned. I smooth it and wait. She breathes peacefully. It doesn't look like she has any pain which is good.

Her eyes open again.

She turns her head towards me. 'Meryl, beautiful girl, there you are. I was waiting for you so we could go for a swim like we used to, remember?'

'Yes Mum,' I say.

'You know the happiest time of my life was that summer we had in France on our own. Remember?' and she really looks at me, like it is really important that I remember.

'Yes Mum, I remember,' I say.

'Good job we didn't invite your grumpy old dad, eh?' she says, looking at Tim.

Tim and I smile at each other.

'We wouldn't have had half so much fun, would we?' she says.

'No Mum,' I say.

She takes hold of my hand with her other hand and pulls herself towards me. 'We were okay on our own, weren't we? We didn't need anyone else, did we? We had The Show, didn't we? We had the whole world, didn't we?' she says.

'You did Mum,' I say, 'You had the whole world.'

'I don't think it matters that I kept it a secret anyway,' she says.

Morag and Granny come in with the soup.

'Kept what a secret, Mum?' I say.

Her breathing is slowing down. She closes her eyes. She takes a deep, deep breath. Then there is nothing. Granny and Morag rush over. She takes another deep breath, and Granny pushes her arm underneath Mum's shoulders, cradling her, their heads together, soft hair gently intertwining.

There is another breath, a slow, deep rasp of a breath and I know it is her last.

'I love you Mum,' I say quickly as that last sag of air leaves her body and I feel Morag's arms tight around me, binding me together, and the room settles into utter silence.

I don't know what I expected, but it wasn't this.

I look at her face and my mother has gone. Her eyes are so tightly closed, sealed shut, her mouth is slack. Granny starts to rock her and begins a low keening. It is a terrible sound. I turn away from it and into Milk filming.

'No,' I say quietly, 'No, not now. Turn it off,' and he looks at me over the handheld apologetically as if he has no choice. 'What is wrong with you?' I ask. 'Are you some kind of robot? Is this what you have to make the first moments after my mother died about?'

He keeps the camera on me but starts to back away.

I get between him and Granny and Mum. 'Get out,' I say, 'Get out now or I will make you.' He keeps filming. I move towards him; each step pushes him closer to the door and further from the bed. I don't want to scream and rant but I feel it building inside me. 'Out,' I say, and he keeps moving back.

We make it into the hall and I shut the bedroom door behind us. 'Do not go back in there,' I say, 'Or you're fired.'

'You can't do that,' he says.

'Watch me,' I say.

I go into my room and head for my walk-in wardrobe. I charge to the pile of junk in one of the closets. I find what I am looking for.

I move into the hall and go back into Mum's bedroom; Granny is still crying and Morag too and so they should be. 'I'm so sorry I say,' and I swing my baseball bat at the cameras and mics placed around the room. I storm into bathroom and dispatch the cameras in there too.

I move into the hall and swipe at the one out there before heading downstairs. 'You wanted this,' I say to the world and Mum wanted this,' I smash the cameras in the dining room, sitting room, playroom and guest suite as I speak, 'but I never wanted any of this, I never wanted to be part of this freak show. Any of you sick fucks who just watched my mother die should be disgusted with yourselves. That was not your moment to share, she was NOTHING to you. She was not REAL to you. She was on your TV!' I rampage through the garden swiping and smashing as I go. The tech guys arrive waving their hands, 'I'll stop, if you pull the plug,' I say to them, they look helplessly at me. 'Thought so,' I reply and head back into the house. I work my way back through the kitchen, opening the fridge and smashing the handle of the bat into the fridge cams, then through to the pantry and utility, swinging the bat around my head like a pillaging Vandal.

I run back out into the garden demolishing the cameras on the terrace and around the borders and under the tree at the bottom, and then I head through into the kitchen garden where the last of the vegetables are quietly nestling in the tidy rows maintained by Morag and Red. Splintered plastic sprays onto the lush vegetation as I swing my weapon over and over, and I frown at the amends I will have to make for polluting their organic haven. I race through to the pool, panting and exhilarated, and feel my arms and shoulders tiring but I am alive and I have the strength to do this. I thank the Lord that Tim insisted all the cams should be easily accessible for maintenance, and that Mum didn't want high looming shots but wanted everyone to feel like they were standing in our home when they watched. I can reach them all with the tip of the bat and a stretch through my shoulders.

I charge back through the house mentally tallying every room and camera that has logged and clocked and spied on our lives for the past decade until I am standing in the courtyard facing the final camera.

I am out of breath but exhilarated. 'Looks like this it then, ship mates,' I pant, 'So, in the words of that cheesy motherfucker Truman, in case I don't see you, good morning,' and I stand tall, 'good evening,' and I pull the bat up high behind me taking aim at the final glassy eye aiming down at me, 'and good night!' I say and I swing hard and true, over and over until I have obliterated the final camera.

'Good job,' I say to myself.

'That equipment cost thousands, hundreds of thousands,' Tim says. He's standing in the doorway watching me.

'Bill me,' I say with deep satisfaction.

'Meh,' he says, 'Who cares, right?'

'Right,' I say.

Despite my mother's best efforts, *The Flora Show* doesn't make it to a decade. We are three weeks and two days short when I commit carnage. I have a tiny moment of regret over that. It's fleeting. Miniscule. Sub-atomic. No. I don't really think it existed. I think I should have felt it but I didn't.

I don't regret a thing.

No one sleeps. I feel like I never want to sleep again. I don't want to wake up and have to remember that my mother is dead.

There are already news vans at the gates and helicopters circling and, until she is buried, this won't be over.

60

Flora

the.real.flora.tatton
daily contemplation:
Flora Tatton 03-04-1983 - 18-09 - 2024

Liked by **PopeALIII** and **15,873,474 others**

nowayback
fly high sweet angel My heart is broke #heavenistheplacetobe

fuckeduphuman
NO WORDS

bobbyboombastic
sending deepest sympathy from across the ocean

1974999
Why does she get to die so young? There is NO GOD #takentoosoon

lilpiggywenttomarket
grief flows today #floshowisnoshownomo

cheesywotsups
RIP saint Flora. Rest easy free from pain
#love #funeralvibes

61

Joyce

Flora never had a wedding, she never had Meryl christened so there hasn't been the opportunity for big rituals that some families have. As I listened to Tim go through the plans for the funeral, I truly considered not attending. What business would I have at such a grand affair with so many hundreds of guests, film stars, actors, directors, media moguls even royalty. I wouldn't know any of these people the way Flora had.

I'm not sure, of course, how well she did know them. There was a steady stream of visitors to the house over the years and they were higher and higher in status as The Show took off. A visit to Flora became part of the circuit to plug your film or book or TV series or perfume or whatever other crap you were peddling to the public. It was like a show I watched from time to time as a child. When I was ill (which was rarely), my mother would usually take me into school with her for the day and I would sit quietly next to her at her desk and colour or read or listen to her teaching, if I could follow the lessons. If I had anything too catching or debilitating, I would spend the day with our neighbour, Mrs Leighton. I wasn't over keen on this arrangement but, looking back, Mrs Leighton was a kind soul who would tuck me under a blanket on the sofa and let me watch the schools' programmes on TV while she got on with her housework, and then, after lunch on trays, we'd sit and watch the grown-up afternoon TV together. One of her favourites was *Pebble Mill at One*, a chat show where they reported on a little on current affairs and had celebrity guests. As we rarely watched TV in my house, and certainly never through the day, I found *Pebble Mill at One* a bizarre idea. For a start they had a pretend kitchen with pictures on the backwall but no sides to it, and the presenters walked from their stools or chairs into the kitchen and someone cooked something, lickety-spit, there and then and they often ate it, standing up. Most odd. The presenters talked to the guests like they were old friends and asked about their families. I found it very confusing and assumed everyone famous must just know each other.

That's what Flora created on her Show. One big real house with an open-door policy. Celebrities were invited on as part of the programme planning but she also did get to know them as the years passed and some genuinely called by. She didn't interview them when they 'dropped in'. No. They chatted or swam in the pool, or she cooked them lunch, or they cooked her lunch, or they tried a craft like trimming a fascinator or paper sculpture or fashioning a Christmas tree decoration. And there were fantastic dinner parties with spectacular guests over the years; dream dinner parties. There was always something going on, like there is supposed to be in a real house in real life, except that it was filmed and, in truth, to some extent, it was fake.

So when the greatest hostess of all time dies, you want to show up for the funeral. You want to be there, whatever you thought of her, or The Show. Most celebrities play the game of 'Leave me alone,' as they turn their best side to the camera. With Flora, at least she was honest. She knew what she wanted and she let everyone know. It was absurd but it was truthful.

She'd made all the funeral arrangements as soon as she found out about the recurrence apparently. Never mind battling against the odds, let's get on and book the most showy final send off. Tim showed us photos of the floral arrangements she'd chosen. I have to admit, they were spectacular, sugar pinks and deep reds of blousy roses mixed with exotic glossy foliage. They were unlike any funeral flowers I'd ever seen.

She saved us all a job, I must grudgingly acknowledge, and that was a blessing, especially for Meryl who, after Flora died, disappeared into her room for a few days. Just needed her own space.

We got through the day, a fleet of horse-drawn carriages with Flora's tiny coffin atop it looking like a child's. It is a surprise to me that she hasn't opted for a glass casket like Snow White. That she hasn't taken the final opportunity to be filmed in some kind of frozen beauty as a constant reminder for all her fans. But no, the casket is willow, simple and 'environmentally on trend,' was how Tim described it. Crowds and crowds and crowds of people line the streets all the way, hurling flowers and weeping openly and there was a thronging mass of people congregated outside the church watching the service on a giant screen. She would have loved that.

The town embraced the event, recognising it for what it was: the media moment of the decade. Every shop front was 'Florafied' for the occasion, her laminated face beaming out from every window or full-sized cardboard cut-outs like a thousand 2D scarecrows. And most were selling merchandise of some sort; the uptick in trade was more than likely a mini Christmas for most of them. Farmers had opened their fields for camping, and some families had Airbnb'd their houses to accommodate the swarms of people who had descended since she'd died. Hoards and hoards all making the pilgrimage to Mecca before the lights went out. It was insanity but for the traders I think they must have known it was all going to be over soon; they were squeezing the last drops out of the cash cow before the milk ran dry.

I won't go into the service. I was burying my daughter. Enough said as far as I'm concerned. No mother should have to live through that. Especially not with hundreds of people they've never met breathing over their shoulders and in the full knowledge that every shred of grief expressed will be televised.

I couldn't wait to be back in the safety of the house. It was an ordeal from start to finish and, though Flora had arranged a grand function at the fanciest local hotel, Morag, Meryl and I just came home feeling ridiculous in our horse drawn carriage like we were in a ludicrous regency drama.

I didn't need to be with anyone else. I wanted it all done with, once and for all.

It's late and Red is making us all cocoa. None of us are sleeping well. Meryl says that the last few days of Flora's life were so chaotic, it just messed with everyone's circadian rhythms and we're finding it hard to get back into any kind of normality.

The cocoa is hot and sweet and Red has added a little cinnamon which is a nice touch.

'I'm completely unpacked,' Morag announces. She has repainted the downstairs guest suite which we've decided she should move into permanently. The energy that woman has is incredible. And she's no fear of going up a ladder either. She and Red have been working away in there for the last two days.

In fact, there's been a lot of shifting around.

No one is in Flora's room but we're talking about Meryl moving in there. It has a beautiful aspect, and it can't just sit empty.

'I'm pleased you've finished it,' Meryl says looking up from her phone.

'It's no bother when you're painting on new plaster,' Morag says.

'Did you have it all re-plastered when you moved in?' Red says.

'Hell no,' says Morag, 'This is a new build, sweet. It's only fifteen, twenty years old.'

'You're kidding?' Red replies, 'It looks so authentic. Like, hundreds of years old.'

'Nope,' Meryl says, 'This is basically *Disneyland*. Not quite made from plastic, it is built from bricks, well breeze blocks probably, but it's all just a replica of a Georgian house. I thought you knew. I thought everyone knew.'

'I had no idea,' they sound amazed, 'It's a good job, innit? A lot of period detail.'

'Yep, you'd never know,' Morag says.

We drink our cocoa.

'When's Milk leaving?' I ask.

'Late afternoon tomorrow,' Red says, 'That's when his flight is. I guess he'll be going just after lunch.'

'I've hardly seen him today,' Morag says.

'He's been in meetings. A lot of things to sort out apparently,' Red says.

Milk is going to LA. Senior Production Exec on some hit reality show over there. Not the same format as The Show, not 24/7. He got a call twenty minutes after Flora died. Vultures. He said yes there and then according to Red. He was always on at Flora to travel to the States more, but she hated the long haul flights; hated the claustrophobia of flying. He's been itching to get out there.

No one has said they're going to miss him, and I think that's sad, and I wonder why that is. Perhaps it's harder to get to know someone who always behind a camera, one step removed from you, who's always looking at you in terms of the shot, in terms of the content. Or maybe they've already said it to him too many times and I just haven't heard.

Surprisingly, the doorbell rings. We used to have a doorcam but no more. No cameras allowed. Now when the doorbell rings it's a nice surprise who will be waiting outside.

'It's late for visitors,' Morag says.

'Very late,' Red says severely, old habits die hard, 'I'll go,' and we smile indulgently at them and each other.

I finish my cocoa, loving the bitter chocolatey dregs at the bottom of the mug and I think it really is time for bed though I'm not in the least bit tired.

'Meryl,' Red calls from the hall, 'It's for you.'

62

Meryl

I pass Red in the hall heading back to the kitchen, 'Let me know if you need any help, okay?' they say darkly.

A young man is standing on the drive, his back to the house, shoulders hunched. He turns and it's Tyler.

'I jumped the gate,' he says, 'Your security's taking a nap. Just for info. Left the van up the lane a bit.'

He kicks and digs at the gravel with the toe of his trainer. I'm stuck as to what to do next. Do I ask him in? Do I yell at him? Do I tell him to fuck off? I kinda want to do all these things.

'Sorry about your mum,' he says, and he twists his mouth a bit and shuts one eye. This is awkward.

'Right,' I say.

We wait.

He looks up at the house.

'Nice place,' he says, 'Looks bigger on TV.'

'Really,' I say, crossing my arms, 'Why're you here Tyler? Did you just pop by to see the house in the flesh or is there a point to this house call at … nearly midnight? What do you want?'

'I don't know,' his voice sounds whiny, 'I miss you, Mare. I been camping nearby. In the van. Trying to get up the balls to come by, see? I wanted to come sooner. Ever since she died but I didn't know how. After everything I did. After all that stupid shit. But I just decided tonight I was going to do it and so … well … here I am.'

'Fantastic!' I say, 'You've passed on your condolences, and you've seen the house and decided it looked better on the small screen, so now you can be on your way. I don't think we have anything else to say to each other.'

There's a tut behind me and I turn to see Morag, Granny and Red hastily retract back into the kitchen doorway.

I step down onto the driveway and pull the door to behind me. 'Follow me,' I say, tetchily, and I trot round the side of the house into the garden. It's dark but the security lights come on, illuminating everything rather beautifully much to my annoyance. I head down the lawn to the oak tree to make sure I am out of earshot of the three witches in the kitchen, who I can see are already peering out of the window. 'Am I never to have any privacy in my life?' I think to myself.

Tyler trots after me.

'I really don't know how I can help you, Tyler,' I turn on him, 'Or have you run out of cash, eh? Half a million not enough? I mean, yes, I will be coming into some money now but you're going to have to wait a little while for another free handout.'

'Meryl...' he looks in agony. He steps closer to me and looks at me with those wonderful, sensitive eyes that I trusted and loved and looked into with absolute faith for so long.

'I'm not interested, Tyler, okay?' I snap, 'You made your position very clear before you left. Let me repeat that, before *you* left, *you* disappeared with my mother's money. What on earth are you doing here? You miss me you say? What does that *mean*? We're kids, Tyler. Go and find someone uncomplicated to have some fun with or take some responsibility for your life. Just don't include *me* in your plans. Okay?'

'Woah,' he says, raising his palms and taking a step back, 'Okay, okay. I was hoping we could talk but you are strung out, girl.' He frowns. 'You're wrong about me. And you're wrong about you and me. I can do responsibility. I just couldn't do all that money. I *loathed* it. It was like ... a chattering monkey in my ear, never shutting up. Once I got in the van and got away, I understood that.'

'Got away with the half mill, you mean,' I correct him.

'I never spent it, Mare,' he says quietly.

What?' I say.

'I never spent it. Not a single penny. I couldn't. It felt like stealing. The whole thing felt like robbery. All that stuff I bought, it,' he searches for the word, 'soiled me. Once I was away from it all I knew I was never going to touch it.'

'Don't tell me,' I say cynically, 'you gave it all to charity, like you did all your gear.' This is going to be the icing on the cake.

'Nah,' he says.

'So where is it then? Because it sure as hell isn't in the account we had.'

'Yeah,' he says, 'That was the other thing I wanted to say. I transferred it back over today. All of it. I wanted to tell you myself.'

I stare at him in disbelief. 'Go on,' he says, 'Check your phone.'

I log on and sure enough the money is there.

I look at him.

'Why? I'd never have chased you for it. It could have changed your life,' I say.

'I didn't want to change my life,' he says, 'I loved it the way it was.'

We stand together and the wind rustles the leaves above us. They're changing their colour and soon the tree will let them go and suffer another winter with bleak, bare branches and nothing to protect it. I hated that as a little girl. When the apple trees in France lost their leaves, I would ask Flora if we could stick the leaves back on or buy the trees coats. She told me the trees were sleeping and didn't mind not having leaves, but I thought the leaves made the trees looked friendly. The bare branches were dark and grasping and dangerous like they could reach down and grab me as I ran under them. The money had stripped Tyler of his leaves; I'd seen a desperate, grabbing side to him that was not pretty.

'What do you want to do?' he says.

And part of me would like to hug this boy before me. Part of me would like to take comfort from the familiarity of this human who understands me and accepts me and who probably is in love with me.

It would be so easy to welcome him back and pick up where we left off and playhouse with Treasure and pretend that none of the bad stuff ever happened.

I look into those eyes.

'I want you to go,' I say.

63

Flora

nowayback
TAYLOR SWIFT IS DA BOMB
#swiftyswiftyswifty

fuckeduphuman
soopermarket trolley with wobbly wheel AGAIN. No words

bobbyboombastic
sending energy from across the ocean

1974999
Why do white clouds always look so goddamn cheerful? #blacklivesmatter

lilpiggywenttomarket
new channel for #floshow woohoo!!

cheesywotsups
back to beeing a vegan #3rdtimelucky #fortheplanet

64

Joyce

My house is sold and I am permanently moving in with Meryl and Treasure and Morag. It's a big step for a Yorkshire lass to up sticks and move to the south but what have I left up here?

As I was packing up, I got a visit from one of the officers who has been dealing with Liz and her charming husband Ricky. The officer was a fan of The Show and, though not obligated to follow up on the case, I could tell she wanted to pop in to pay her respects as much as anything.

Morag and I have gone over and over how I could have been so stupid to have been taken in. The officer filled in many of the blank spots for us. It appeared that Liz had moved away from the area years ago and was living in Lancashire. She was an avid fan of The Show, a 'superfan' was how the officer described her. The fact that she was such a fan was a help to the police. Once she started talking about it, she couldn't stop; told the police everything they wanted to know and more. She and her husband had hatched a plan to dupe me of the money when Flora received her first diagnosis and had moved back over here to stay with one of their four (!) daughters. The surly waste of space we met at the door was Liz's son- in-law apparently. Yes, so she has one daughter living in the town who agreed to put her up if she split the money with her.

Nice that Liz shared that detail with the police; I don't know if that made the daughter an accomplice.

Apparently, Liz had all sorts of information gleaned from The Show about me and what she thought I would respond to. Hence the half sugar, the gardening, the history, all the private details of my life the wretched choices my daughter made has made public.

Hats off to Liz though, she'd put in her time. They live in a one-bedroom flat in Darwen. No sign of a garden there. She looked everything up online, just to fool me. And I was fooled. Hook line and sinker as they say.

Everything had nearly gone tits up when Flora invited her to the house. Liz was beside herself at the thought of meeting her in person. She'd ended up taking tranquilisers to deal with it all such was her excitement. What a ridiculous situation.

She's got a record.

Done time for fraud already. Bank cards and persistent shop lifting, but nothing on as big a scale as this. She also crowed to the police that she'd taken a few 'souvenirs' from the house. Said she couldn't resist. They'd found thousands of selfies on her phone taken all over the place. How the cameras didn't pick this up, or see her taking anything, I just don't know. I suppose people only see what they expect to see.

So the whole interception and arrest has gone down very well with the press. I think that's the only reason the police were interested at all. Technically, I'm not sure a crime had actually been committed until she took the cheque, so it was good of them to put the effort in. But like I say, it was a big scoop for whoever's in charge of the police in our area nowadays.

It doesn't really stop me from feeling a fool, however.

Morag says I mustn't dwell on it and that it won't happen again. I know how much of Flora's estate she's packaged up to make sure I'll never want for anything. And it frightens me. I need to think long and hard how to keep that money away from all the other potential Liz's in the world.

Anyway, Morag's right. I mustn't dwell.

Meryl is back in college, and we need to be organised if she is going to get the grades she wants. I've brought down a few bits and pieces, but I hadn't much I wanted, or needed, to hang on to.

We can't make a decision about Flora's room, so we've put her old bed back in there and left it as it was. It's comforting for all of us to go up there from time to time and spend a moment in there with her. There's still the lingering scent of her favourite perfume and it is still the most glamorous room in the house. We'll leave it as it is for now.

I'm in one of the upstairs guest suites now Marsha has moved into the annexe with Shy and Red. Shy says he is looking for something else but the way he trails around after Marsha and Treasure and ploughs up and down the pool every morning with his easy crawl, I can't see that his search is much of a priority.

So many more people in my life now, more than I would ever have thought possible. We are, for now, a happy community.

I miss her though.

I miss her terribly.

65

Meryl

'She left you control of her estate, so all the footage we have, all the past episodes, to some extent, you have the final say over what we can do with them. The network wants to set up a dedicated channel. There's definitely the desire; people are having withdrawal symptoms already so we're running them ad hoc at the moment.'

Tim is here for a final planning meeting. It's just me and him. We're in the dining room looking out onto the garden There was a frost last night, the first one of the year and it looks pretty outside. A little bit magical.

'Even if you're not overly keen, Meryl, it's always going to keep the royalties trickling in for you and Treasure. The network will keep monetising too, they're talking about adding in a sister shopping channel and really you don't need to do anything.'

He must be able to see that I look a bit dubious. 'Think about people's jobs, Meryl. She's keeping people in work, that's all and she's keeping people happy. TV is full of old re-runs. Just let it play out until everyone gets tired of it or they move onto the next thing. What's the harm?'

'Okay,' I say, 'but I have other things to be worrying about. I can't be dealing with this stuff all the time. It's my A level year.'

'Why don't you leave it up to me?' Tim says.

'I don't think you have that great a track record,' I say, 'There's a conflict of interest with you. You want to please the network too much.'

'A little offended, Meryl but I take your point,' Tim concedes.

'I'm going to talk to Red about it,' I say, 'I think they always have our interests as their top priority, and I want to keep them around.'

'Good call,' Tim says.

'Okay,' I say, 'Anything else because human biology is calling my name. Lots of work to catch up on.'

'Funny you should say that,' Tim says, 'Look Meryl, this isn't easy to bring up, but the night Flora died, that stuff she was saying, about me…' he trails off.

'Go on,' I say.

'Okay,' he seems to gain a bit of confidence, 'look Flora and I, we did, have a fling,' he looks a little embarrassed, 'and when she said all those things about secrets and being your dad, well, I've given it some thought and had a look back through some old diaries.'

'My, my,' I say, 'Quite the Sherlock Holmes.' I'm not sure I like where this is going though.

'It's just that, by my reckoning, it is possible.' And he looks at me.

I look at him.

'That I'm your dad, Meryl,' he says uneasily.

'Oh,' I say.

It is clear that neither of us know what to do with this information.

I think about his blonde, wavy hair and mine too, but Mum was blonde as well. I'm tall, he's tall but mum was too.

Do I want Tim to be my dad? Do I want a dad at all?

'Look Tim,' I say, 'That's great and all but I'm nearly eighteen I mean what are we going to do, if it's true, which it very well might not be?'

'How do you mean?' he says.

'I've not got much need for a dad, have I? Okay there's the walking down the aisle scenario where I may find myself lacking but frankly, I'm heading out of my childhood, Tim. I don't need to be taken to the park or taught to drive or any of the stuff dads do. Hell, I don't even know what it is dads *do* do. Mum was always such a big personality I never felt I needed another parent. One like her was enough for any kid.'

'Okay,' he says, cautiously.

'What I'm saying is, Mum kept it a secret and I'm okay with that. Are you? We're just guessing anyway. She was pretty spaced out at the end, wasn't she?' I chuckle.

'You're right,' Tim says, 'She was. She could have been saying anything.'

'Exactly. So I'm happy to leave things as they are if you are?' I venture.

'Fine,' Tim says firmly. He stands up and offers his hand for me to shake.

'Tim …' I say and smile at his hand.

'Sorry, Meryl. You really are an extraordinary young woman. For the record I would have been very proud to be your …'

'Tim,' I say, firmly, 'Let's leave it at that, shall we?' and I usher him from the dining room to the kitchen.

'Tim!' Morag says, 'Let me get you some shortbread and a coffee, I've just put on a fresh pot. Now, is there any news on the romance front?'

'Funny you should say that Morag,' Tim starts and I dart back out and run up the stairs and close the door of my room, smiling at the thought of poor old Tim taking on my paternity; he certainly wouldn't know what had hit him.

Unzipping my rucksack, I heave out my books and flip open my biology textbook as I settle down at my desk, breathing out slowly, as I relax into the quiet and security of homework.

My phone pings.

It's Tyler.

Acknowledgements

Thanks to Graeme for your continued help with listening to my ideas and reading and re-reading and throughout the birth of this book. You are and always will be my love.

Thanks to my Mum, Sue and my brother, Rory for your excellent proof-reading and editing skills. You are my team and very much appreciated.

The answer to the cryptic clue on p.131 is 'meathead'.

Also by this author

The Emperor Reversed

Long listed for the prestigious **2024 Mslexia Novel Prize**, Jane Barrie's second novel. **The Emperor Reversed**, has been as well received as her first.

Karen and Archie look like they have it all from the outside; a long marriage, a beautiful home, successful careers, not to mention three beautiful children. When an horrific accident changes everything, it soon becomes clear that all may not be as it seems for this idyllic family. Told from three very different points of view, **The Emperor Reversed** is a forensic analysis of love, control and revenge. Once again, Jane Barrie explores the darker underside of intimate relationships with unflinching, pinpoint accuracy, never flinching from revealing the reality of the worst and the best of human nature. Another compelling read you won't want to put down.

Reviews for **The Emperor Reversed**

'I couldn't put this book down... really well written and a brilliant story line with unexpected twists and turns ... Brilliant read... looking forward to a third novel please.

'I read this book in two days and thoroughly enjoyed it. It's both extremely dark and very funny and having three main characters tell the story from their perspective works so well and adds brilliant twists. Full of suspense and the way it's written really makes you feel you know the characters.

Absolutely loved it and have been thinking about it long after finishing.'

'This is a compelling story, brilliantly told. Jane Barrie creates wonderful characters, ordinary yet extraordinary, and then pulls us this way and that, as their lives ravel and unravel, and where perspective is everything. It plays games with your mind and emotions. It is dark and troubling but fabulously funny. If you read **A Rust of the Heart** you will devour this. If you haven't, why not? Another brilliant, brilliant book.'

'I've read that second novels, particularly when the first was successful, often fall flat. Not this one. Actually I think this is even better than **A Rust of the Heart**. The writing seems more assured and though (hopefully) very few readers will have lived through a marriage like this we can all still understand it...

I bought this book on publication but then had no chance to read it until Christmas. I'm glad about that because it is a fascinating read and I'd have hated to have to go through piecemeal. It really is one of those once started, difficult to stop, books. I enjoyed it, a lot, and the only spoiler I'll give is that I'm so glad the children of the marriage came out of it well, in particular the lovely, but vulnerable, Joe.'

A Rust of the Heart

Meet Jen, eldest child, undervalued and overlooked, sharp-witted and sharp-tongued. Her desire to be the centre of attention never leaves her. Follow her story through engaging and often amusing windows into her world, decades apart over fifty years. She is not afraid to say what others often think as she navigates through a life filled with envy and dissatisfaction. Watch as Jen tries to escape her dysfunctional family; a failed actor father and reluctant mother intent on turning a ruined castle into a B and B plus her magnificent, younger sister who is the apple of everybody's eye, much to Jen's annoyance. Will she ever find happiness? Or fulfilment?

Sharply evoked characters and clarity of language plus a story with unexpected twists and turns make for a lively, page-turning read in this debut novel by Jane Barrie.

Reviews for **A Rust of the Heart**

'Highly immersive and disturbingly relatable. With rich characterisation and a plot that will keep you guessing. A definite 5 out of 5 read.'

'Intriguing plot, with well-drawn characters. Explores a family dynamic through the eyes of a seemingly unsympathetic protagonist, full of local Cumbrian colour. Highly recommended.'

Definitely a page turner, can't wait for Jane's next book!'

'Brilliant debut novel from Jane Barrie. Really enjoyed trying to work out what the main character would do next. All the characters were very well described, the family dynamics were spot on.

'At the centre of the story - exactly where she'd want to be - is Jen. Deliciously spiteful, furiously intolerant, it's difficult sometimes to dislike her as much as she deserves. Amidst the tragedy and heartbreak, the writing is laugh out loud funny; Barrie handles her minor characters superbly, setting them each like jewels within a well-crafted vignette. This book is recommended - and I'm interested to see what this new writer does next!'

'To be honest, I'm still not entirely sure what to make of this book, but there are a few aspects of which I can be certain. First, it's compelling and addictive. The characters get under your skin, and you have to keep going to find out what will happen to Jen and her family (I won't say friends, don't think she has any) in the ensuing decades. Second, it's very well written. Third, for a first novel, it's really impressive. Fourth, don't start it when you are busy elsewhere. You need to clear the decks and be able to keep going. I can't wait to see what Jane produces next.'

Find more reviews on Amazon and order your copy of A Rust of the Heart and The Emperor Reversed here.

A final word ...

If you enjoyed **Floor Show**, please do leave a review on **Amazon** or **Goodreads.com**. This makes all the difference in reaching a wider audience.

Follow Jane on Facebook **@Jane Barrie Writer**, or on Instagram **@janebarrie**, or check out her website **janebarrie.wordpress.com** to read her blog and to keep up with news of her next novel coming out Spring 2025

Printed in Great Britain
by Amazon